"You saved my life."

Matthew glanced over his shoulder. "At best, I saved you from a broken tibia. More likely, a sprained ankle. And some embarrassment."

"Well, it's the embarrassment that would have devastated me," Marlee said. "I mean, none of my outfits would look as good with a cast."

He paused, glanced over his shoulder again. She was standing by the bumper of her delivery van, shading her eyes with her hand, grinning like the cat that ate the canary.

"You can thank me by moving your van."

"That's why I'm out here."

"And you can park it in front of your own shop from now on. If you're feeling really grateful."

"Hmm. Nope, I think I'm good. It wouldn't have been *that* embarrassing. My outfits look cute no matter what I wear with them."

She tossed her keys in the air, caught them, then turned on her heel and got inside the van.

Dear Reader,

Marlee and Matthew were the first couple to come to mind when I started creating the Haw Springs miniseries. The feisty florist and the pragmatic pediatrician. Soft petals meet hard science. Irreverent pluck versus studious quirk. Their individual stories were right there in my grasp, but I wasn't sure how those stories would ever possibly merge. They wouldn't likely gravitate toward each other, so their paths would never naturally cross.

I realized that I needed time to really understand these two guarded individuals. So I spent time with them in other Haw Springs stories, got to know them and finally I realized that what they needed was a little push to get them started on the path to romance. I knew that if they simply were forced to spend some time together, they would reveal their love. Their story about breaking down the walls they've built, and discovering their true connection, is one of my favorites. As you spend time with Marlee and Matthew, I hope you will also find that falling in love with the florist and the doctor is as easy as...well, falling off a ladder.

Jennifer

THEIR SWEETHEART SCHEME

JENNIFER BROWN

If you purchased this book without a cover you should be aware that this book is stolen property. It was reported as "unsold and destroyed" to the publisher, and neither the author nor the publisher has received any payment for this "stripped book."

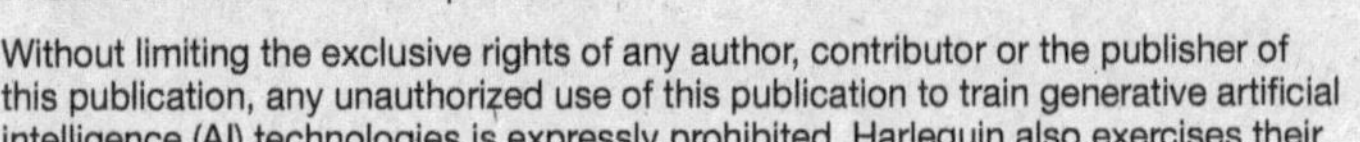

Recycling programs for this product may not exist in your area

ISBN-13: 978-1-335-46047-9

Their Sweetheart Scheme

Copyright © 2026 by Jennifer Brown

All rights reserved. No part of this book may be used or reproduced in any manner whatsoever without written permission.

Without limiting the exclusive rights of any author, contributor or the publisher of this publication, any unauthorized use of this publication to train generative artificial intelligence (AI) technologies is expressly prohibited. Harlequin also exercises their rights under Article 4(3) of the Digital Single Market Directive 2019/790 and expressly reserves this publication from the text and data mining exception.

This is a work of fiction. Names, characters, places and incidents are either the product of the author's imagination or are used fictitiously. Any resemblance to actual persons, living or dead, businesses, companies, events or locales is entirely coincidental.

For questions and comments about the quality of this book, please contact us at CustomerService@Harlequin.com.

TM and ® are trademarks of Harlequin Enterprises ULC.

Harlequin Enterprises ULC
22 Adelaide St. West, 41st Floor
Toronto, Ontario M5H 4E3, Canada
www.Harlequin.com

HarperCollins Publishers
Macken House, 39/40 Mayor Street Uppe
Dublin 1, D01 C9W8, Ireland
www.HarperCollins.com

Printed in U.S.A.

Jennifer Brown cut her storytelling teeth by letting her imagination run wild in the fields, forests and farms of her youth. Her love of weaving romance and nostalgia into stories that feature simple small-town living runs deep. Nearly all of her novels—young adult, middle grade, women's fiction, inspirational romance and heartwarming romance—feature connection between people, a sense of belonging and a love of community. Jennifer lives and writes in Liberty, Missouri. Visit her at jenniferbrownauthor.com.

Books by Jennifer Brown

Harlequin Heartwarming

A Haw Springs Romance

The Cowboy's Dream Family
The Veterinarian's Perfect Match
Snowed In for Christmas

Love Inspired Inspirational Mountain Rescue

Rescue on the Ridge
Peril at the Peak
Hunted at the Hideaway

Love Inspired Inspirational The Protectors

Kidnapped in Kansas

Visit the Author Profile page
at Harlequin.com for more titles.

For Scott, the one who stands at the bottom of the ladder, always ready to catch.

Acknowledgments

I am hardly a gardener, but I've put together a few bouquets to acknowledge the people who've been by my side in Haw Springs.

To my agent Cori Deyoe of 3 Seas Literary Agency, I present a bouquet of gladiolus, goldenrod and zinnia to thank you for the integrity, strength, encouragement and lasting affection you've provided me throughout the years.

To Johanna Raisanen, I give you coreopsis and iris for your always-cheerful trust. For the entire Harlequin team, here are heaps and heaps of hydrangea to express my gratitude. Tied with iridescent ribbon, of course, because you are all so shiny and awesome.

For my family, no bouquet, but an actual red rose garden, for all the love in the whole world.

And for my readers, I offer big bouquets of marjoram, the flower of happiness and joy. May you experience nothing but delight in these pages and beyond. Thank you for reading!

CHAPTER ONE

MARLEE WEST THREW her delivery van into Park and jumped out without paying even the slightest bit of attention to her parking job. She had way too much to do to worry about things like parking, especially in sleepy Haw Springs on a beautiful late spring day, where shoppers walked from home and parking spaces were plentiful. She preferred the spot directly across from her flower shop's front door, a straight line for carrying and loading big, heavy arrangements.

Keys jingling in hand, she jogged across the street and barged into Blush & Bloom flower shop with such vigor her snoozing shih tzu, Poppy, raised her head and gave a singular, startled bark.

"It's just me, Poppy," Marlee said. "You can stop pretending to be a watchdog."

As if she understood, Poppy gave a lazy wag, her tail thumping against her little dog bed, then lowered her chin and went back to her slumber. Poppy never met a stranger in her entire life;

watchdog would be the last duty she would ever take on, anyway.

"You're about out of iridescent ribbon."

Morgan, Marlee's sister, stood behind the counter, her robin's-egg blue T-shirt blending in perfectly with the sage-and-pink palette of Blush & Bloom. Even at their busest, Marlee's flower shop felt cozy, elegant, unrushed. And Marlee liked it that way. As high-energy as she was, she liked to lean into the slow and easy Haw Springs mentality. Even though prom weekend was neither slow nor easy for any flower shop.

Morgan held up a mostly empty cardboard spool with one hand, her fingers squeezing floral tape around the stem of a rose with the other, holding a puff of baby's breath in place.

"Again? Don't these girls realize that they're all going to look the same?"

Morgan chuckled. "They probably want that. Don't you remember high school at all? You wanted to match your date, yes, but more than that, you wanted to have what all the other girls had. And you definitely didn't want someone showing up with something so ridiculously beautiful that it made your carefully curated ensemble look shabby in comparison. Remember Michelle Stevens and...*the pearls*?" She said the last words in an ominous tone.

Marlee set her chin and narrowed her eyes in pretend irritation as she joined her sister behind the counter. "Those pearls. How could I forget? A rich, generous grandmother in London? How could the rest of us compete with our little mall-purchased rhinestone necklaces? Yeah, that will forever be known as The Great Accessory Disaster of Haw Springs High School. She single-handedly changed the prom glam game forever."

"Exactly." Morgan rolled the spool down the counter toward Marlee's computer. "So you'd better start ordering."

"I won't get it in time. I'll have to drive up to the city this afternoon and buy out a craft store again. Which means…" Marlee paused, woke up her computer and stared at the screen. Four more orders had trickled in while she'd been gone. The kids who waited until the very last minute to order their corsages were both the bane of her existence and her bread and butter. Right now, she was feeling the bane aspect. "Another late night for me." She laid her head on her sister's shoulder. "Or for *us*?"

Morgan shook her head. "I promised Decker I would help him get ready for the new session that starts next week. And, remember, you promised to help us as soon as prom season is over. Since I helped you." She sang this last part, set the taped rose on the order printout and ruffled Marlee's hair.

Marlee sighed—she'd been doing a lot of that since her assistant, Kimberly, had suddenly and suspiciously grown ill with a weeklong mystery bug, the third time since Christmas, and the worst possible week imaginable for her absence. Just about every corsage and boutonniere that was going to show up at Haw Springs High over the weekend would be made by Marlee herself, and that meant anyone at Haw Springs High who planned to attend the dance was going to be walking through her door in the next forty-eight hours. Just when she thought she was on top of things, she also received an anniversary order and three birthday bouquet deliveries. She had been forced to call in Morgan for reinforcement.

But Morgan had her son and her own life, not to mention her own job, working for her husband, Decker, who ran a successful equine therapy ranch for children on the autism spectrum up on the ridge on the outskirts of town. Marlee was not one to look a gift horse in the mouth; if she only had Morgan for the afternoon, she would be grateful. If she had to stay up all night, she would stay up all night. She would let herself collapse into sleep on Saturday evening, when the kids were dancing in the gym with their iridescent corsages shimmering under the black lights. A missed night of sleep along the way wasn't the biggest deal in the world. Better than a flower shop with no customers.

She could remember her early, lean days when she wasn't sure she would ever have enough business to keep Blush & Bloom open. If it hadn't been for her parents, who kept her afloat in every possible way, she may not have made it through that first year. She would have given anything for too many orders back then. *Work hard, and then work harder* had been her motto. So she did, and she was finally beginning to reap the rewards. Now that she was established, she wasn't going to complain. Working hard was just part of her fiber now. And the more work she had, the faster she could pay off her parents, who loaned her the money to support her dream.

"Late night for us, then, Poppy. I know for a fact that you don't have anything else going on. And it's not like we have anything—or any*one*—waiting for us at home." The dog gave more sleepy thumps against the cushion with her tail but didn't rouse. "You think you're tired now. You just wait until midnight gets here. Then we'll talk about tired," Marlee muttered.

Morgan expertly tied the roses she'd been wrapping onto a wrist elastic and set it in a box filled with tissue paper. "Another one down." She wrote the name and date on the box. "Garrett Shelly, you are going to have one happy, iridescent date."

"Purple velvet," Marlee said as she began gathering materials to start the next order.

Morgan placed the box on a shelf. "Someone ordered purple velvet?"

Marlee shook her head. "No. I had purple velvet ribbon in my corsage at my senior prom. Keith wore a purple vest. Remember? My dress was white and purple with those velvet floral appliqués. Michelle may have had her pearls, but I had purple velvet ribbon in my corsage. I was way too cool for iridescent. Or for pearls."

Morgan laughed out loud. "Your little sister definitely thought you were cool. I'll give you that. And your dress was perfect."

Marlee walked the length of the counter as if she were walking a runway, playfully tossing her hair over one shoulder and then the other. "Hair, perfect. Shoes, perfect."

"Your date, though, a little less than perfect."

"You had to go there?" She came back to the corsage she was working on. "You can sure say that again. He taught me a very important lesson, though."

"That high school romance is fleeting?"

"We dated all through college, too, remember?" Marlee said sourly.

"Okay, that young romance is fleeting?"

"That romance, period, is fleeting, and not worth the time. It's all a fairy tale. I prefer to live in reality, thank you."

Morgan got out a new box and lined it with green tissue paper. "Oh, here we go. I shouldn't have said anything." She began reciting the words Marlee had drilled into her over the years, "*There is no such thing as a perfect match. Romance is a paid highway with a hefty toll. For every minute of butterflies in your stomach, you earn an hour of tears on your cheeks.* I'm missing one. What was it again?"

"There is no such thing as Mr. Perfect," Marlee supplied.

"Yes, that's it. *There's no such thing as Mr. Perfect—only Myth-ter Perfect.*"

"What?" Marlee asked. "Keith is a great example. I thought he was Mr. Perfect. He also thought he was Mr. Perfect. But we were both wrong. Mr. Perfect doesn't exist. It's Myth-ter Perfect. A myth."

"It's ancient history," Morgan said. "He was definitely not your forever, I will agree to that. But that doesn't mean your forever doesn't exist out there somewhere."

"Maybe. But he's going to have to exist in Haw Springs. Because we both know I'm never leaving here." Marlee cut the stem of a peach rose short and began preparing to wrap it. "So, you know... he doesn't exist."

"He might, and you would never know it because you're too stubborn to put yourself out there," Morgan said. "Because you're so convinced it's all a myth."

"Blah, blah, blah. Not interested. Been there, done that. Have the scars to prove it."

"Scar, singular."

"Scars, plural."

"Scar that turned into scare."

They stared at each other for a beat. The two sisters were close. *Sometimes too close,* Marlee thought, when Morgan was calling her out on something. And Morgan was almost never afraid to call her out.

The truth was, Morgan could very well be right. Maybe what it all boiled down to was that Marlee was just plain scared of romance. Maybe that was what happened to someone when they were dumped the way Marlee had been dumped by Keith. Instead of coming home from a romantic dinner with the diamond ring she'd fully expected, she'd come home with a broken heart, the whole ugly scene forever seared into her memory.

I thought you were going to propose to me, Keith. Why did you bring me here just to break up with me?

I wanted you to know I had no hard feelings.

You? You *had no hard feelings? Ha! Six. Years.*

We were kids. We're adults now. It's time to move on and...and live our adult lives. Independently.

Ah. So you want to be independent of me. Well, I'll help you out with that. No time like the present.

Come on, Mar. Don't leave. We already ordered. It's expensive. Let's keep this amicable.

She laughed out loud at the memory, breaking the tension with her sister. "The last time I saw

Keith, he was *amicably* wearing an entire family-style bowl of fully dressed, *expensive* Italian salad in his lap. Remember? He looked very *independent* sitting there alone with his mouth gaping open."

Morgan giggled. "I've always wished I had been there to see that."

"I wish it had made me feel better. But it didn't."

"I know. You were a mess when you came home."

"I was a mess for a while. But I haven't even thought about Keith for years until today. So, see? Growth. I'm not a mess anymore. Now I just no longer believe in the big romance myth."

"Decker isn't a myth."

Marlee sprayed adhesive on her corsage and sprinkled it with silver glitter. "Well, good for you that you found the one non-myth out there." She saw the hurt on her sister's face and set her corsage on the counter. "Hey." She wrapped one arm around Morgan and gave her a squeeze. "That sounded sarcastic, but it wasn't. I love Decker, and I know that he is the real thing. I think he's perfect for you. And for Archer. I mean it. Can we just talk about something else for a while? Something other than my love life?"

"Lack of," Morgan corrected her, but grinned as Marlee gave her a light shove. "Okay, okay. I'll let it be."

"Thank you. New subject, please. Tell me something interesting about today that has nothing to do with prom or corsages."

"Well… Dr. LaSalle is outside, sniffing around the van," Morgan said, nodding toward the front window.

"Ugh. No. Not that subject." Marlee dropped her corsage into a box and quickly folded it. "He's going to complain about my parking again. Poppy. Go watchdog the van."

Poppy opened one eye for the briefest moment, then went back to sleep.

"Terrible watchdog."

"He doesn't look happy," Morgan said.

Marlee propped her elbows on the counter and rested her chin in the palms of her hands. "Why must someone who looks so pretty be so difficult?"

Matthew LaSalle, the handsome pediatrician who'd opened a clinic directly across the street from Marlee's shop, was standing on the sidewalk outside his clinic, hands on hips, staring at her delivery van. She knew the posture well enough to know that his next move would be to storm across the street and demand that she move her van out of "his" parking spot. This had become a daily ritual, with the doctor insisting that the spots in front of his clinic were reserved for his patients, and Marlee arguing just as vehemently that in downtown Haw Springs, a spot was a spot was a spot.

To be fair, the spot she most loved to park in was directly in front of his clinic, and he might have been able to make an argument that it kept his patients from being able to see his front door. It was an argument he tried to make pretty much every day. An argument she rejected based on principle. He *could* ask nicely.

Marlee remembered Matthew LaSalle from school. He was two grades above her, quiet, quirky and seriously studious. The cute boy that all the girls overlooked. After graduation, he'd gone off to college, and she'd honestly forgotten all about him until he reappeared in Haw Springs and opened a clinic. Now, he was a quiet, quirky, studious pediatrician with a chiseled jaw and a runner's form. She did not mind the view across the street one bit and often found herself idly standing at her front counter, admiring him as he buzzed around the front of his clinic.

Buzzed around her van.

Buzzed from her van toward her shop.

And usually that was about when she stopped admiring the view.

He was quirky and cute, and incredibly rigid.

The kind of rigid that had a way of destroying a perfectly good crush.

"Here he comes," Morgan said under her breath, just as the phone rang. "Oops, I'm busy. I've got a phone to answer."

"Coward," Marlee said.

"Just being smart," Morgan said as she brought the phone to her ear.

The flower shop door opened and a middle-aged woman with a bored-looking teen daughter entered.

"Boutonniere?" Marlee asked.

The girl rolled her eyes and made an exasperated noise.

"Too young, no date," the woman said. She checked to make sure the daughter wasn't listening, then leaned forward over the counter and whispered. "Sore subject."

"Oh." Marlee raised her voice to address the girl. "You're not missing out on anything. Dates are overrated."

The girl gave a perfunctory smile—the kind that screamed *I'm humoring you*—and returned to ignoring them both as she poked around on her cell phone, occasionally holding it up to take a selfie.

"Anyway, I need a centerpiece for my parents' anniversary dinner. Something with pink carnations, if you can. That's what she carried in her wedding bouquet. It's a big anniversary, so I want it to be perfect."

"I can do perfect," Marlee said, pulling out her order pad with one hand and sliding a catalog in front of the woman with the other. She flipped open the book and pointed to a pink bouquet. "What about something similar to this?"

The woman made an appreciative noise as she bent over the catalog.

The door opened and Dr. LaSalle stepped in, white coattail flapping. He stood behind the woman and the teenager with his arms folded, tapping his foot impatiently.

Marlee gave him an extra warm smile. “I’ll be right with you.”

Secretly, she loved that he was going to have to wait in line to complain. Maybe, if he had to wait long enough, he would just give up and leave her alone.

She took her time flipping the page on her order pad and even sharpened her pencil while the woman hemmed and hawed. The teenager began drifting around the shop, fiddling with this and that, and bending to pet Poppy, who was suddenly wide-awake now that attention was being doled out. Every two feet, it seemed, the girl would pause to snap a photo and type something into her phone. *Her own personal paparazzi*, Marlee thought.

“And do you have one of those bubble vases?” the woman said. “You know what I’m talking about?”

“Bubble vases…” Marlee thought longer than she needed to; she knew exactly where the bubble vases were. She pulled a bulbous-looking vase from under the counter. “Like this?”

“No, no,” the woman said. “The ones with the

little bubbles. They were popular in the '70s. They had those little nubs all over them?"

"Oh, you mean a hobnail vase." Marlee tapped the eraser of her pencil against her chin, mentally running through her inventory. She'd opened Blush & Bloom when she was twenty with little more than an idea, some natural talent, a few catalogs, and her parents' garage for a storefront. She'd worked hard and fast to build her business and, as a result, she'd accumulated a huge inventory in a short amount of time. Her backroom storage area was practically caving in with vases and pots and trinkets and decor.

That didn't include all the cabinets and shelves that lined the shop itself. There were a lot of things hiding in nooks and crannies. Sometimes it took days for her to locate something that she unequivocally knew was *around here somewhere*. "Where would I put a hobnail vase?"

Marlee trailed off, the woman and her daughter and Dr. LaSalle completely forgotten for the moment. She turned slowly, eyeing the shelves, trying to channel Past Marlee, who would have put it wherever it was least likely to get in her way. There was obviously not a huge demand for hobnail vases, and she hadn't seen one lying around in years. But the last time she saw one, she was pretty sure she saw it…

"Up there." She pointed to a corner shelf that stretched all the way to the ceiling. She gave the woman a smile. "I'll get it down." And then, to Dr. LaSalle, "I'll be another moment."

"I have patients," he said, coming to the counter.

"Thank you so much," Marlee said, pulling the rolling library ladder to the corner. "I appreciate your patience."

"No, not patience. *Patients*. People waiting to see me."

"Oh, you should go to them," Marlee said. "I'll come over there as soon as I have a moment. Maybe Monday? It's prom weekend."

"Do we have any black roses?" Morgan called, the phone tucked against her chest.

"Who on earth would want that?" the woman said.

The girl made a noise. "You're so old-fashioned. Black roses are so pretty. Dramatic."

"No, we don't," Marlee said, "but we do have blue roses and black glitter. I can make it work." She ascended the ladder.

"This can't wait until Monday." Dr. LaSalle came around the counter. "I need to speak with you now. If you don't mind."

"This will only take a minute," she said. "Whew, there's a lot of dust up here. Morgan, remind me to write *dusting spray* and *rags* on my shopping list. When Kimberly gets back, she and I have to do some deep cleaning here."

Dr. LaSalle was standing at the bottom of the ladder now. "I don't need a long conversation.

I'm just wondering if we can come to some sort of agreement about the parking situation."

Marlee held up a finger, enjoying his discomfort a little too much. "Just one more sec." She'd reached the highest she could go and still needed to stand on her tiptoes to peer back into the depths of the corners. She wasn't skittish by any means, but she didn't love the idea of blindly plunging her hands into dark hidey-holes that hadn't been disturbed in years and could very well feel like a home invasion to a cranky spider family.

"You do have a parking space along the side of your building here," the doctor continued, placing his hands on one of the lower rungs, as if to steady the ladder. "It's technically closer than where you've been parking. We've been through this. And I can't help thinking that maybe you're doing it on purpose."

"I think I might have two back there," she called to the woman, ignoring the doctor. "I'll bring them both down." She reached in and snatched the dusty vases, then hugged them to her chest with one arm while she held on to the ladder with the other.

Poppy had managed to con the teenager into picking her up. The girl was now posing for selfies with Poppy licking her cheek. Cute. But Poppy could get pretty wiggly when she wanted to. And the girl was only holding her with one arm. And loosely, at that.

"Be careful," Marlee said, leaning away from the ladder to try to get the girl's attention. "She might wriggle right out of your arms."

The girl either didn't hear her or was possibly ignoring her.

"I mean, you have way more parking next to your shop than I do in front of my clinic," Dr. LaSalle said. "It makes no logical sense. I'm just asking you to be fair."

"Sweetie, can you please hold my dog with two hands?"

"Celia, put the dog down," the woman said without looking up from the catalog. She turned the pages rapidly. "I'm thinking a white vase would look amazing. Do you have white?"

"Just one more picture," the girl whined. "She's so cute, and my followers are eating it up."

The woman absently waved her hand at the daughter. "You and that influencer nonsense."

"It's not nonsense. I have over two thousand followers now."

"You could park three vans on the side of your building if you wanted," Dr. LaSalle continued. "You're actually making it harder on yourself with where you're parking."

Marlee's head swam from all the activity surrounding her. So many voices, so many different conversations.

"You don't understand what it means to be an influencer," the girl said.

"You're thirteen. You have no influence."

The girl gave an overexaggerated look of being slighted. "How could you say something like that to me? You know it's my dream."

In the midst of all the chaos, Marlee hadn't realized how close her toes had gotten to the edge of the rung.

And then the dust got the best of her. She sneezed.

Her left foot slipped off first, but the movement was too swift for the right foot to take up the slack, and it slipped off as well. And then she was falling, the fingers of her free hand grasping for the side of the ladder but finding only space. The vases both tumbled from her arm and shattered on the floor. She let out a little shriek, her eyes squeezing shut as she fell.

And was caught around the waist by two strong, warm hands.

She opened her eyes and gazed down into Dr. LaSalle's face. *Not a bad last thing to see before plummeting to your death*, she thought, and then smiled with relief.

"Gesundheit," he said. Calm and cool.

Marlee's heart pounded. She'd never noticed his eyes before. Serious and curious, but with a spark of life that made him look a little dangerous. The muscles in his arms strained against his white coat as he held on to her, and she had a wild urge to reach down and wrap both hands around one of them, just to see if her fingertips could touch.

Marlee gripped the ladder and pulled herself away from Dr. LaSalle, finding her footing on the rungs again. It took a moment, and a couple of swallows, to find her voice. Adrenaline coursed through her, making her sweat.

It was the slip, she told herself. It was scary, and her body was reacting to that fear. It had nothing to do with the fact that she could still feel the heat of his hands against her waist.

"Are you okay?" he asked.

She nodded, glanced at the glass shards on the floor. "I'm good. Are you okay? The glass didn't get you, did it?"

"I'm totally fine." He ducked his head in a single nod, and stepped back from the ladder, appearing shy for the first time that Marlee had ever seen. She didn't hate it. But it made her feel awkward as she climbed down the last two steps of the ladder.

"Thank you. If you hadn't been here, I probably would have broken something other than the vases," she said. "Fortunately, you probably know how to set a broken bone, am I right?"

"I'm a pediatrician," he said.

She shrugged. "I would think a bone is a bone is a bone. Besides, I have small bones. Childlike, even."

She was trying to be funny, but was only making it weirder and sounding argumentative. He crossed his arms in his usual pose and glanced out the window again.

"Right," she said. "I'll get my keys."

CHAPTER TWO

MATTHEW LASALLE WASN'T accustomed to zaps of electricity. Matthew LaSalle was accustomed to routine. He was accustomed to two cups of coffee—one regular, one decaf—and a quick scroll of the news to start his day, and two cups of tea—both decaf, because lack of sleep equals years subtracted from your lifespan, and that's just a fact—and a solid, slow novel to end it. He was accustomed to patterns and intentions and parking spots that unequivocally belonged to him.

Okay, maybe not as unequivocally as he would prefer, but reasonably belonged to him, at the very least.

He was accustomed to shirts with collars and colorful neckties that distracted kids while he peered into their ears, and research reviews at lunch and carrying his laptop in an old-fashioned traveling doctor satchel because it was cool. Or at least his version of cool.

Which, he recognized, was maybe not traditionally cool. But he prided himself on not being traditional and had learned to embrace it before he was ten years old, so…yeah. Cool.

But Matthew LaSalle was not accustomed to zaps of electricity.

Yet that was exactly what he felt when he reached up to steady Marlee West as she began to fall off the ladder. *Zap!* Right through him, as if he'd reached up and touched a live wire. It had taken everything he had not to snatch his hands back in surprise.

Reaching for her was pure instinct. He would have steadied anyone who'd started to fall off a ladder in his presence.

But it had to be her. Why did it have to be her? The woman who interested, perplexed and maddened him on a daily basis. She ran around like she wasn't accustomed to much of anything. One of those seat-of-your-pants types. No schedule, no discipline. The type that frustrated him to no end.

Generally speaking, Matthew LaSalle noticed things. He noticed the scent of strep throat in a closed exam room before he even reached for a test strip. He noticed when his plants were thirsty. He noticed when Lynette, his receptionist, had her roots touched up, he noticed when she replaced the M&M's in her candy dish with jelly beans and he noticed when trash pickup was running an hour behind.

So, of course he'd noticed Marlee West. Way back in high school, he noticed her. She was hardly the kind of person who went unnoticed. She was small in stature, but huge in personality. She was loud. She was bold. She was always talking, always laughing that big, full-throated laugh of hers that drew a grin from him even when he was irritated that she was laughing. He had a suspicion that it was her diminutive stature that caused her to be so large in just about every other way. Compensation and all that.

He, on the other hand, was not as noticeable in school. In fact, he did everything he could to remain unnoticed. He was there to work, to learn, to build a future. He was busy owning who he was, because he liked who he was, which meant he stayed under the radar to keep teen ridicule at bay. He was pretty sure Marlee didn't even know there was a radar.

Besides, Marlee was a couple of years younger than him, so he'd never quite had a reason to approach her, anyway. They hadn't had any of the same classes. They didn't hang out in the same circles. They didn't do the same things—while he was marching across the football field with his trombone, she was cheering on the bull riders at the junior rodeos. While he was dissecting frogs with earnest concentration, she was releasing chickens in the field house as a prank.

But he'd noticed her. Because noticing things was what he did.

And he definitely noticed that zap. What *was*

that zap, anyway? It was lingering. He shook his head as he walked back to his office, hoping it would fall away. It wasn't falling away, though. Probably because she was following him.

She trailed him out of the flower shop and across the street.

"Again, thank you," she said.

He waved her away without so much as turning around. He didn't have a patient waiting, as he'd claimed, but his next appointment would be arriving soon, and he hated getting behind schedule. And he did not need his attention to be divided by that silly zap. "It was nothing."

"You saved my life," she said, breathless from trying to keep up.

He glanced over his shoulder. "At best, I saved you from a broken tibia. More likely, a sprained ankle. And some embarrassment."

"Well, it's the embarrassment that would have devastated me," she said. "I mean, none of my outfits would look as good with a cast."

He paused, glanced over his shoulder again. She was standing by the bumper of her delivery van, shading her eyes with her hand, grinning like the cat that ate the canary. Joking. Always joking.

He wasn't sure what to do with it. This was the middle of a workday, not open mic night at a comedy show.

He stood there awkwardly for another second

and then said, "You can thank me by moving your van."

She held up her keys, letting them dangle. "That's why I'm out here."

"And you can park it in front of your own shop from now on," he suggested. "If you're feeling really grateful."

"Hmm." She tilted her head and scrunched up her lips, thinking. Then, "Nope, I think I'm good. It wouldn't have been *that* embarrassing. My outfits look cute no matter what I wear with them."

He started to turn away but thought better of it. He squinted at her. "What is it?"

She blinked in confusion. "What is what?"

He pointed at the van. "You. And the van. Why are you always fighting me on this? Why don't you just park it by your shop?"

She had the gall to let irritation brush over her face. "This *is* by my shop. If you didn't notice, my shop is right across the street."

He gestured toward the front door of the clinic. "But it's literally right in front of my clinic. I have a lot of parents coming in here carrying a child. Or juggling multiple kids. Or just one toddler and a half dozen bags and toys and bottles." It wasn't true that he had a *lot*, exactly. He had a few, at best. But he was banking on her not noticing that little detail about his clinic. He doubted she noticed many details about, well…much of anything.

"Same," Marlee said, setting her jaw defiantly.

"Plus, older people who maybe can't walk as far without assistance. Do you have a lot of elderly people coming into your pediatric clinic, Dr. LaSalle?"

"Do you have a lot of expectant mothers, Miss West?" He felt himself twitch. He wasn't sure how far he wanted to take this argument. He wasn't really an arguer. Plus, he had a feeling that few people took on Marlee West and won.

"Do you have a lot of…anyone?" Marlee asked, and it was this barb that made him flinch just slightly. *Ouch.*

So she did notice.

His lack of patients was something that had been grieving him since he opened the clinic. He grew up in Haw Springs, and like everyone who grew up in Haw Springs, he saw Dr. Tidwell, the iconic, lovable general practitioner. The thing was—so did his mother. And, he was pretty sure, his grandmother before her. Dr. Tidwell was eighty if he was a day, and when Matthew made the decision to come home after medical school, he did so on the assumption that Dr. Tidwell's retirement would be forthcoming. He'd been smart about it, completing a combined Medicine-Pediatrics residency, in the hopes that he could start off as a pediatrician and transition to general practice as soon as Tidwell hung up the old stethoscope.

But, so far, no such luck.

And he'd begun to fear that he didn't have the time, or the money, to wait him out.

His practice was lean.

He was hardly running out of parking spaces. Not to legitimize her argument.

"That's what I thought." She tossed her keys in the air, caught them, turned on her heel and got inside the van. She rolled down the window and leaned out. "Thank you again!"

Matthew, perplexed and frustrated, watched her, and then continued his course into his office, trying to let everything go. Trying to let Marlee West, and that lingering zap, go.

He snuck in through the side door, hoping to go unnoticed. Maybe Lynette hadn't realized yet that he was running behind. Or maybe she'd noticed, but had figured he was in his office, poring over books, trying to identify a difficult rash or a cough that sounded uncharacteristic.

Instead, she was standing in his office doorway to intercept him, her arms crossed, her cardigan pulled snug around her. She was wearing her glasses, peering at him over the top of them, the chain that held them around her neck dangling by her cheeks.

"Your eleven o'clock is here early," she said.

Matthew liked Lynette. She was a friend of his mom's, and had been in his life since literally the day he was born. A retired elementary school secretary, she was kind and sweet, unflappable when it came to children, and unafraid not to take any nonsense from anyone.

Including him.

"I'll be right there. I was—"

"I know where you were," she said. "Next time, why don't you let me go over?"

"Because…" He faltered.

This wasn't the first time Lynette had volunteered to walk across the street and give Marlee West what-for. She was protective of Matthew. But there was something about the idea that rubbed him the wrong way. At first, he told himself it was that he wanted to fight his own battles.

But over time he'd begun to suspect that it was something different, something more, that had kept him from allowing her to go over there.

He suspected that somewhere along the line, he'd begun to enjoy his little spars with Marlee West. That he didn't mind seeing her midway through his day.

That he wanted to battle her himself, only closer and in person.

Until today, the battle had been partly frustrating, and partly…fun.

"Oh," Lynette said, placing one hand on a hip and blocking his doorway. "I see."

"No," he said, edging past her to get to this satchel. "You don't *see* anything."

She threw up her hands. "Matthew, she's hardly

a troll. Who wouldn't see? You like her. It's a good thing. I promised your mom that I wouldn't let you just lock yourself in your office with blinders on all the time."

"I don't do that."

"No," she said. "You occasionally come out to go over there and...*not see* her."

"I'll have you know, it was a good thing that I was there. If I hadn't been, she would have been severely injured falling off a ladder. She might have broken an ankle."

He pawed through his bag, giving the inventory a once-over, as if it could have changed between his last appointment and this one. It was a way for him to center himself. A way to mentally prepare to see a patient. His eleven o'clock was a new patient; he had to be on his game. He literally couldn't afford to blow it. This day had gone off the rails in so many ways. He had to get it back on track.

"I'll let the invitation stand," Lynette said. "If you want me to take care of the parking situation once and for all, just say the word. If you're enjoying going over there—if you're working on a plan of some sort—"

"There's no plan. The plan is to get her to stop parking in front of my clinic. That's it. That's the whole plan."

She held up a finger to stop him. It worked. "Either way, your eleven o'clock is waiting for you, and it's not like you to keep someone waiting."

He took a breath, his thoughts finally settled, and let it out. "Lynette, listen. It's not a big deal. She parks on my side. I don't know why. I go over there and handle it. I come back here. I see my patients. Sometimes I get a little behind. It's not a big deal."

"Okay, if you say so."

"Thank you for your offer. And tell my mom I said hello."

She raised her eyebrows innocently. "Who said I would be talking to your mom?"

He followed her out the door and down the hallway, where she turned right to return to the reception desk and he turned left to go to the exam room. "And tell her I love her."

Matthew LaSalle noticed things. But he was feeling a little off-kilter, as if he hadn't noticed everything he'd meant to notice this morning. His thoughts were clouded.

His heart was still beating faster and harder than the norm. He hadn't gotten a good inventory of his satchel. There was a light line of sweat in his hairline.

And in the back of his mind was the surprised look on Marlee's face when she opened her eyes to see who had caught her. She'd smiled, so warm and trusting and grateful.

It wasn't a big deal.

It wasn't a big deal.
It wasn't a big deal.
So why did it feel like it was?

CHAPTER THREE

MARLEE'S ALARM HAD dragged her out of a deep, deep sleep. She emerged into reality, feeling as if she'd only just closed her eyes moments before. She was vaguely aware of soft, rhythmic movement nearby, along with the faint tinkle of Poppy's tags as she steadily groomed her paws, leisurely sprawled across the empty half of Marlee's bed, as if it belonged to her and Marlee was sleeping in the empty half of *her* bed. Marlee blinked the sleep out of her eyes. Poppy stopped, the very tip of her tongue sticking out from between her lips. She peered into Marlee's face, as if to make certain that she wasn't mistaken, then wagged and hopped up, ready to start her day. She pranced in place, then leapt to the floor, her effort to lead Marlee to the door.

"I wish I had your energy," Marlee groaned. "How can you be so instantly perky?"

Poppy pranced in place, showing off. She hopped in a circle, then jumped back up on the bed and then down again.

"Yeah, yeah, I know you've been waiting on me." Marlee yawned. "To be fair, you slept for most of the day yesterday, and all evening while I was finishing up those corsages. You are way more rested than I am. Not the best assistant in the world, I might add."

Poppy let out an impatient bark.

"Hey, Little Miss Antsy. Give me a second. I just woke up. Sheesh." Marlee sat up and yawned again, the blankets pooling around her waist. Her fingers were red and sore. Her arms hurt. Her neck ached. Her feet throbbed. She never wanted to look at another corsage for the rest of her life.

She couldn't count the number of times she'd heard someone claim that being a florist must be easy work, *just standing around sniffing flowers*. But there was a lot more to it than most people knew.

For example, sometimes—like at least twice a year, every year, until you died—you stood around *sniffing flowers* while you wrapped them in miles of iridescent ribbon, your feet going numb and your fingers freezing into painful claws. She kicked the blankets off and instantly noticed an angry bruise on her shin. And then sometimes, while *sniffing flowers*, you fell off a ladder while looking for a vase. A vase that, in the end, became shards of broken glass on the floor. She flopped back against her pillow.

"Ugh. I don't want to get up."

Poppy let out another bark, and then returned

to the mattress, zeroing in on her target; she set to exuberantly licking Marlee's face as if to say, *I'm done playing around.*

"Okay, okay, I'll get up."

She stood, tied her robe around her waist and dropped her cell phone into her robe's pocket. Poppy eagerly led her to the back door, doing a little doggy dance as if one more second could cause her bladder to burst.

Marlee opened the door and let the little dog out, then stood and enjoyed the early morning fresh air while Poppy scurried around the yard in her usual circuit, sniffing the ground along the fence line, under the bird feeder and in a circle around the base of the birdbath. Marlee closed her eyes and took a deep, cleansing breath.

There was something different about morning fresh air than any other time of the day. When Marlee was younger, she would have sworn that there was something actually in it—something that would wake a person just as swiftly as a gulp of caffeine. There was a sweetness to it that she liked to think of as *eau de small town.* It was the scent of hay and grass with just a hint of woodsmoke. And something farmy lurking beneath. It filled her soul.

When she was feeling extra energetic, she would sometimes take Poppy for morning walks, timed so that the sun would rise while they were out. She always came home in the best mood when she did that. It was the perfect start to her day.

Today wasn't that day. In fact, if Kimberly didn't call in sick, Marlee just might choose to go back to bed for a while.

She shut the back door and scuffed around the kitchen, putting on a pot of coffee and then pouring and eating a bowl of cereal while she waited for it to brew. Finished, she took her cup to her favorite spot in her whole house—the window seat in her bedroom. It was her little reading nook, which she covered with fluffy cushions and pillows, and hid from the world behind gauzy, sheer curtains. She curled up on the window seat and idly thumbed open her email to see if any last-minute orders had come through overnight.

She took a sip of coffee as she waited for her email to load.

And then nearly spit the coffee across the room when it did.

"What the…?" she said, staring at the number of notifications.

When it came to any given school dance, she could count on stragglers. There were always those two or three truly last-minute dates secured or last-minute people who somehow managed to get through life on procrastination, emergency action and apologies.

But this was more than a couple of stragglers. This was dozens. This was…confusing.

She opened the first order.

"Oak Hollow?" she said aloud. "Since when do they order from me?" She opened another order. "Oak Hollow." And another. "Riverside? They're an hour and a half away from here. Why would someone come all that way for a..." She scanned the order. "A basic corsage?"

Her thumb shook as it wavered over the phone screen, her brow furrowed. Something definitely wasn't right. Oak Hollow was close—maybe halfway between Haw Springs and Riverside—and sometimes teens would get on a bandwagon. It wasn't without reason that someone might have seen her work and decided they wanted something out of the ordinary from what all their friends were doing.

But Riverside was a different story. It was a bigger city. They had choices. They were equidistant from Haw Springs and Kansas City, where they probably had hundreds of choices. Why would they choose her?

It had to be a mistake. She would need to get to Blush & Bloom, see if she could make sense of it on her computer.

Her phone buzzed in her hand, and she nearly dropped it, realizing only at that moment that her body was on high alert. She answered on speaker, continuing to scroll through email while she talked.

"Good morning," a singsong voice said on the

other end. Her best friend, Ellory DeCloud. "How does a lavender peach blossom latte sound?"

"Sounds…flowery," Marlee said, distracted.

Ellory made a disappointed noise. "And here I thought you would be my customer most likely to love it."

"It has to be a mistake," Marlee said in wonder.

"No, I actually had you in my mind as the ideal customer while I was making it," Ellory said. "I thought it would be a great spring cross-promotion between us. I guess I was wrong. I'll scrap it. You don't even want to try it?"

"What?" Marlee said, snapping out of it. "Oh. No. I mean, yes. I will definitely try it. It sounds great, and I love the idea of cross-promoting. I was just trying to make sense of something."

"Make sense of what? Are you okay?"

"Yeah. I think so." Marlee thumbed out of her email. "You know what? I have to get on my computer, anyway, so I'm going to toss on some clothes and come try that coffee, okay? I'll tell you all about it when I get there. Maybe you can help me make sense of what's happening here."

Marlee got dressed at lightning speed, let Poppy inside and fed her breakfast.

"I'll be right back," she said, patting the dog's head lightly, but Poppy was already curling up in her dog bed and settling in for her midmorning nap. She, too, had probably had enough of the flower shop for one week.

The Baked Bean was Ellory's creative and trendy coffee shop right next door to Blush & Bloom. The shop, originally named The Dreamy Bean before Ellory added baked goods to her menu, stayed true to its theme, with cloud-and-rainbow decor that made it feel somewhere between ethereal and cartoonish, and a pervasive scent of dark roast, cinnamon and vanilla that enveloped you like a hug. Every month, Ellory experimented with a new flavor, and Marlee was often the first recipient of said flavor. Black licorice and orange spice cold brew in October, mint cookie mocha in March, lavender peach blossom in May. They were all delicious as far as Marlee was concerned. Ellory had a gift.

Ellory was a transplant to Haw Springs, and she and Marlee had hit it off immediately. Ellory was drawn in by Marlee's energy, and Marlee was thrilled by Ellory's dreamlike quality.

When Marlee arrived, Ellory was sitting with Mr. Crowley, an elderly regular who walked to The Baked Bean every morning for a cup of coffee, a bite to eat and an actual paper newspaper that Ellory subscribed to specifically for him. And, of course, for Ellory's company, which she was more than happy to provide. Ellory had once confided in Marlee that Mr. Crowley was sort of a grandfather figure for her.

She must have sensed that something was wrong because she stood when Marlee walked in, alarm etching across her face, leaving Mr. Crowley mid-sentence. "What?" she asked, before Marlee could say a single word. "What's wrong?"

This was the reason Marlee loved Ellory the most. It wasn't just about the proximity of their shops to one another, nor was it the free experimental coffee flavors chosen just for her. It was the connection the two had. She would do anything for Ellory, and she knew without a shadow of a doubt that Ellory would do anything for her.

She held her phone in the air. "I actually don't know. Nothing is wrong, exactly. But something isn't right. I have all these new orders. They came in overnight. Like, twenty corsages."

Ellory reached out and gave Marlee's hand a quick squeeze. "That's great! Prom is this weekend. Makes total sense." She frowned as Marlee shook her head. "But…it doesn't make sense? Why? I don't understand."

"It doesn't make sense because I've filled all the prom orders from Haw Springs. These orders aren't for Haw Springs' prom." Marlee pulled up her email and opened a random order, then turned her phone face out so Ellory could read it. "Oak Hollow."

Ellory peered at the phone, her brow furrowed, and then looked at Marlee, shaking her head, not understanding. "Oak Hollow is close by. I think their prom is next weekend, from what I hear. Maybe their florist went out of business."

"They didn't ever have one," Marlee said. "They always just go to Riverside. I've been trying for years to figure out how to get them to come to me instead."

"Congratulations," Ellory said. "Looks like you got them. What did you do?"

Marlee shrugged. "That's the thing. I didn't *do* anything. And look at this." She pulled up the Riverside order. "I don't know what happened. I'm nobody in Riverside. How did people hear about me overnight? And there are probably three places in Riverside where they can get flowers. Why come here? Twenty new orders." Her phone made a little noise, and she glanced at it. Another email alert. "Twenty-one."

Ellory wrapped Marlee in a hug. "You're worrying over nothing. It makes sense. You work so hard, and you're so talented. It's about time people noticed." She put her hands on Marlee's shoulders and pushed her out to arm's length, so she could look her in the eye. "This is good news. I'm excited for you. Don't be freaked out."

"I'm not freaked out," Marlee mumbled.

"You seem a little bit freaked out."

Marlee's phone dinged again. "Twenty-two!" she cried, admittedly sounding more than a little bit freaked out.

Ellory thought for a second, then gasped and snapped her fingers. "Wait. You said they came in overnight? I have an idea. Let me see your phone."

Marlee turned it over and waited, her stomach in knots while Ellory typed and scrolled. Suddenly, she stopped. "Oh. Oh!" She pushed her hand to her mouth and let out a little giggle. "Oh!"

"What?" Marlee asked, her stomach dropping even further. "*Oh, oh, oh* what?" She scurried to look over Ellory's shoulder. Those *oh*'s were definitely freaking her out.

"You're all over social media." Ellory's giggle grew longer, and then louder as she handed the phone over to Marlee.

"What? How? I don't even have social media." This had been a point of contention between Marlee and her marketing expert sister, Morgan, who insisted that a strong social media presence was a necessity for twenty-first century business promotion. Marlee was determined to avoid it as long as possible. All of her customers were right there in Haw Springs. Saying hello over the oranges at the supermarket was all the business promotion she needed. She didn't have the time, nor the stomach, for sounding interesting online. Her eyes landed on the photo. And, worse, the caption. "Oh, no. Is this for real? You think people saw this?"

Ellory glanced at the post. "I don't think it, I know it. A lot of people saw this. Do you see how many hearts it got? Over a thousand in less than twenty-four hours. And a lot of people shared it, too. I'm surprised you're not getting orders from California."

Marlee made an anguished noise. "How would I fill an order in California?"

"Don't freak out. You got a business boost. And, you have to admit, it's a really cute photo."

The photo was a selfie of the teenager who had been in Blush & Bloom the day before. But it had been zoomed and cropped so that only about half of the girl's face and one Poppy paw showed in the very corner.

In the background, she had captured Marlee's slip on the ladder. Only it didn't look like a slip, because Matthew had caught her. Instead of capturing a fall, it had captured Matthew reaching up, his hands on her waist to steady her. He gazed up at her, the surprise on his face looking a little more like longing. And she gazed down at him, her eyebrows arched, her mouth slightly parted in a soft smile. Relief looking for all the world like adoration. The only way someone could know that something was wrong in that moment was the slight loosening of her grip on the vase in her hand.

The caption on the photo read: *Forget prom, I just want someone to look at me the way he looks at her. #RelationshipGoals #cutestcouple #dreamydoctor #HawSpringsflorist #Blushand-Bloomromance*

"Okay, fine," Marlee said. "It's a cute photo. But what happened wasn't at all what it looks like. I was falling off the ladder. And Matt—Dr.

LaSalle—just happened to be there, complaining at me like always. It was hardly a romantic moment, and he for sure wasn't looking at me in any sort of way."

Ellory arched one eyebrow at her friend, grinning.

"And I wouldn't exactly call him dreamy," Marlee said. "Some days I would describe him more like a nightmare."

Ellory's eyebrow arch deepened.

"A parking nightmare. Just when you thought it was safe to park, *The Parking Nightmare on Main Street*, barging through a front door near you."

Ellory let out a bark of laughter that caused everyone in the shop to look up. "I remember when I thought Rowan was a big, old grump," she said. "But it turned out he was the grump of my dreams."

"Yes, your husband was a Scrooge. But that's very different from a general grump. And that's beside the point," Marlee said. "I don't understand how one girl can get so many people to look at her post. Explain that."

"Well," Ellory said, taking Marlee's phone and scrolling some more. "Someone with a whole lot of followers must have gotten a hold of it. Once that happens, these kinds of things tend to spread like wildfire. Ope. Yeah. There it is. Oh, my."

"Oh, my what?" Marlee grabbed her phone out of Ellory's hand and stared at the screen.

The first comment read: Hey @ModernVowMag, cute doc and flower shop together?!?!?! What are you waiting for?

Followed by a comment from the popular relationship and wedding planner *Modern Vow Magazine* itself: We will reach out! Then they shared the post on their own page with the caption: *We say "I do" to this couple. Feature coming? We hope so!*

"Wait, is this real? *Modern Vow Magazine?* That can't be real. Is it real?" Marlee's hands trembled, struggling to hold on to her phone. It buzzed again with another order. She couldn't look away. "What does this mean?"

Ellory had sneaked behind the coffee bar and began making a cup of coffee. "Girl, it means you went viral. And it sounds like you're about to do a spread for *Modern Vow Magazine* with your adorable doctor boyfriend." She pushed a cup across the counter; Marlee's nose lit up with the scent of lavender.

"Viral? How is it possible to go viral when I don't have social media?"

"That doesn't matter," Ellory said. "The right person at the right time captured just the right moment and had the right thing to say about it." She pointed at Marlee's phone. "That teenager knows what she's doing online. She's probably over the moon about it right now."

Marlee had no trouble imagining the girl's excitement. Being an influencer was her dream, she'd said. This photo would undoubtedly help her along that journey.

Ellory had made herself a cup of coffee, too, and came around the counter with it. She tapped it against Marlee's cup in a toast. "Congratulations, my friend. You and dreamy doctor are the it couple of the season, whether you want to be or not."

Ellory sipped her coffee, but Marlee stood like a statue, her phone in one hand and her steaming drink in the other.

The *it* couple.

The *it* couple?

Whether you want to be or not.

Well, she most definitely did not.

No way.

Not even a little bit…

…did she?

CHAPTER FOUR

MATTHEW LIKED GROWING up in Haw Springs. He liked the way the air smelled, sweet and floral, undercut by something animalistic and earthy. He liked the thrum of a summer evening, the busy hum of insects and whinnying of horses giving way to the songs of frogs by the ponds. He especially liked the certainty that if he stopped by his parents' house on a Saturday night, there would be meat loaf and mashed potatoes and a place set for him at the table, whether he was coming or not.

Tonight, he was coming. He was hungry for meat loaf, and even hungrier for friendly faces.

The truth was, Matthew never even considered living anywhere other than Haw Springs. While he was in school, he pined for returning home and would spend his long nights bent over homework, fighting daydreams of sitting on his parents' front porch, a sweating glass of iced tea resting on his thigh, faceless children that shared his blood running around in the yard, shrieking under the cold prickle of hose water against their backs, just as he had done as a child. As his classmates vied for prestigious hospital positions in big cities, he never even considered anything but a future in private practice in his beloved hometown.

When Matthew went away to college on the East Coast, these were the moments that he missed the most. Some days, when he was so sleep deprived, he thought he would possibly just fall to the floor, mid-step, out like a light, it was only the thought of coming home permanently that kept him going. He would daydream so vividly he almost thought he could smell the hay on the air right in the middle of the hospital. On the day he graduated, his bags were already packed to come home before he even donned his cap and gown.

Only, in his daydream, there was room for a private practice in his hometown. There was a living to be made, because he would be the only doctor making it.

His head was heavy with worry that he would be forced out. But as he opened his parents' screen door and let himself in, those worries faded away into the scent of meat loaf that immediately drew out a deep hunger.

"There he is!" his mom called, coming at him with arms raised.

"Hi, Mom," he said, accepting a hug and a kiss on the cheek. "You got enough for one more at the table?" He knew she did. Far more than enough. Asking was part of the ritual.

"Of course we do, pal. Come on in." His dad's voice floated in from the living room, where he was watching a baseball game. "Royals are up two."

Matthew unwound himself from his mom and then unwound himself from his lab coat, which he dutifully hung on a peg on the coat-tree by the door, and followed his dad's voice.

"What inning?"

"Third. Have a seat. Eat some pretzels. Long day?"

Matthew sighed. "Not long enough." He popped the soda open, and the two of them waited through two full at-bats before he spoke again. "Three ear infections, that's all. In and out."

"Jerry, huh?" his dad asked without looking away from the TV, as his mom appeared out of nowhere and pressed a cold soda into his hand.

Matthew nodded as his dad popped open the soda. A player smacked the ball and both he and his father hooted as the player ran to second base. Matthew grabbed a handful of pretzels and settled back in his chair. "Yep. Jerry," he finally said.

Jerry Tidwell, MD. He was a family doctor in every sense of the word. Even Matthew and his sister, Sarah, saw him all the way through high school. Dr. Tidwell was a thousand years old but still sharp as a tack, and with the bedside manner of a kindly and funny grandpa.

Matthew didn't want Dr. Tidwell to retire. But he kind of needed him to. Or to at least let up the stranglehold he had on Haw Springs' newborn population.

"Have you advertised in Oak Hollow?"

"They've got their own version of Jerry," Matthew said. "Only younger. Dr. Karen Mallinson, a family practice superhero. After a full, back-to-back day of seeing patients, she'll show up to help repaint the nursery at Second Methodist and bring chocolate chip cookies to share with the other painters. She's untouchable, and for good reason."

His father grinned and glanced at him. "How good are you at baking?"

"Not good enough."

"What about Riverside?"

Matthew waved his father's suggestion away. "Who's going to drive an hour and a half with a sick kid?"

"Someone who wants the best care for their child, that's who." Matthew's mom stood in the doorway, a dish towel hanging from one hand. "It's ready if you're ready."

It's ready if you're ready was Matthew's mom's way of saying, *Come to the table before it gets cold, no matter what inning it is.* He and his father dutifully stood, just as the front door burst open and Matthew's younger sister Sarah barreled in.

"There better be enough meat loaf for me," she called, her approach to…well, everything in life, really…slightly more assertive than Matthew's. Sarah was a nursing student in her third year. She drove to Riverside daily to go to school and didn't seem the least bit fazed by the hour-and-a-half commute.

And of course there was enough meat loaf. There always was. A hundred family members could walk in, and there would be enough meat loaf. He didn't know how his mother did it, but she did.

They filed into the kitchen, the baseball game muted but still playing. If Matthew's dad leaned slightly to the left, he could keep up with the score. Everyone sat in the chairs they'd been sitting in for Matthew's and Sarah's whole lives. Matthew's mom said a quick blessing, and then they dug in, all formality gone, Sarah babbling on about something she'd learned in class, quizzing Matthew, just as she'd always loved to do. And him batting down the questions, answering them easily—*boom-boom-boom*—just as he'd always loved to do. Tradition. It was how things were meant to be.

Matthew noticed things. And he was actively noticing that this was exactly the way he loved his life to be, when his phone buzzed in his pocket.

He ignored it. Maybe sometime down the road, he would need to check, just in case it was an urgent situation with a patient. But that moment wasn't now. He continued eating.

His phone buzzed again.

And then again.

Okay, this was highly unusual.

Frowning, he dug his phone out of his pocket and stared at the screen. He'd missed three phone calls, all from the same number—one that wasn't in his contacts. As he watched, a voicemail popped up.

Everyone stopped eating and stared as he lifted his phone to his ear.

"Sorry," he said. "I'm sure it's nothing..." He trailed off as a woman's voice filled his ear.

"We've been getting so many of those spam calls," he heard his mother say.

But Matthew's mind trailed off, too, as it took in exactly who had been calling him. It was *her*. His skin prickled at the sound of her voice, light and lilting in that life-is-such-a-funny-joke way of hers. He could practically see the wrinkle in her nose that she got when she wondered aloud why it was such a big deal where she parked.

"...got your number from my sister..." she was saying. Morgan McBride, who had his number from an event that he helped her with a year before. He should have known he'd regret making that connection, even though it resulted in four new patients for him, including Morgan's autistic son, Archer. He scooted away from the table and left the room to listen harder.

"Oooh," he heard his sister coo from the table. "Matthew needs privacy."

"Anyway, so the weirdest thing happened… you're probably not going to believe it because honestly I don't believe it. This is just…" A delighted laugh. "You just have to see it to believe it, maybe? I don't know. I never expected anything like this. The kid really is an influencer… and, oh I just noticed, there's Poppy's paw. I'm rambling. I swear I'm not normally a rambler. This has got me rambling and you probably think I'm crazy. Well, you already think that." Another laugh that sounded somewhat unhinged. Matthew found himself smiling at her delight, while also feeling that prickle on his skin again. She probably hadn't meant to actually call him. This call was likely meant for someone else. Morgan had misunderstood and had accidentally given her his phone number instead of another. He heard her take a deep breath and let it out in a happy sigh that had just a twinge of nerves to it. "Just call me, okay? Soon. Or not? I don't know. Ellory says soon. Or you can come by the shop. I'll be here pretty late tonight. I've got…" Another nervous giggle. "Okay. Thanks, bye."

Matthew pulled the phone away from his ear and stared at it, as if it held answers to the million questions that were running through his mind at that moment. She was right—he did think she was a little…well, crazy wasn't the right word. Excitable, though? Maybe. Energetic, for sure.

"Is everything okay?" his mom called from the kitchen.

"Royals scored," his dad said, not caring in the least about Matthew's phone call.

Matthew gave his phone one last look and then pocketed it. "That's great," he said, shoving his curiosity away, trying to ignore the buzzing just under his skin. He would have to call her later, after dinner. But, until then, he would be on edge. "Everything's fine. Just a, uh, I guess a business phone call. I'll deal with it later."

He returned to his spot, and the conversation thankfully turned to Sarah. He nodded and *mmm-hmm*'ed in all the right spots as he ate his meat loaf.

It had grown cold while he was on the phone.

But he was too distracted, and way too curious, to care.

CHAPTER FIVE

MARLEE WAS A stress-pacer and always had been. She'd done more pacing the length of her shop than working in it at this point. She couldn't stop pacing after her conversation with Ellory.

Which was bad, given that the orders kept coming, and Oak Hollow's dance was in one week. She already knew that she couldn't ask Morgan for help. Ellory was swamped, trying to get her food menu up and running. And she felt bad asking her parents for help. She'd done enough of that just to get the shop off the ground. They'd put in just as much blood, sweat and tears as she had, and had ponied up a lot of money on top of that. As long as she still owed them, she felt guilty even asking them for the tiniest favor. Her parents were the best. They'd given everything to their daughters. They deserved a break.

So she had to get these orders processed herself.

Her phone made a noise again, and she jumped to look at it, on high alert. It was from Annie Allbrook, Haw Springs sweetheart, whose wedding was right around the corner.

What do you think of pink? the text read.

Pink is great! Marlee responded.

Or maybe purple. Yes, definitely purple.

Purple is great too!

But maybe teal.

Annie's wedding to McBride Ranch's hand, Ben Werth, was the talk of Haw Springs. It seemed Annie had invited the entire town, plus out-of-town family members. It was going to be huge, which was great news—a big order—for Marlee. The only problem was, Annie had changed her mind on flowers a hundred times, and would likely change it a hundred more before the wedding date arrived. Eventually she would have to come to a final decision, and Marlee would have to execute the plan, but how could she do that if she was inundated with orders? She would have to somehow get Kimberly to come back to work. Maybe even hire another assistant.

Still. The orders. It was exciting to have them. It was exciting to think about hiring new people, having a full staff, maybe even branching out with shops in Oak Hollow and Riverside and possibly even Kansas City. She could become a franchise.

She didn't know what that entailed, but she could figure it out. The giddy dreams had started to set in, bidden or not, and she couldn't help but let them excite her.

Nervous excitement. Terrified excitement.

"Stop pacing, start working," she said aloud. Poppy trotted after her as she paced the length of the store one more time. "You're right. I should feed you first," Marlee said.

She went to the back room to retrieve a can of dog food. Her limbs felt electric, her heart buzzy, her head swimmy, but in a good way. She giggled as she opened the can and scooped the food into Poppy's bowl. In all her pacing, she had begun to cobble together a plan. It was crazy, maybe even insane, and it required Matthew LaSalle, of all people, to cooperate with her.

But if it worked…it could really work.

When she reemerged into the shop, Matthew was standing there, looking just as perplexed as she felt. She wondered if he'd heard her laughing in the back. Perhaps he was thinking that she was losing it more than just a little bit.

Perhaps she was. Because, seriously, if she was in her right mind, would she have asked him to come over? Dr. LaSalle, the man she most actively ducked and dived to avoid?

He wasn't wearing his white lab coat, a sight she hadn't seen since high school, and she couldn't help noticing the way his shirt tugged against his biceps. He'd also taken off his tie and unbuttoned the top button of his shirt. She didn't mind this more casual version of him. It was disarming in a way that she needed at that exact moment.

He held up his phone and wiggled it in the air. His clothing might have looked more casual, but his face still carried his nine-to-five annoyance. So much for being disarmed. "Did you mean to call me, or was that meant for someone else?"

Marlee realized that in all the pacing, she'd never quite worked out what she was going to say to him when he arrived. How she was going to convince him to do what she wanted him to do. She wasn't even sure she had convinced herself yet. Or that she'd even worked it out completely. She forced her feet to move toward him.

"It was for you," she said. "Sorry if I interrupted something."

He tucked the phone into his back pocket. "You didn't." No explanation. He wasn't doing much to calm her nerves, that was for sure.

"Good. So, um…have you seen it yet?"

He crossed his arms, frowned. "Seen what?"

She pulled out her phone and walked toward him. "I didn't mention it in my message?"

"You didn't mention anything fully in your message."

She let out a breath. Her thoughts were so scattered. She was still trying to wrap her head around what happened. Leaving the message for

Matthew was like an out-of-body experience. She didn't know what to say to him, only that something needed to be said.

She pulled up the screenshot she'd taken of the post and handed her phone to him.

"'Forget prom, I just want…'" He trailed off as he read, then continued "'Hashtag Blush and Bloom romance'? What is this?"

Marlee realized that her hands were shaking. Adrenaline? Nerves? Yes, and yes. "Look at the comments. There are…a lot."

He thumbed to the next photo, and the next, a frown deepening as he stared at the phone, his head slowly shaking. She could tell he was receiving this just as unbelievably as she had. "You posted this?" he asked, handing the phone back to her. She could swear a blush had pinkened his cheeks. "Why?"

"No, it wasn't me," she said, taking the phone back. "Until twenty minutes ago, I didn't even have social media. I don't love it. I don't have time for it, and never really saw a need for it. All of my family is right here, all of my friends, my customers. Everyone is in Haw Springs."

"Same," Matthew said, then mumbled, "Sort of."

"This was posted by the girl who was in here yesterday." She pointed at the half of the girl's face that was showing in the photo. "She said she wants to be an influencer. I didn't take her seriously, but maybe I should have, huh?"

He glanced around the shop, as if the girl might still be there. "I didn't notice her, I guess," he said.

Marlee turned off her phone and dropped it into her apron pocket. "Well, apparently a lot of people do notice her. Online. And we, um, went viral." She shrugged as if to apologize, though she wasn't sure why.

"We went viral," he repeated.

"It means—"

He held up a hand to stop her. "No, I know what it means to go viral. But I wasn't looking at you the way she's suggesting. She's put a spin on it."

"I know," Marlee said, although if she was pressed to describe exactly how he was looking at her in the photo, she might also have described it as a *way* of some sort. And was that very different from some sort of way? She wasn't sure.

"I was looking at you like I wanted you to move your van."

"I know," she repeated.

"I was looking at you like I didn't want you to fall from a ladder and become seriously injured."

"I know," she said once more.

"This is what's wrong with social media, you know," he said, pointing toward her apron pocket. "There's no context. People think all kinds of untrue things, just because they saw it in writing somewhere. Regardless of who wrote it or why."

He started to pace, covering the same ground she had been covering before he'd arrived. Ah. So he was also a stress-pacer. Finally, something they had in common.

"I know that too," she said softly, trailing after him. "It's just…"

He stopped, turned to face her. "It's just what?"

She grabbed the phone out of her apron pocket again and tapped it alive. She pulled up her email and turned the screen to face him. "I've gotten a ton of new business."

Marlee had the whole spiel worked out in her head, but now that she was close to him, in the radius of his grumpiness, she felt shy and unsure. Her voice didn't want to work. Her hand shook, forcing her to grip her phone tighter. Truthfully, she didn't know Matthew LaSalle all that well. She only knew the displeased side of him. She had no idea what would appease him, other than moving a van from one parking spot to another one twenty feet away. Was he that simple? Not likely.

He let out a breathy laugh and rolled his eyes. "My point exactly. People don't know you. They believe this nonsense and now suddenly they want to be part of it. Thanks for showing me. I'm sure it'll blow over quickly."

He started toward the door. Marlee's heart leapt into her throat, threatening to choke her voice into nonexistence. *Say it with your chest, Marlee*, she heard Morgan's voice say in the back of her mind. *You've never been intimidated by anything or anyone. So just come out with it.*

"You could get a ton of new business, too."

He stopped, but didn't turn to face her. She took this as her chance, swallowed, and kept going. "If we…leaned into it?"

Slowly, he turned. "Leaned into it. What exactly are you saying?"

She hurried toward him, still cradling the phone in her hand, as if presenting evidence. "I'm saying if we go with it—just for a little while—maybe it can be lucrative for both of us. I'm not trying to be rude or anything, but I've noticed that your clinic is hardly swarmed by patients."

"It takes time to build a practice. People aren't going to choose a doctor based on something they saw online. I don't sell flowers."

Marlee felt her hackles try to rise, but she tamped them down. Getting angry and fighting wouldn't get her what she wanted. She had to stay calm and get on his good side. If he had one. Which she was beginning to doubt. She shrugged off the comment and moved on.

"It's not a criticism. It's the point I'm trying to make. It takes time. Or—" she wiggled the phone screen at him again and gave a hopeful grin "—a little help?"

"So we *go with it*. What do you mean, *go with it*?" he asked.

She shrugged. She hadn't really thought this

part all the way through yet. She wasn't sure what exactly *go with it* could mean. "You know…make it look…real?"

His frown deepened. "Make it look real how?"

"We could post a couple of photos? Morgan said we could kind of like…thank the girl?" She hated that she was ending everything like a question. She stood taller, tried to exude confidence. "I opened an account. We can do it there. Morgan said I could just use the same hashtags and people would see it."

"But it's not real."

"I know," she said, this time the words coming out more exasperated than anything else. "I know it's not real. But we could make it look that way." She pointed to the ladder photo. "That wasn't real, but it sure looks like it is, and you can see it. I can see it. If you told yourself that this couple was in love, you'd believe it, too." She felt her cheeks grow warm. Something about saying the words *in love* gave her a squicky feeling deep down. This could be a terrible idea. She could be treading into an alliance that was more exasperation than anything.

"No," Matthew said. "It doesn't feel right. I'm not doing it. It's a lie."

"You said yourself, everything out there is a lie. People believe it because they want to believe it. Maybe because they need to believe it."

"Why would someone need to believe a fake

love story between two people they don't know and will probably never meet?"

"I don't know. Maybe because sometimes it can be hard to believe that love exists out there for anyone."

"That's bleak."

She bit her lip, trying not to show the wave of emotion that was threatening to wash over her. *They. Right. Not you, though, Marlee. You certainly wouldn't be part of the cynical* They *who don't believe.* "Maybe," she said. "People can be bleak."

They stared each other down for a beat too long. Marlee began to feel uncomfortable, but just as she was about to give up, she felt something shift.

"I'll never park in front of your shop again," she said. "One photo. Two, tops."

He let out a low chuckle and shook his head at the floor, hands on hips. "Wow. You're playing hardball now."

She dropped her phone back into her pocket. "You'll never have to do anything else. I promise. We post a couple of photos, get some new business, and then the internet will get bored of us and move on to another couple."

"And if it doesn't? We're just in a fake relationship forever?"

She shrugged. "We can fake break up if we need to. Anytime. Just say the word."

He raised his eyebrows. "That easy, huh?"

"I have dozens of new orders to fill, and I didn't do anything to get them. Yes. That easy." He hesitated, so she pressed on. "New patients. People from Oak Hollow coming over to see the cute doctor the internet is raving about."

He shook his head again, but this time in resignation. "I don't think it works like that, but…if it keeps you out of my parking spot—"

"It's not your spot, but that's beside the point."

"If it keeps you from parking in front of my clinic, and it's just one photo—"

"Maybe two."

"*One* photo. Fine. I'll do it. I'm going to regret this, I'm sure. But I'll do it."

Marlee resisted the urge to wrap her arms around his neck. She started typing into her phone.

"What are you doing?"

"Texting Morgan to get over here. We've got a photo to take."

"Tonight?"

Marlee hit send and grinned at him. "Right now. The internet moves fast, Dr. LaSalle. And I've already got an idea."

CHAPTER SIX

MATTHEW KNEW THAT he would regret agreeing to this crazy internet ruse, but he didn't expect to regret it so immediately.

She didn't even give him a minute to wrap his head around what he was about to do. As a rule of thumb, Matthew didn't allow himself to get pressured into instant deals like this. Even as a teenager, excited about buying his first car, he still left a deal on the table to go home and think it over before agreeing. When he'd gone back the next day, the car had been sold out from under him. But he didn't regret his reticence in the slightest, because thoughtful in decision-making was the smart way to be.

Okay, maybe that wasn't totally true. That car was worth every penny the seller was asking. He'd ended up with a worse deal on a worse car. But he'd gone into that deal with eyes wide-open, and that was the important part.

This deal, he'd just blindly agreed to, disappointing himself with how little he'd fought it.

It's something about her, the little voice in the back of his mind nagged at him. *Maybe you wanted to be in this deal because of her. Maybe you find her irresistible and you don't altogether hate the idea of the world thinking you're together.*

Inwardly, he balked at the very idea. *Not a chance.*

If nothing else, her little scheme was proof that she would never be the right partner for him.

You should walk away, Matthew. Tell her you've changed your mind. Tell her she's crazy for even considering doing this. Tell her you believe in the slow growth of a practice built on solid medicine and word of mouth. Tell her these things and walk away. Stay true to yourself.

But the truth was he didn't have time for solid medicine and word of mouth to build his practice. He wouldn't be able to keep living off his savings for much longer. He would be forced to move closer to one of the bigger cities, open up there.

These were things he wished he'd thought of when he decided to pursue medicine for a career. He was the king of pros and cons lists. He should have pro-and-conned his career choice. A huge con? The possibility of failing, and having to live somewhere other than Haw Springs, the town he loved so dearly.

But would it have mattered if he had pro-and-conned it? Would he have chosen something different? And what would that different thing even be? He knew from the time he was a small child that he was good at puzzles and science. He knew that he was curious about all the ways the body could be invaded, and the consequences of that invasion. It didn't take long for him to put together that what he was truly fascinated with was medicine.

It was his calling.

Maybe that's what was behind his dour feelings now.

"You're falling behind." Marlee pulled him out of his thoughts by plopping another handful of fading roses on the counter between them. "Are you afraid of the thorns or something?"

He picked up a rose and pulled the flower off the stem. Ironically, he pricked his finger with a thorn in doing so, but he was determined not to dignify her question with a response, so he said nothing as he began to pull apart the petals and drop them into the bucket she'd placed between them.

"Good," she said. "Keep going."

"How many of these are you planning to rip apart? Seems like a lot of money. Roses aren't cheap," he said.

"As many as it takes," Marlee said. "These are kind of dying, anyway, so it's fine. Think of it as placing an ad. That would cost money."

"A Super Bowl ad, maybe," Matthew said.

She grinned as she dropped a fistful of petals

into the bucket and continued to the next flower. "With Super Bowl returns, I hope."

He furtively wiped away a bead of blood that had appeared on his thumb and picked up a new rose. "Have you thought about what will happen if you get too popular? It's just you here."

She nodded. "It's not supposed to be. I have an assistant. Kimberly."

"I've never seen her."

"She's not the most reliable. It's a whole thing. There was a florist here before me."

"King's Flowers. I remember."

She looked up. "Prom?"

"Uh… I didn't go."

"Oh."

"I didn't want to," he said, clarifying. Why was his throat so dry all of a sudden? He never cared about this in the past. Now he sounded defensive, and he knew it and hated it, but he couldn't stop himself. "I was pretty focused on school. I didn't do a whole lot of dating. Or…any dating…really."

"Well, it seems to have paid off," she said. "All that focus on school. You're a doctor."

He sniffed. "Yeah. A starving doctor, maybe." It was like his mouth was on overdrive, running without his consent. Why did he feel like he had to fill the void when he was with her? Like she was judging him? Like he even cared? He didn't. He didn't care. Mostly. No, not at all. He didn't care at all. But he did keep talking. "I don't mean that. I'm not actually starving. It's just been slow, and… I mean…" He trailed off, wishing for all the world that he could rewind to five minutes ago and redo the entire conversation. "Anyway. King's Flowers."

"Oh. Yeah. So Monica King. I don't know if you remember her. Really vivacious and eccentric and unique."

Oh, he remembered Monica King. Everyone remembered Monica King. She was a Haw Springs icon, a town fixture, floating around the square in big, floppy hats and muumuus and jingly jewelry, sometimes literally dancing to a song that only she could hear. Like a flower that had loosened itself from its stem and ridden the wind beset with a twinkling glee that nobody else truly understood.

"I remember," he said. "She died, though, right?"

"Yeah, years ago. And it was sort of expected that her daughter, Kiki, would take over the shop."

"That's right. But she didn't, and they closed it down."

"Because Kiki didn't really want anything to do with flowers. No passion there whatsoever."

"So enter Blush & Bloom?"

"Eventually, yeah. I bought the old storefront, which had been empty the entire time I was in college, and I started slow, and then when I got momentum under me, I hired Kimberly King."

He glanced up. "As in…?"

"Kiki's daughter. Monica's granddaughter. She's got Monica's esoteric personality. And her natural gift with flowers. But she's got her mother's passion for the business. So she's drawn to the art of flower arranging, but not exactly drawn to working."

Matthew chuckled. "And you're stuck with her?"

Marlee took a deep breath and dropped the last of the rose petals into the bucket. "I wouldn't say stuck with, exactly. I like her. She's fun and funny and really artistic, and a naturally talented florist. But also, yeah. Kind of stuck. I mean, what do you do when the descendant of floral royalty wants a job? You hire her. And then when she treats her job like it's an option instead of an obligation, you live with it."

He shook his head and dropped the last of his petals into the bucket on top of hers. "Maybe you live with it, but I don't think I could."

Marlee waved her hand. "She's a good kid. And I like that she's got that dreamy quality about her. Not everybody knows from birth what they want to do with their life. I sure didn't."

Matthew eyed Marlee curiously, as he came to realize that he really didn't know her at all. There was some depth there that he would have sworn didn't exist. *Not exactly fair of you, Matthew*, he told himself, and he felt a pang of guilt for not noticing who the woman he had been battling might actually be.

The door opened and Morgan McBride swooped in. She held up her watch. “Decker’s giving Archer a bath, which means I have exactly thirty minutes to knock this out. I think we decided on a rain of rose petals, yes?”

“Yep. We’ve got the petals.” Marlee jumped up and clutched the bucket to her chest. She beamed at Matthew, but he could have sworn that her smile looked nervous along the edges. She came around the counter and grabbed his hand. And there it was again, that zap.

“All right, love of my life, come with me.”

“Nope, don’t call me that,” Matthew said, but he let himself be pulled along, anyway.

CHAPTER SEVEN

THEY DIDN'T GET it done in thirty minutes. In fact, they barely even got things started in thirty minutes, partially because it seemed that Matthew questioned everything. Every. Single. Thing.

First, he decided that he needed a tie and trotted across the street to his office to fetch one.

And then he didn't like the potential optics that something was going on during work hours, so he took the tie off.

But then he didn't feel as though he was representing himself accurately, so the tie went back on.

And then off again, for what appeared to be no particular reason whatsoever. Which was when Marlee flung it across the flower shop, where it hung from the branch of a fiddle-leaf fig. Which he found to be completely unacceptable. Because *you don't treat a good tie that way.*

Morgan fought valiantly to keep them on task, but when her alarm beeped, she shrugged and gave Marlee a quick hug. "I tried," she said. "But now I've got to get Archer to bed. You'll have to finish this on your own. Just set the timer on your camera and go crazy."

"What part of Matthew LaSalle says *go crazy*?" Marlee whispered. They both turned to watch Matthew as he fussed with extracting his tie from the tree, straightening it out along the counter.

"The part where this was your idea," Morgan whispered back. "Besides, he's kind of cute."

"Cute like a rock in your shoe," Marlee said.

"Cute like you sure do protest a lot. And I remember what a crush you had on him when he first opened his clinic."

"That was before I got to know him."

"I don't think you really know him just yet," Morgan said. "Give him a chance. This is all new to him."

"It's all new to me, too," Marlee said.

Morgan wrapped her sister in a hug. "Again, your idea. So you're at least a day ahead of him. Let him catch up."

"Are we sure we want to stage the photo right here, with a dog bed in the background?" Matthew called. "I'm not sure if a dog bed speaks to our image."

Marlee gave Morgan a thin smile. "Let him catch up," she repeated. "Right."

Morgan's phone buzzed. She jumped and checked her watch again. "Gotta go."

"Coward," Marlee said to her back.

"You try dealing with Archer when his routine has been altered, and then tell me who's the coward," Morgan said. "Love you!" She blew a kiss and was gone, leaving Marlee alone with Matthew.

Marlee took a deep breath to steel herself, and then pasted on a smile as she turned to face Matthew. "What's wrong with the dog bed?"

"It's just kind of ugly. Not very…"

She waited for him to finish, but he didn't. "Not very what?"

"Nothing. Romantic, I guess." The tips of his ears were red. Everything about this plan appeared to make him uncomfortable. But at least he was thinking in the right terms. Marlee took it as a positive step forward.

"I don't know. Poppy's pretty cute. And her paw is in the original picture. Maybe we'll catch the eye of some dog lovers while we're at it. Bring Poppy in as part of the relationship that our followers will be…following… I suppose."

"But, why, if this is about promotion? Neither of us are selling dog food or veterinary care."

Marlee didn't really have an answer for that. Her gut told her that Poppy was cute and social media would love her. But it wasn't a hill she was willing to die on. Plus, she was starting to fear that, with every new question, she was losing Matthew's willingness to participate.

"Okay," she said, bending to pick up the bed. She flung it behind the counter. "What else?"

He raised his eyebrows and held his hands up at his shoulders as if he was innocent and had no idea why she would even be asking him that. "Far be it from me to tell you how to do this."

"Really? Far be it?"

"What?"

"Nothing. Let's just get on with it."

"Well, that sets a romantic stage," he mumbled.

Marlee fussed with a rabbit statue on a small table, then propped her phone against it, lining it up to take in most of the shop. She could crop things out later. Phone in place, she brought the bucket to Matthew and held it out for him to take a handful of rose petals. She gave an obviously fake smile. "Good thing we're not actually romantic, then, isn't it?" She shook the bucket. "Do you mind?"

He grabbed a handful; a scattering of petals dropped to the ground at his feet. Marlee sprinkled more directly from the pail onto the floor, then took a handful of her own. With the petals cradled against her, she shuffled to the phone and poked around, setting the timer to take a photo blast. Once set, she raced toward Matthew.

And they both froze, facing each other nervously, petals dripping from their closed palms.

"Uh," she said.

"Are we…?" he said at the same time.

Flash.

She let out an exasperated breath. "Okay. It's a start. We should do something, though."

"Definitely," he said. "Like what?"

Marlee's mouth went dry. In all of her planning, she hadn't even thought of what exactly their faked photo would look like. Only that there would be rose petals and it would be romantic and swoony and would stop every social media scroller in their tracks.

And now that she thought of it in those terms, it all seemed so silly. Ugh.

Not to mention, in order to look swoony and romantic, she might have to actually get swoony and romantic. Or at least in the same airspace as Matthew. Which seemed completely strange and impossible now. She barely knew him.

"Maybe," she said, about to finish the sentence with the words *this is a bad idea*, but he spoke at the same time.

"We could look like we're dancing." He put his arms out as if to take her into them.

She stepped back involuntarily. Suddenly shy. *What?* Since when was she shy? "Um. Sure. Okay. That's a good idea. Should be pretty easy to fake a slow dance, right?"

Wrong.

Three tries, three stepped-on toes. Six more tries, six wasted handfuls of flung rose petals. And at least a million mumbled *sorry, so sorry,*

I'm sorry. And they still had nothing but a dozen wasted photos.

"What if you tried to spin me?" Marlee asked hopefully.

But then there was a whole argument about whether to spin toward or away from the camera. Ten failed photos.

Followed by a discussion about spin speed. Ten more photos, including one where Marlee was spinning out of control toward the camera, a wild, panicked look on her face.

And yet another side argument about whether they match right hand to right hand or use opposite hands. Ten photos of them each holding up the wrong hand. In three of the photos, Matthew had his tongue poking out the side of his mouth in concentration.

"We're terrible at this," Marlee said, looking forlornly into her rapidly emptying bucket. "We're going to run out of petals, and we still don't have a successful photo."

"What if we just don't try as hard," Matthew suggested, the words coming out as if it pained him to say them at all. Marlee guessed that *not trying hard* was not something in Matthew La-Salle's daily repertoire. She guessed that he probably tried harder than he had to pretty much 100 percent of the time.

"What do you mean?" she asked.

"What if we just…smile?"

She gave a mocking little grunt, as if she couldn't believe he would suggest such a thing. "Just smile?"

He shrugged. "Why not? I'm not suggesting we sit for a portrait. I'm suggesting a simple smile, as if we're enjoying each other's company. What's so wrong with that?"

"What's so wrong is…well it's… I mean, you can't just…" But she realized she had no real argument about what could be so wrong with smiling. Everything else they had tried had been an utter failure, so who was she to act like she knew what would work? "Fine. We'll give it a try. Can we at least throw the last of the rose petals first?"

"Definitely."

So they did.

And when Marlee threw hers, she didn't realize how close she was to Matthew's face; her thumb jabbed him right in the eye.

"Oh, my gosh!" She spun and grasped his shoulders as he staggered backward, clutching his face. "I'm so sorry! I thought we were farther… Are you okay?"

The result: another ten unusable photos.

"Let me get you some ice," Marlee said, sweeping decorative pillows off a wooden bench and walking him backward to sit down.

"I'm fine, I'm fine," he said, resisting just slightly before sitting, his palm still pressed over one eye.

"At least let me get you a tissue," she said.

She bustled behind the counter and into her tiny office at the back of the store, where she dug ice cubes out of a desktop ice machine. She deposited a few cubes into a paper towel and then brought them back to him.

"I'm so sorry." She sat on the bench next to him, their knees touching as she angled herself toward him. "Here, let me..."

"Really, you don't need to," he said, taking the paper towel from her and pressing it against his eye.

Marlee sagged a little, her forearms resting on her thighs. Suddenly, she felt very tired. This was part of why she'd resisted social media to begin with. Her life was simple. Quiet. This was going to make it so much more complicated than it needed to be.

"This was a dumb idea, wasn't it?" she asked.

"Dumb? No. Overeager? Maybe." He lowered the paper towel and exaggeratedly blinked. "No retinal detachment that I can ascertain. Of course, I'm not an ophthalmologist, and I have no equipment here. But I think it's just a standard poked eye. We can try again."

Marlee glanced at him. "Your eye is so red."

"I'll angle it away from the camera."

"Well, that will look strange, me facing the camera—*smiling*—and you giving a mug shot silhouette."

"So don't face the camera."

"And we're just facing each other smiling? Weird."

"No, no, you're not getting it. Forget the smile. Here." He set the ice on the bench and jumped up, going back to their staging area. When she didn't join him right away, he turned and beckoned. "I can't do it alone," he said. "Come on." She got up and joined him, wary and unsure. "I'm going to face this way," he said, turning his body. "And you're going to face me." She did. "Now, watch. I put one arm here, and you hold my hand here." He snaked an arm around her waist and pulled her to him. "And now, turn your face to the camera, but don't look directly into it."

Marlee had to admit, it didn't feel altogether wrong. Maybe a little awkward, but definitely not more awkward than what they had been doing.

"I know what we need," he said. "Music."

"Good idea." Marlee pulled away and went behind the counter to turn on the radio she kept on a shelf under the cash register. Soft music trickled out. Yes, that did seem better. She set her camera's timer one more time.

When she came back to him, he was stiff and bumbling. Of course he was. He was Matthew LaSalle. But they went back to their positions easily, and with no bickering. He pulled her in a little tighter than before. She leaned her head against his chest, feeling his heartbeat softly thud against her cheek. Without talking, or even thinking about it, they began to move to the music.

For the briefest moment, she was lost in the rhythm and the calm of his heartbeat, swept up in a cloud of what could be, and without thinking, closed her eyes and bit her lip in a soft, content smile.

And that was the photo they used.

CHAPTER EIGHT

THAT WAS FRUSTRATING. And confusing.

Frustrusing, if he could be so bold as to create a new word himself.

He hated every second of that photo shoot. Except for the moments that he absolutely loved. And he couldn't pinpoint those moments; he only knew they were there, like the feeling of being watched when you're in a room all alone. Everything about this little experiment was so unlike anything he would ever get involved with that it almost felt like an out-of-body experience. Like he was a puppet being led by a very powerful hand. A hand named Marlee West.

He sat at his desk and stared at the photo that Marlee had sent him. The one they posted the night before on her new social media accounts. The one where she looked soft and serene and as if she might be holding back a little secret that made her extraordinarily happy. She certainly didn't look like a powerful hand.

Yet somehow…

He stared harder at the photo. His head was bent toward her, as if he were smelling her hair or maybe getting ready to kiss the top of her head. He had been doing neither. In actuality, he had been praying that the tears from his injured eye wouldn't drip onto her or show in the photo. He'd also been actively hoping that this photo would be the one, so he could go home, hang up his tie and go to bed. He needed a good night's sleep.

Yet after a good night's sleep, he didn't feel any better about what he was doing.

Probably because he didn't get a good night's sleep. He got a tossing-and-turning night's sleep as images of Marlee and the sound of the song that had been playing while they danced ran through his head on a loop. He told himself that it was the stress of lying that kept him awake.

In general, Matthew was not in favor of lying. Lying was exhausting, and he believed it took a heavy toll on the human soul. Even as a child, he would not resort to even the smallest fib to save his own hide when he'd done something wrong. He would own up and accept the consequences, because he believed that this was what a good person did, and because he felt the physical weight of even the tiniest secret.

He stared so hard, the image began to blur.

Did this mean he was no longer a good person? No, he didn't believe that at all. Nor did he believe that Marlee was a bad person. Yet they had lied, and it felt no better to him now than it had when he was seven.

"Why did I go along with it, then?" he asked himself aloud as he closed out the photo and set his phone on his desk. He rubbed both palms over his face. He was tired. His eye ached like a dull bruise when he touched it.

And there was a ripple of excitement somewhere deep inside him. Some enjoyment of this lie. Some anticipation that something good could come from it. He sighed and rubbed his face again. This was not the best morning for a slow morning. He really needed to see some patients to take his mind off Marlee and photos and social media and whatever that bitten bottom lip might have meant.

"You okay?"

He snapped out of it. Lynette stood in his office.

"Huh?"

"I don't see you slumping around very often. Are you good?"

"Oh. Yeah. Just…tired."

"Up too late?"

"Yes and no. I just didn't sleep well."

"I don't suppose that would have anything to do with slow dancing on a carpet of rose petals with the love of your life, would it?" He felt a jolt from deep within.

"You saw it?"

"From the looks of things, everyone in Haw

Springs saw it. You should probably call your mother before she sees it."

"You think she'll see it?"

"She's my best friend. Of course she's going to see it, because I'll show it to her."

He felt a pang of something deep within him. He hadn't even thought about the possibility of his family seeing the photo. Of them knowing about the ruse. Would he even be able to tell them that it was a ruse? Would he have to lie to them, too?

Regret. The pangs he was feeling were definitely pangs of regret. Why did he let himself get talked into this?

"Do we have any coffee?" he asked.

Lynette's eyes grew big. Matthew never drank coffee during the workday. He didn't need it. She'd often joked that he seemed to be *supercharged from within, fueled by possibility and purpose*. True, he did tend to wake up one minute before his alarm even had a chance to buzz.

She sank into the chair across from him. "So the photo is real? I had been sort of telling myself that it was faked. Artificial intelligence or… or… I don't know what. But, when? How? Why?"

"What are you, a reporter now?"

She poked a finger his direction. "Nope. You're not going to distract this conversation. It was only a couple of days ago that you were vehemently trying to convince me that you didn't like that woman. Was that all a lie?"

He opened his mouth to explain, but all that came out was an aggrieved sigh, followed by the word "Coffee," spoken in a tone too close to a plea for his liking.

"I'll brew a fresh pot. But this conversation is not over. Not by a long shot." Her voice trailed behind her as she made her way to the reception area.

He let his upper half sag onto his desk, his head dropping into the cradle of his folded arms. "I'm sure it's not."

He knew that Lynette's reaction was only the first, and perhaps the mildest, of the reactions he would have to face. He could still get out of it, right? He could tell Marlee that this had the potential to really blow up in their faces. Surely she would understand that. Any reasonable person would understand that. He could talk some sense into her, get her to take down the post before too many people saw it.

"Yes," he said aloud, pulling his head out of his arms. "I can just talk to her. Tell her I've changed my mind."

That'll upset her, his mind so generously offered.

"Then she'll have to be upset," he said.

She needs the business, and so do you, his mind argued. Yes, of course, he already knew that. It was, after all, the weakness that she'd used to her advantage when talking him into this.

"I can get business." He stood and paced the length of his office, the afterimage of the photo still burned into the backs of his eyelids. "I don't have to participate in dog and pony shows to get business. No, I don't. She doesn't, either. I'll just make her see that. And I'll tighten my belt and wait for word of mouth to—"

He heard a *whoop*, some excited, muffled chatter and a door opening. Next thing he knew, Marlee was standing in his office doorway, her face flushed, yet bright. She wore a hot-pink shirt, adorned with whimsical hearts and flowers, and a white skirt. She looked like an exclamation point, Matthew thought. Or maybe like she was surrounded by a whole cloud of exclamation points. He felt an involuntary smirk tug at the corners of his lips. Contagious exclamation points, apparently.

"Have you seen it?" she asked breathlessly.

"Yes," he said.

She waited a beat, and then, obviously dissatisfied, maybe even dumbfounded, shook her head. "And?"

"And…what? It's a pretty good photo."

"Pretty good? It's great. How can you be so—you know what? Never mind. I'm not talking about the photo itself. Did you see this?"

She rushed toward him, a swirl of pink and white and enchanting energy, aiming her phone at his face. He couldn't wait until he got back to a time when people stopped brandishing phone screens at him.

"This," she said. "*Modern Vow Magazine* wants to do a feature. On us."

"*Modern Vow...*?"

She dropped her phone to her side, exasperated. "Remember? It's the relationship magazine. From first dates to weddings, engagement parties, everything in between. They reached out. They actually want to feature us."

"People still read magazines?" Matthew was aware of the magazines on the tables in his waiting room, but he'd never paid attention if anyone ever actually picked one up. And he supposed he saw magazines in doctor's office waiting rooms as something different, unique. Nobody had magazine subscriptions anymore, did they?

"They have online content, too. That's beside the point. They have a readership of...millions, I would guess. This could be it. My—*our*—big moment. I'm actively designing a wedding right now. My arrangements could be seen worldwide." Now she began to pace, but quickly, as if she had way too much energy to contain in one spot. "Can you imagine? I could get orders from countries on the other side of the world. I have no idea how that would work, but who cares? This will change my whole business model. I would have to figure out how to ship. I would have to create a whole new website. A better website." She turned to him.

"Do you know how to create a website? I was doing good to create the website that I have. How am I going to create a new, better website?" She returned to pacing, but Matthew wasn't sure if she even took a breath. "You know what? It doesn't matter. I'll figure everything out when I have to. Right? We both will. It could get busy, sure. It could get really, really busy. But who needs sleep, am I right?" She let out a semimaniacal giggle and turned to face him again. "What?"

He must have had a look on his face. A skeptical one, no doubt. He didn't mean to be skeptical. He didn't want to rain on her parade. But, well, he *was* skeptical, as uncomfortable as that might make each of them feel. And he felt like, in her excitement, she wasn't asking all of the questions. Including a very important one. "How is getting into a bridal magazine going to bring me more patients?"

"Oh. Right." She nibbled a fingernail, thinking. "You never know. It's not about *where* or *how* you get internet famous that's important, it's *that* you get internet famous."

"Internet famous?" There was the skeptical tone again. "I don't want to get any sort of famous. I just want to be able to pay my rent. People from countries on the other side of the world aren't going to come to Haw Springs to get their baby's first checkup. I'm sorry, I just don't see how these dots connect."

And just like that, he could see those exclamation points fall away from her. She sagged, depleted, and he felt horrible for being the reason.

"You're right," she said. "I hadn't thought about that."

He didn't want to be right. "I'm sorry."

She held up a finger. "What about books? Podcasts? Daytime talk shows?"

"I didn't go to medical school to write books and be on daytime TV," he said. "I went to medical school so I could come back to my community and make a difference."

"But there's more than one way to define 'community,'" Marlee said. "And more than one way to make a difference." She took a deep breath and came toward him. The pleading look in her eyes was almost more than he could bear. "Listen. I know this is a lot. And maybe it's a lot for me, too, and I'm all swept up in the moment. It's just that I've never really had a moment to get swept up in. Morgan was always the star," she said. "She was the better student, the better rule-follower, the better sister. She's the younger sister, but she got all the firsts. She got her business degree while I was still changing majors, she got married first, she moved away first, became a savvy businesswoman first and she gave my parents their first grandchild." She let out a mirthless chuckle. "And now she's even remarried. Before I ever got off the starting blocks, she's starting over. She lapped me." She flopped into one of the chairs across from his desk. "But, you're right, it's unfair of me to ask this of you. Forget I said anything. I'll tell *Modern Vow* no."

For a moment, Matthew was unsure what to do, or where to go. Was he supposed to stay near her side? Was he supposed to go to his chair on the other side of the desk? Was that too far? Was it too clinical?

Was there anything he couldn't overthink?

In the end, he slowly lowered himself in the chair next to her, angled in such a way as to not be too close.

She kept talking. "I was a good kid, don't get me wrong. I never did anything to give my parents any sort of real grief. I stayed in Haw Springs, even though I was so curious about the world. I just…never had a plan like Morgan did. I never quite got there. I was wilder, a free spirit, an artist. I wasn't the best student or the best rule-follower or even the best sister. I never moved away, I never graduated college, I never got married…" She swallowed, and Matthew was sure he saw something there. Something painful that was buried, but not too deeply. She turned up her palms. "No grandchildren."

"You still have plenty of time for all of that. It's not a race. And you're incredibly successful. You own your own business. That's a big deal."

"Except…" She turned her body so she was

facing him more fully now. "I'm telling you this, because my parents paid money for me to live at home for a long time. They paid money to get me out of my small messes. They paid money for me to go to college and not finish. And, when I finally figured out what I wanted to be, they gave me money to help open the shop. They gave and gave and they continue to give, and they would continue to give for the rest of their lives, if I needed it. But, for once, I want to be the one who does things right. I want to make my own way, and pay them back, and show them—show everyone, I guess—that I may be a flighty, free-spirited dreamer artist type, but I can be savvy and I can do hard things and I…well, I suppose… I can matter."

You matter, he wanted to say, but the words didn't quite come out, because he wasn't sure how it would sound coming from him. He didn't really know her. Who would he be to try to motivate her?

But the exclamation point cloud, the dewy excitement, the matter-of-fact crease between her brows as she tried to explain why this was so important to her. He didn't just notice them; he felt them.

And, suddenly, he realized he *wanted* to know her. He wanted to learn more about her wild days, her free spirit, her art. He didn't want to fall in love, and he didn't think he was in any danger of that. But he did want to learn about her. As a friend. An interested third party.

A business partner, maybe?

Or maybe he was justifying what he knew he was going to do, anyway.

He sighed. "Okay. We'll meet with the magazine. What do I need to do?"

CHAPTER NINE

MARLEE SAT ON Morgan's patio, a glass of iced tea on the table in front of her. It was barely the end of May, and it was already getting hot. She gazed out over the pasture, where Archer was getting a one-on-one lesson from Decker's right-hand man, Ben, when she heard Annie scream. What started as a startled *whoop* turned into something much longer and louder, almost siren-like. Marlee's eyes darted around, trying to spot Annie, and finally found her as she raced across the field toward the house, pausing only to wildly wrap her arms around Ben's neck for a quick, rough hug that knocked off his cowboy hat.

Annie had once confided to Marlee that being on the spectrum meant that she grew up her entire life feeling like she didn't quite belong. She'd told her that she'd feared she would forever be alone, because she would never find anyone else like her, and would also never find someone who could accept that she was different.

Annie was sweet and kind and exuberant. Everyone liked her. She had friends. But, in a way, she was right. She was not understood. Not totally.

Until, that was, she met Ben while they were both teenagers volunteering at McBride Pathways. For Annie, it had been love at first sight. Ben was also on the spectrum, was brilliant, hardworking and caring. And Ben understood her completely.

He didn't have a hard time connecting with people. He connected with lots of people, all the time. But he had a hard time expressing that connection, so everyone else thought he had a hard time connecting.

Annie had understood this about Ben within the first day of meeting him.

She thought he may have even had a crush on her. She was positive that she had a crush on him.

It wasn't until years of volunteering later that Ben finally proposed to her, in a homemade sled, during a blizzard that swept through Haw Springs at Christmastime. She'd said yes and leapt into his arms before he even got the words out.

Their love was sweet and pure, and Marlee was thrilled with the idea that the entire world was, in a way, going to have an opportunity to witness their wedding.

Finally, Annie let go of Ben and raced toward the porch, her boots thunking on the hard ground. Her hat, too, had fallen off twenty yards or so back, but she had been too excited to stop and pick it up.

"Sounds like *Modern Vow* reached out to her," Marlee said.

"Is it true? Is it true? Is it true?" Annie called as she approached the patio.

Marlee nodded, grinning. She had intended to ask Annie's permission rather than just tell her that *Modern Vow Magazine* was going to feature her wedding florals in their fall issue. But Morgan had let the cat out of the bag, and Annie's excitement was all the confirmation that Marlee needed. It was also contagious. "It's true," she said.

She set her glass down milliseconds before she was nearly tackled out of her chair by the same neck-hug that Ben had just received.

"Morgan, did you hear?" Annie asked. "My flowers will be in a real magazine."

"I heard," Morgan said. "Congratulations, Annie."

"So you're okay with it?" Marlee asked, feeling a huge weight lifted from her. She'd sort of already promised the *Modern Vow* reporter access to her entire process of planning for, arranging, and delivering the flowers at Annie's wedding. She didn't really have a backup plan for what to do if Annie wasn't okay with it.

"Are you kidding me? Yes!" Annie squealed. "I can't believe it! A real magazine!"

"I can't believe it, either," Marlee said. "Can I show you some new ideas that I have?" She pulled out her phone and opened her photos. She and Annie had met half a dozen times already—sometimes purely by accident at The Baked Bean, but now Marlee worried that their ideas were boring compared to what they could be. They needed some *oomph*. Some…modernizing. "I think we can really jazz things up."

Annie's eyes grew big. She hopped on her toes, her hands pressed together under her chin. "I would love that." She dragged a chair next to Marlee and sat, leaning over so she could see the phone screen.

"What about Ben?" Morgan asked. "Have you asked what he thinks?"

Annie leaned back in her chair dramatically and adopted a deep voice meant to mimic Ben's style of speaking. "I'm going to marry you, not a flower. Do whatever you want, darlin'."

Morgan laughed. "To be fair, that sounds exactly like something Decker would say."

Annie grinned, proud of her imitation of her fiancé. "Oh, but wait," she said, leaning into Marlee. "I have a question."

"Sure," Marlee said.

"I didn't know that you and the doctor were in love. Wait. That's not a question. Are you and the doctor really in love?"

Marlee's eyes darted to Morgan, who seemed to be enjoying this line of questioning just a little too much. Morgan and Ellory already knew, and that was two people too many, as far as Marlee was concerned.

Marlee wasn't sure what to say. It was one thing to pretend on the internet, but another thing altogether to have to lie to someone's face. Especially someone she liked. And she liked Annie an awful lot. She chewed her bottom lip, thinking, but there didn't seem to be any way around it. Either lie, or risk being caught. She could not risk getting caught. The stakes were getting too high.

And as much as she liked and wanted to trust Annie, the truth of the matter was, the more people knew, the more chances of someone slipping up and everything blowing up in their faces.

Still, it was hard to lie out loud. Marlee simply nodded, trying to give her most eager look.

Annie gasped. "He's so cute!"

"I know," Marlee said. She didn't have to lie about that. He was cute.

Annie lowered her voice. "He's kind of weird, though."

Marlee laughed out loud. Another truth. "That he is, Annie. That he is."

"Maybe your wedding will be the next wedding. Morgan and Decker. Ellory and Rowan. Me and Ben. And now you and Dr. LaSalle."

This time Marlee felt Morgan give a single breath of laughter next to her; she gave her a subtle elbow jab.

"*Your* wedding is the next wedding," Marlee

said, trying to reroute the conversation. "I would never want to distract from that. It's going to be the biggest, most beautiful wedding Haw Springs has ever seen. With the best flowers. And the press."

Annie giggled excitedly, bouncing around in her chair a little, and leaned over, wide-eyed, as Marlee showed her all the new design ideas she'd been thinking about. Annie loved every single one of them. Marlee was grateful to have such an easy client for what had become a huge event.

"Do you think the magazine will actually come to my wedding? Not just take pictures?" Annie asked.

"That would be amazing, wouldn't it?" Morgan asked, reaching over and giving Annie's arm a light stroke.

Annie's eyes grew wide. "The whole magazine? That would be a lot of extra potato salad. My Aunt Lorraine is making the potato salad by hand."

"Don't worry," Marlee said. "They probably won't want to come to the actual wedding. But if they do, it would only be the writer and a photographer, probably."

Annie was in the scared zone, though, and barely heard her. "What if they really like potato salad? I should warn Aunt Lorraine so she can make sure she buys enough potatoes."

"I don't think that will really be necessary,"

Marlee said, but Annie was already on her feet, wandering away, looking concerned.

Marlee gave Morgan a worried glance. The last thing she wanted was to stress Annie out about her wedding.

"Hey, Annie?" Morgan called when Annie had left the patio. Annie turned around. "It's going to be great. You'll have plenty of potato salad."

Annie nodded.

"And if there's anyone you don't want at the wedding, including the magazine people, then we will make sure they're not there," Marlee added. "Even if you decide at the last minute."

"I want them there," Annie said. "I so, so do."

"Then we'll tell them they can't eat all the potato salad," Morgan said. "Or, even better, Decker and I won't eat our portions. They can have ours. Problem solved."

Annie beamed. "Okay. If there are leftovers, I will bring them to you and Decker right away."

Morgan held up her hands. "Problem solved."

Annie threw up her hands like Morgan's. "Yes! Problem solved. Don't sweat the small stuff. Right?"

"Don't sweat the small stuff," Morgan repeated. "It's your wedding!"

Annie beamed. "It's my wedding! And I love Ben."

"We all love Ben," Morgan said. "And we all love you."

"And she loves the doctor. And everyone loves potato salad," Annie said. "But that's small stuff." She gave an exaggerated wave with her hand, as if to wave the very concept of potato salad away. Marlee loved the way Annie dealt with things. She wished she had Annie's forthrightness. Her ready acceptance of things, and willingness to let it show when something wasn't right. She wished she had Annie's openness.

But, then again, if she did, she probably wouldn't be in this situation. It may be tricky, but the fact of the matter was, she was poised for big things to happen.

And, even if she let the small stuff be, it was still going to feel big.

CHAPTER TEN

MATTHEW'S FINGER WAS still on the doorbell when the door whipped open and Marlee reached out and grabbed his arm, pulling him inside, as if she'd been just inside the door waiting for him. He nearly tripped over the threshold, and then again over the dog, who was barking at him with gusto, her front paws hopping across the ground with every effort to scare him away.

"Hey, you know me, remember?" He started to lean toward the dog, hand out for a sniff, but Marlee had grabbed hold of his elbow and yanked him away.

"Whoa. What's going on?" he asked, tripping behind her as she whisked him through the foyer and through a tidy, modern living room.

"It's a disaster," she said, depositing him into the kitchen. "Total disaster."

"What's a total disaster? It looks clean to me. Oh." He blinked at the disaster, aka the kitchen.

The entire room looked as if it had been plucked from the house, shaken like a snow globe and plopped back into place. Dishes were piled in the sink, drawers were left half open with towels and hot pads hanging out of them, carrot peelings clung to the countertop and onion skins skittered across the floor. "This is no problem. We can clean it. We have time." He checked his watch. "Ten minutes. Okay, that's tight, but we can make it if we work together." He began to roll up his sleeves. "I'll do the cleaning while you finish up dinner. What's…for…dinner?" He looked around, trying to find a discernible dish, but found none.

And then the smell hit him. He made his way to the stove, where a pan filled with smoldering, unidentifiable food greeted him. He realized now that the light coming down from overhead was yellowish from the smoke that had likely poured out of the oven when she pulled out…whatever blackened thing this was. Tendrils of smoke still snaked their way through the cracks of the shut oven door. Something had boiled over on the stove and was still giving a little hiss.

"Are we having…charcoal? With a side of lava?" It was a joke, but she didn't laugh. Instead, she tipped her head to the side as if to say, *Read the room.* Feeling like a heel, he tried to save the moment. "Charcoal is my favorite!"

It didn't work.

Marlee's eyes were big and watery. He wasn't sure if they were watering from the turbid air or from emotion. “We’re going to have to cancel,” she said.

Yep. Emotion. Definitely from emotion.

He wasn’t used to seeing this kind of emotion from Marlee. Usually she was spirited, ornery. A little abrasive, even. When she was irritated, she had a tendency toward mockery, as if she were daring the universe to cross her.

What he was seeing in her now was defeat, and it was…unsettling.

“What? Cancel? Why?”

“Why?” she asked, her voice clipped. “Did you just seriously ask why? Look around, Matthew. Look at it. It’s a total catastrophe. I can’t feed that to anyone, much less to a reporter. My kitchen looks like a bomb hit it. My whole house smells like a firepit.” She lifted a listless lock of hair. “And my hair has cheese sauce in it. At least I hope that’s cheese sauce. Could be anything at this point. Do you know why? Because I was so busy trying to make everything perfect, I forgot to shower. They’ll take pictures, and I’ll be in them, unshowered.” She dropped her hair, her chin quivering. She was about to cry.

Matthew was not good with criers over the age of five. Maybe eight. Certainly not adults. Adult criers made him very uncomfortable. He always felt as if he should console them, but he was never sure what was the most appropriate way to do it. Pat on the shoulder? Patronizing. Side hug? Awkward. Full-on hug? Overkill. He was especially unsure how to handle it with his fake girlfriend, moments before a reporter was set to arrive. Was there a handbook that covered this? He very much doubted it. But he also very much needed one at this moment.

"There, there," he said, unmoving, his hands pushed deep into his pockets. Perhaps the most awkward thing he could have possibly done. And he could see in her face that she felt the awkwardness, too. She looked somewhere between astonished, disgusted and crushed. He held back a chuckle as he gazed down at the atrocities on the stovetop. How on earth could someone burn something this badly? "I'm sure it's not as bad as you think."

"It's so bad," she said.

"It's not," he said. "It's salvageable. It's…" He squinted at the carcass. "Well…what exactly is it? Or was it?"

She groaned. "It was pot roast."

His eyebrows shot up and he leaned farther over the pans. "That was pot roast?"

She let out a little whine. "And potatoes and carrots."

"Right," he said, tilting his head to the side and squinting. "I see it now." He didn't. There wasn't enough tilt-and-squint in the world for him to see it. "We could probably scrape it off." He plucked a potato out of the flakes of burnt grease and cut it in half in hopes of seeing fluffy white potato flesh under a thin crust of burn. But the potato cut like a piece of hard candy, the pieces flying off the counter and sailing across the floor. "Okay, scraping probably isn't the best option. Maybe we can cut off the top layer of the meat?" But one look at the meat told him that even if they cut the burnt layer off, the whole thing was probably going to taste like a cigar. He didn't know what else to do. How to spin it. He just had to keep her from crying. "We can pivot. No big deal."

"No. We should cancel, and honestly, we should just get out now. Admit that we were lying, take our internet punishment, then wait for it to blow over so we can go on with our lives. No harm, no foul. A couple of days of feeling like jerks and we're back to normal."

She turned and picked up a dish towel and began swiping at the counter, as if to begin cleaning up.

Honestly, that plan didn't sound altogether too bad to Matthew, but he knew that it wasn't how she really felt. Not down deep. She wanted him to say it was salvageable, and maybe even salvage it himself, so she wouldn't have to.

"You're being irrational," Matthew said.

Probably not the reassurance that she had in mind.

The words had popped out before he could register that he'd been thinking them. His sister had *regretted to inform him* years ago, after he'd said the same thing to her, that it was never, ever going to be the right thing to say to someone. But especially not to someone who was clearly upset.

In other words, he had, as usual, chosen the exact wrong thing to say in the moment.

Way to go, LaSalle. You did it again. This is why you shouldn't be in a relationship—not even a fake one. Because you get comfortable, you start being yourself, and then you learn all the ways that you really need to change.

"Excuse me?" Marlee asked, her towel paused in mid-swipe. His sister had been right. "Did you just call me irrational?"

He held out his hands, as if warding off a bear. "I'm just saying why call the whole thing off because you burnt dinner? We'll pivot. You clean up, and I'll go grab some burgers. When the reporter gets here, we can all have a laugh at what happened." He reached into his pocket for car keys, but just as his fingers brushed metal, the doorbell rang. He was too late to sneak out.

He and Marlee gave each other panicked glances.

"That's them," Marlee said.

"What do we do?" he asked, all of his calm, rational planning flying out the window.

"I don't know," she said. "How would I know? Look around. I haven't exactly been on my best game today, have I? I'm not prepared for this."

"Well, we can't just leave them out there," Matthew said.

"Can we, though?"

"Actually, you're right. People don't answer doors all the time. The worst thing that happens is they go away, right? And that's really what we both want, isn't it?" He scratched the back of his head. "I don't know. I don't know what we want anymore. Not in the slightest. What do we want?"

"How was any of what you just said helpful in any way?" Marlee asked.

"It wasn't. I told you I'm not good in a crisis."

"You never told me that. And *you're a doctor.* This all started because you literally caught me out of thin air. I was plummeting to my death. I'd call that something of a crisis."

"You're blaming me now?"

"No, I'm just saying that you should know exactly what to do."

The doorbell rang again.

"Fine," Matthew said. "We can't just leave them out there. We have to answer the door."

"And then what?"

"We'll improvise."

There was a knock. Marlee let out a sigh.

"Let's just…get this over with." They moved toward the door, slowly, stiffly, side by side, as if they were going to their executions.

"They're going to see right through us," Marlee whispered. "I'm in no headspace for lying today.

I'm not even in the headspace for checking on a potato."

"Oh, the potato? It's done. You can take it out of the oven now," Matthew said, and this time, she cracked a smile.

"We haven't talked about how we're going to sit or anything," she said.

"I was sort of guessing the normal way. On our backsides. Knees out front." He didn't know where all these one-liners were coming from, but he could feel her relax a little next to him, and he felt his own stomach loosen from being clenched in anticipation. This was it. No turning back now.

"Are you going to be a stand-up comedian all night, or is this lovely part of your sparkling personality reserved just for me?" Marlee asked. "When I want you to be fun, you're a horrible drag. *Move your van, move your van, your van is blocking me, wah, wah, wah.*"

Matthew grabbed her hand and twirled her, as if they were dancing, then let her hand drop again. It was the only thing he could think to do to get her out of this mode. When she spun to face him, her scowl was gone.

"It's just for you," he said. "I plan to be a right grouch for the reporter. I want her to go away wondering what on earth you could ever possibly see in me."

"Oh," Marlee said. "Then just be your normal self." Only this time, she gave him a little wink.

"I suppose I walked right into that one," he said.

"I suppose you ran into it headfirst." She grabbed the doorknob, just as the doorbell rang for the third time.

"I suppose I did."

She looked back at him and sucked in a shallow breath. "Are we really doing this?"

Not that he had ever truly been on board, but now that he was standing in Marlee's foyer and the reporter was separated from him by a few inches of wood, ready to report on their romantic bliss, he felt energized, inspired. They were about to make a huge mistake—he knew that with every fiber of his being. But maybe they would have some fun in the process.

He simply shrugged and said, "I don't see why not. What could possibly go wrong?"

That was the comment that finally made her laugh. *Huh.*

"Let's get famous, then," she said, and opened the door.

On the other side of the door stood a squat woman carrying a shoulder bag stuffed so full and heavy, her right shoulder drooped a solid two inches lower than her left. She wore a large pair of glasses—much too large for her face—and had a pencil tucked behind one ear, as if she'd expected to have to stop, drop and note-take immediately upon meeting them. She wore a khaki dress, like something out of a safari, with black-and-white-striped tights and combat boots. Several steps behind her stood a hunky photographer, looking bored in a pair of ripped jeans and a plain white T-shirt, his jaw working a wad of fluorescent green gum. He had a large camera draped around his neck and carried a bag.

"Marlee and Matthew?" the reporter asked. "I'm Janquil Thomason from *Modern Vow Magazine*. This is Tyler." She gestured toward the photographer, who gave a single nod.

"Come in, come in," Marlee said, and then became a fidgety flurry, brushing off the front of her shirt, running her hands through her hair, waving away invisible smoke. "Pardon the, um, smoky smell. We've had a bit of a, um..."

"We were busy staring into each other's eyes and accidentally let dinner burn," Matthew blurted. Oh, he was going to be so bad at this. Janquil and Tyler gazed at him curiously, as if they couldn't tell if he was being serious or not. Marlee's attempt at a curious gaze had a distinct underpinning of rage and warning. Matthew let out a chuckle to let them know he was "kidding," and was pleasantly surprised when they joined his laughter.

Marlee wrapped her arm through his, as if this was the most natural thing in the world for them. "He's so sweet. The truth is I got distracted and burnt dinner, but of course he'll take the blame for me. He always does. You're so good at protecting me, aren't you, sweet…um…s?"

Sweetums? Was there no end to this humiliation? He raised one eyebrow at her. The ornery smile he was so accustomed to quirked one corner of her mouth. He gave a little head tilt. *Oh, is that how we're playing this?*

He patted her hand. "I've got your back, sugar… cone."

Oh, no. Sweetums was bad, but sugar cone was so much worse. He could feel the rage and warning deepen as she gripped his arm tighter and tighter, her fingernails digging into his skin.

"Sugar cone," Janquil said as she wrote in a tiny notebook she produced out of nowhere. "Cute. Different, but cute. I'm sure there's a story there."

"I'm sure there is," Matthew said.

Marlee let out another gaspy laugh. "He's so adorable, isn't he? He's going to get us burgers. We can chat while he goes. See you soon, sweetums. Cheese on mine, please." She patted his arm a few times and steered him toward the door.

"Actually," Janquil said, brushing past them and barging right into the house. "We ate before we came, anyway. We don't need dinner. We can just chat, hmm?"

Marlee and Matthew exchanged worried looks again.

"Absolutely," Marlee said. "Let's just chat."

She let go of Matthew's arm and swept around

him to lead them into the living room, which Matthew was only now realizing had one small love seat and one rocking chair. A part of him cursed her for having such sparse furniture and wanted to rant, *Who calls this a living room set?* But then he remembered the futon and recliner in his own tiny living room. When you lived alone and didn't do much in the way of hosting, what more did you really need?

Or, in his case, if you didn't host anyone, ever.

He could hear the voice of Tamara, his ex-fiancée in his head. *Where do you expect people to sit in a room like this?* she'd asked more than once, while trying to convince him to change his ways. *On each other's laps?*

I don't, he would respond. *This is my kingdom, my castle. This is the furniture that I like.*

In the end, he'd given in to her demands and purchased a sectional that had dwarfed his tiny apartment.

He hated that sectional.

When he graduated med school and moved back to Haw Springs, he left that sectional in the apartment. *Furnished*, he told the landlord. *What a steal.*

It'll be a steal for the dump, the landlord countered.

Even better, Matthew had said over his shoulder as he walked out of the office, leaving the sectional, the apartment and Tamara to be part of his past.

I'll charge you the moving fee, the landlord had yelled.

Worth it! Matthew yelled back.

He guessed that Marlee would have understood his furniture choices. She wouldn't have expected him to fill his apartment with an expensive couch to seat nobody.

But now, with Janquil taking up residence in the rocking chair, leaving only the small love seat for him and Marlee, he supposed he could see Tamara's point.

He gestured for Tyler to take the cushion next to Marlee.

"All good, mate," Tyler said. "I'll be moving around, anyway." He lifted the camera for emphasis.

"Right," Matthew said. "Of course."

Marlee, looking almost as nervous as he felt, sat on the love seat and patted the cushion next to her. He sat, suddenly overly aware of everything about her.

Was her voice always so melodic? Was that soft undercurrent of vanilla always radiating off her? Did she really giggle this often? Was her leg, currently pressed up against his, always this warm?

He found himself fidgeting now, the way she had done on the porch. But she seemed to be relaxing into the ruse, her posture perfect, her ankles crossed, her eyes sparkling and smile wide as she small talked. He found himself watching her, admiring the show.

"So let's get down to it," Janquil said, opening her notebook. "How did you two meet?"

They turned to gaze at each other. Marlee let out that little giggle again. But he could see the alarm in her eyes. In all of this, they'd never even thought to put together a backstory that made sense. The most basic thing, and they'd overlooked it.

Now they were going to have to lie on the spot.

"You tell them, sweetums," Marlee said.

Matthew felt his entire body turn to ice.

He wasn't good at lying. He was pathetically terrible at it. He had been hoping to follow Marlee's lead throughout this entire con, smiling and nodding while she wove tales and made them appear to be romantic without ever having to be romantic.

He realized now what a mistake that plan had been.

His ears started buzzing as his mind raced to find a story that sounded both believable and romantic. Again, Tamara's voice piped up in his head. *You're a terrible storyteller, Matthew, did you know that? You give details like you're reading a police report. You're a real snooze-fest. Let me talk from now on.*

He could pull the plug. Right here, right now.

Be done with the whole thing. Marlee would be livid, but she would get over it. And if she didn't, oh well. It wasn't like they were even friends. He could save himself the humiliation of being a horrible storyteller and end it.

Right here.

Right now.

He could feel all eyes on him. He had to speak.

He smiled and his mouth opened and words came out of their own volition. He wasn't in charge anymore.

"I'm afraid you're not going to like what I have to say."

CHAPTER ELEVEN

NO. WAY. THERE WAS no way he was about to out them. After all this work, he was going to end it before it could even properly get off the ground. She knew she made a mistake in choosing Matthew, of all people, to fake a relationship with.

Marlee felt her heart sink, pounding as it fell, sending reverberations throughout her whole body. She was sure that if Janquil and Tyler looked at her hard enough, they could see the booms move her frame.

She watched in wide-eyed horror as Matthew continued.

He shrugged. "I'm just not the best storyteller, and it wasn't very romantic. She double-parked her delivery van in front of my clinic."

Marlee let out a breath that she hadn't been aware she'd been holding. Thank goodness. Thank *goodness.* And brilliant—he was going with the truth. They had met over him complaining about her parking, and it had been anything but romantic.

"To be fair," she interjected, "I didn't even know that he'd opened a clinic there." That was a lie. In fact, she'd been very aware of the handsome doctor across the street. She'd watched him intensely the entire time he was moving in, as if he were her new favorite reality TV show. She'd admired him from afar, all the way up until she met him. That's when the long-distance crush ended.

He nodded conspiratorially with Janquil. "She knew. Anyway, so I went across the street to her shop, and there she was. Making a wreath."

"Funeral wreath," she said somberly. "For Mrs. Akins. Haw Springs' beloved public librarian."

"It was stunning," he said. "Pink and orange, if I remember correctly."

Marlee stared at him in awe. How odd that he remembered that detail, she thought. She had all but forgotten about the flowers in that wreath. But now, she could see them vividly in her mind. "Orange Asiatic lilies and carnations," she said, the words sounding faraway to her ears. "And hot-pink spray roses, with some yellow chrysanthemums and huckleberry."

"There was something blue in there, too," he said, maintaining eye contact with Marlee.

"Um." She found it hard to concentrate with him staring at her like this. "Blue delphinium. I think. Wow."

He gave a tight, nervous grin, then cleared his throat and broke the gaze. "I will admit I was a little irritated that she'd double-parked in front of my clinic, because she'd done it every single day since I moved in."

It took Marlee a moment to gather herself together, shake the...whatever had just happened between them. She gave an exaggerated wink to the room; Tyler's camera clicked. "*A little irritated*, sure. He was practically frothing at the mouth."

"I was not frothing at the mouth. I was spirited."

"Oh! Spirited! Great word for a ranting and raving lunatic."

"Ranting? Raving? More like eloquently stating my case."

"Loudly."

Matthew scratched the back of his neck, going pink. "Okay, with a little bit of volume. And if I remember correctly, you also had volume. And offered to stuff that wreath over the top half of my body."

This elicited a chuckle out of Janquil. Marlee felt the nerves and awkwardness drain away as she, too, laughed at the memory.

Yes, it had gotten spirited between them.

"So did you know right then that she was the one?" Janquil asked, pencil poised over the pad, her fingers twitching as if to write the words she knew he was going to say before he said them.

By now, the pink that had crept up Matthew's neck had turned scarlet and moved to his ears.

Marlee felt a twinge of guilt over what this lie was going to do to him over the long haul. Surely he was feeling all sorts of stress over this.

He grew very serious, his eyes locked on Marlee's as he talked. "I knew that she had this incredible energy about her, this bravery, as if she was unafraid of anything the world had to throw at her. And that she was smart as a whip and this hugely talented artist." His voice softened. "Who wouldn't fall in love with that person?"

Now Marlee felt her own face redden.

"And you called her an artist," Janquil said. "Not a florist. Marlee, do you consider yourself an artist?"

Marlee opened her mouth to answer, but Matthew shifted position so that he was facing Janquil. "Oh, but there is no other word for it. If you'd seen her building that wreath, if you'd ever seen her build anything, the way she approaches it, softly biting her bottom lip, turning her head this way and that, thinking of the perfect way to arrange things, it's like you can see her gathering her soul into something that the world can see and touch. It's just the same as watching a sculptor. Only…well, you know, flowers are beautiful all on their own. She could get away with just throwing them together, much more easily than a sculptor could get away with throwing lumps of clay together. But she doesn't. She takes something already beautiful and makes it sublime. Spend a moment with one of her creations, and I assure you, it will start talking to you. It will tell you things that you never knew possible or maybe confirm for you what you thought you already knew." He shifted again. "I'm sorry to interrupt, my love. Er, sugar cone."

He reached over and squeezed Marlee's hand. She knew he was putting on a show, but in the moment he sounded so sincere, as if these were things that he actually believed about her. Her mouth still hung open, and she realized with a start that everyone was looking at her, expecting her to answer the question that Janquil had posed. Only…she could no longer remember what that question was, she was so discombobulated.

"Can I get anyone something to drink?" she asked, whisking her hand out of Matthew's and standing. Trying to do whatever she could to distance herself from whatever had just transpired and clear her head.

"We're good," Janquil said, without even consulting Tyler. All business, she pressed on. "So you went over to complain about a double-parked van and there was this beautiful artist at work and the whole world was swept out from under you," she said. "Marlee, what about you? What was your experience?"

Marlee dropped back onto the love seat. Her mind was still swimming after listening to him; how on earth was she going to even begin to compete with what he'd just said? She couldn't. She'd have to go an entirely different route. Go with the truth.

"I despised him," she said.

This elicited a nervous chuckle throughout the room, which, oddly, put her at ease. So she continued.

"I thought he was rude and entitled and brash." Again, she and Matthew locked eyes, but she could have sworn she saw something different in his. Surprise. Displeasure. And maybe, just maybe, a little bit of admiration? She turned back to Janquil. "I mean, I thought he was handsome. Anyone can see that. But he was difficult and prickly and exactly the opposite of me in just about every single way. I vowed then and there that he and I would never be friends. That I would oppose him in every way that I could. So I continued to park my van there, day after day."

"She wanted me to come in and complain," Matthew said, his eyes blazing with competition.

She laughed. "Oh-ho! I did, did I?"

He nodded. "It was the one surefire way that she could guarantee seeing me every day. She parked. I came over and complained. We fought. Day after day. She made sure of it. Tell me that's not a crush."

"So who made the first move?" Janquil asked. "How did it turn into love?"

"He did," Marlee said quickly, before he could

say anything. She gave him an arched-eyebrow look meant to say, *I won*. "He made the first move."

"But she wanted me to make a move," he said. "She didn't exactly fend me off."

Tyler circled the room, the camera clicking and clicking. Aware of this, Marlee snaked her hand across the love seat for Matthew's and clutched it, a lump growing in her throat as she did so.

This was all just so weird, and for some reason, she hadn't anticipated any of it. She'd been so excited for the big picture, she didn't even consider any of the details.

"What did that look like, Matthew? Your first move. The one she didn't fend off."

"Uh..." He gave a laugh that Marlee somehow knew meant he had no idea. He hadn't thought that far ahead and was buying time. She only hoped that Janquil and Tyler, and his camera, saw it as shyness. "I came over to complain. Again. And she was, uh, moving things around. Just refreshing the shop. You know."

"Sure," Janquil said.

Click went the camera.

Marlee thought she saw a bead of sweat on Matthew's temple.

"So I walked in there like I was really angry. But, of course, I was excited to see her again. So I started in on my usual speech. *Move the van. It's not your space. You're hindering my business.* So on and so forth. But I could see that she was struggling to move a bench. She was dragging it along. Huffing and puffing. Knocking things over. Her hair was in her face. She looked spent. I wanted to help. But I also just wanted to be close to her. So I jumped in and grabbed the other end of the bench. And we got the bench into place without even talking about it—like we were just on the same wavelength. And, after, she was grateful. She thanked me. And I started to say something about the best way for her to thank me would be to park in her own parking space. But I was overcome with something else. I didn't want to argue with her anymore."

"So you were overcome with what, exactly?" Janquil asked.

"Longing."

Once again, Marlee matched his gaze. They held it for so long, she felt compelled to break whatever it was that was transpiring between them.

"I was overcome with thirst. That bench was heavy. I needed water," she said, and there was laughter all around.

"Did he kiss you?" Janquil asked, after they'd finished laughing.

"No!" Marlee and Matthew said together.

"He asked me on a date," Marlee said. "And I said yes."

Janquil frowned. "That's it? After all that explanation, I would have expected a grander gesture. He knew you were the one the first time he came over to the flower shop to complain," she said. "Yet you say he simply asked you on a date and you said yes. That's pretty boring. Standard. I expected more from a viral couple. Are you guys standard?"

For the first time since Janquil and Tyler arrived, Marlee felt a stab that maybe they were looking for more than she was going to be able to give them. They wanted a *Story*. Of course they did. The internet lived and died on stories, big and small. Things that made people keep returning to read more, for one reason or another.

"Standard? Oh, absolutely not," she said, but her eyes pleaded with Matthew to help her out.

"I created a rooftop garden for her," Matthew said. "We had dinner for two atop the clinic, among a jungle of beautiful flowers. She can name them. I can't."

"Sunflowers, lavender, daylilies, petunias, geraniums, nasturtiums, hydrangeas, the *standards*," she added without thinking, surprising even herself. "Plus, of course, roses on the table. And twinkle lights everywhere."

"Sounds magical," Janquil said.

"Oh, it was." What Marlee could see in her mind's eye was exactly that—magical. *As fake as movie magic*, she thought. *The Myth itself, in convenient floral arrangements.*

"Can we get up there? For photos?" Tyler asked.

Marlee felt Matthew stiffen beside her. She jumped in to rescue him. "We had to dismantle it," she said quickly. "The landlord was worried about pests and water damage."

"I'm sure you took pictures, though," Tyler said. "Maybe we can edit them. Enhance them to look pro."

"I was too lost in the perfect evening to even touch my phone," Matthew said.

Marlee gave a vigorous nod. "Same."

Janquil peered at them over the top of a pair of readers that balanced on the bridge of her nose. Her pencil was frozen in the air above her notebook. She looked skeptical. "Surely you went up there more than once."

Marlee and Matthew exchanged glances. "I'm afraid not," she said, searching his eyes for inspiration. What on earth would be the reason for not returning to such a magical setting?

"The landlord lives up on the hill," Matthew said. "He saw it right away and called me about it the next morning. It was dismantled before she and I even talked about a second date."

Janquil's skeptical stare softened, her mouth going into a sympathetic straight line. "That's a shame," she said. "Would have made a great photo. I'm sure we'll find others."

"Already got some," Tyler said, bored.

Janquil pressed on. "So it was love after first date?"

"Definitely," Marlee said. "Who wouldn't fall in love with him after all that?"

"I was already in love with her," Matthew said. "I just had to admit it."

He gave Marlee's hand another squeeze, and when they glanced each other's way again, his flicker of a smile seemed sincere. If she hadn't been the orchestrator of the ruse, she might have been confused into believing that what they were describing was real. That what he was feeling was true. That they'd really fallen for each other in a magical rooftop garden.

Which was why she was so shocked when, after standing on her front porch waving goodbye to the departing Janquil and Tyler, Matthew took a deep breath, turned to her, and said, "I'm out."

CHAPTER TWELVE

"WHAT?" MARLEE'S JAW hung open in shock.

Gravel dust still hung in the air, having been stirred up by the rental car tires. Janquil and Tyler were headed to their hotel in Riverside for the night. As far as Matthew was concerned, that wasn't far enough away. He didn't trust either of them one bit.

"I said I'm out. I thought I could do this, but it turns out, I can't. I'm done." He headed back inside. He was hungry. And tired. All the lying had taken a mental toll on him. "I'll help you clean up first."

Marlee followed him into the house. "What do you mean you can't? That went really well. I think they believed everything we said."

"Oh, they bought it all right." He rolled up his sleeves as he walked through the house. Loosened his tie, and then removed it, hanging it over the back of one of the kitchen chairs.

"Well, then, what's the problem? You were brilliant. Your idea to use mostly true events almost even fooled me into believing you. It felt so real."

He cleared one side of the sink and began running hot water into it. "And that's the problem. It felt too real."

"Too real? What does that even mean, too real? Is the idea of being romantically involved with someone like me so off-putting that you can't stand the idea of it sounding too real, even when you know it's a lie?"

Matthew dunked a pot into the water and let it fill up. Whatever had been in it had incinerated there. It was going to need a lot of soaking and a lot of elbow grease to get clean. "No, of course not," he said.

"Then what is it? Because you are a natural hopeless romantic, Matthew LaSalle."

He turned and pressed the small of his back into the counter. She was standing a little too close—he could feel that zap pulling at him—but he tried to ignore it. "That's what it is. I don't believe in romance. I don't believe in love. I don't believe in relationships. I don't want anything even approaching the things we were so casually describing. So, yes, it was too real. It felt like I could open myself up to such things. And I just can't."

"Hello, have you forgotten? I'm not expecting you to," Marlee said. "Just because you were believable doesn't mean I believe that we're in love. I know what reality is, and I know what it isn't.

And you're not the only one who doesn't want those things, I might add. So, you're good. No danger here."

"Felt dangerous," he muttered, turning back to the sink. He grabbed a sponge and plunged his hands into the pot.

"Stop," Marlee said, reaching around him and turning off the water. "I have a dishwasher for that."

"You can't put this stuff in the dishwasher."

"Why not?"

He felt his eyes bug. "Because you'll clog up the filter in your dishwasher, and it probably won't even come off, anyway." He turned the water back on.

She turned the water off again. "How is it going to clog up my filter if it's not going to come off?"

"You know what I mean."

She arched one eyebrow at him. "Is the soap too real?"

"Do you take anything seriously?"

"Yes. But definitely not dirty dishes."

"And lies, apparently."

She crossed her arms, her brow furrowing. "And apparently you don't take lying all that seriously, either. Since you're so good at it. Seems like maybe you've had a lot of practice."

His mind blipped to Tamara, and how he'd lied to himself for months on end, telling himself that he was still himself, that he could marry her without losing who he was. In that regard, then yes, he'd had plenty of practice.

"I didn't exactly have a choice in the moment," he said. "You threw it at me so fast and so hard, if it had been a ball, it would have given me a concussion."

Her phone beeped and she pulled it out of her pocket. "Well, you certainly had a choice before now. Before any of this started, you could have said no."

"I did."

"And then you said yes."

"Have you ever tried to say no to you?"

She gave him a disgusted look as she unlocked her phone. "What kind of sense does that even make? About as much sense as the dishwasher getting clogged up by…" She trailed off as she scrolled on her phone.

"What?" he said, leaning in to see what had taken her attention. He had a moment of wondering what it must be like to look at everything through the silky curtain of hair that hung over her shoulder.

"Oh," she said. "Oh!" She barked out a laugh and thrust her phone at him. "Guess you are pretty good at lying."

Her phone was open to social media, and a post from *Modern Vow*, which featured a photo of Matthew and Marlee on the love seat, holding hands while exchanging a knowing look. The post read:

We're still swooning from our time spent with these two Haw Springs Sweethearts. Watch for all the romantic deets—first "I love you," first kiss, and when they plan to say, "I do"—in our upcoming feature, which we're tentatively titling "Love in Full Bloom." Just saying, he wouldn't have to ask us twice. We might even be willing to throw ourselves down a ladder if it means this Dreamy Doctor would catch us at the bottom.

"'First kiss'?" Matthew read aloud. "What first kiss?" He glanced at Marlee, who was still laughing, although her laugh had a little maniacal edge to it. "And they're expecting us to get married?"

"Well," Marlee said, taking her phone back. "Not without a proper engagement." She pressed her lips together as if to hold back laughter.

As usual, her lighthearted attitude was beginning to mystify him. Which, he knew, would inevitably aggravate him. It was as if he and she communicated in two completely different languages.

"Two hours ago, you were ready to pull the plug."

"That was before we got engaged," she said.

"You know what?" he said, tossing the sponge back into the sink. "I think it's time for me to go."

"Oh, come on, Matthew. I was just teasing."

"Maybe I don't think it's funny."

"Maybe you should lighten up a little bit, then."

He gave her a long look. How many times had he heard that in his life? From his sister, his teachers, his friends, Tamara, even his own mother. A *plink* sound came from her phone and she glanced at it.

"Maybe I should," Matthew said. "But maybe this isn't the way." He headed to the kitchen chair where he'd left his tie. He retrieved it and draped it around his neck.

"Maybe," Marlee said. "But I wouldn't be so sure if I was you."

"Is that so? Well, then, I guess it's good you're not me."

Wordlessly, Marlee held her phone out to him again. When he didn't take it, she simply raised her eyebrows and nodded.

With a sigh, he took the phone. "I don't know what you're hoping to achieve here. I've seen it and I don't care." He broke off as he took in the comments that had already begun to pile on to *Modern Vow*'s post.

I knew there was a doc there, but I didn't know he was a pediatrician! I'm due in three weeks and wasn't sure what I was going to do with my baby.

There's a pediatrician in Haw Springs now? I live in Oak Hollow and have been wishing for one nearby since my oldest was born.

No more driving to Riverside for all those ear infections!

I hope Dr. Romance has lots of openings, bc he's about to get swamped.

Well, Matthew thought. *That changes everything, now, doesn't it?*

He hated to admit it, but it did. He didn't want to be that guy. He didn't want to be for sale, willing to give up his ideals just because it might be lucrative for him. But it wasn't as if he were greedy—it was about a little thing called making ends meet so he could stay in the town where his heart belonged.

Marlee had predicted a boom in business and here it was, on the verge of possibly booming. The thing was, when Matthew imagined getting new patients, he imagined Haw Springsians finally cutting the cord with Dr. Tidwell; he hadn't even considered bringing in patients from surrounding towns.

This could be what established him in the community. He knew he was good at what he did. He knew that he was the right combination of serious and playful with the kids, knowledgeable and personable with the parents.

And now, apparently, he was also romantic, and maybe even a little...*dreamy*?

He handed the phone back to Marlee, who took

it and went back to scrolling with more than a little bit of glee etched across her face.

"So," she said, typing with her thumbs, "Decker has a ranch for kids on the spectrum. It's called McBride Pathways. Up on top of the ridge, overlooking Haw Springs Valley."

Matthew nodded. "I helped them with a fundraiser when I first moved back."

"Oh, that's right. You worked with my sister, Morgan, on that."

"And now enjoy having your nephew, Archer, as a patient."

"Right. Well, their next session begins next week, and will kick off with a big open house. Part fundraiser, but mostly just to make the kids comfortable with the ranch."

"Good idea," Matthew said, waiting for the *and*.

"And—" there it was "—we are going to volunteer to help out."

"*We* are?"

She kept typing. "Together."

She hit Enter and showed him what she'd written.

Thank you, @ModernVowMag for joining us in our little love nest! We can't wait to show you all our favorite, most romantic spots, and let you in on all the insider secrets! Join us at @mcbrideranch for the open house? We'll be there together. Say you'll come?

Oh, and P.S. ladies, we would love to see your babies in Haw Springs...but remember, Dr. Romance is mine!

While Matthew stared with incredulity that she would put those things out there without even asking—*because you would say no, Matthew, and you both know it*—*Modern Vow*'s response popped up.

We'll be there!

He let his arm sag to his side. "They'll be there."

"Yay!" Marlee golf-clapped as she grinned at him. "We've got a date. Dress comfortably. It gets hot on the trail."

He set the phone on the table and silently walked away.

Yay, he thought as he descended the front porch steps, his tie still slung around his neck like he'd just ended a terminally long day.

Yay. They're coming.

CHAPTER THIRTEEN

MARLEE LOVED THE energy of the first day of a Pathways session. The kids were eager and excited, the volunteers bustling. Even the horses nickered and swished their tails with a little extra vigor.

This was her second year of being part of the excitement, by leading a workshop on safe versus unsafe vegetation on the trail. The kids were always surprisingly into it, and she loved seeing their interest in building bouquets of edible flowers and making bookmarks and prints out of leaves and bark. She liked to think that she might spark something in one of them that could, somewhere down the road, turn into a passion.

Today, there seemed to be an even heavier thrum of energy as she set up her table, which was located under an oak tree between the barn and the house, away from the horses and the riding trail. There were more campers than usual, and more parents sticking around, standing in clumps, chatting, their heads swiveling this way and that.

It seemed to Marlee that they were looking for something, or maybe some*one*, a theory that was confirmed when Morgan appeared at her table.

"Any ETA on the most sought-after pediatrician Haw Springs has ever seen?"

"He's the only pediatrician Haw Springs has ever seen," Marlee responded. "And no, not yet. Are people really looking for him?"

Morgan nodded. "It's crazy. Some of these people have been bringing their kids for years and have kept to themselves, hardly ever uttering a word. All of a sudden, they're all chitchat and jabber. Our best friends."

Marlee felt a wave of nerves wash over her. Her sister, who knew her better than she knew herself, frowned.

"Everything okay?"

Marlee beckoned her to come closer. "What if he doesn't show up?"

Morgan opened a baggie full of flower clippings and spread them over the table. "Is there a chance of that? He said he would do a little Q and A with the parents about children on the spectrum."

"I don't know," Marlee said. "He hasn't exactly been on board with our…little project. And he was flat-out upset after our dinner date."

Morgan smirked. "Doesn't there have to be a dinner in order for it to be considered a dinner date?"

"Okay, okay," Marlee said. "Our interview. Better?"

"Have you talked to him since?"

"No, that's the thing. Not a word. He hasn't even come over to yell at me about my van. I've parked it obnoxiously close to his clinic. Like, basically on his sidewalk."

"Why would you do that?"

"To get him to yell at me!"

Morgan's smirk deepened to a knowing grin that Marlee didn't like one bit. "No," she said, "don't. It's not that."

"Seems like it could be that. Has the myth grown into something more of a tall tale?"

"Can you not?" Marlee went back to her work, plumping a bouquet of edible flowers in a small vase that she would later use as an example. "And to answer you directly, no. It's just…" Marlee glanced over her shoulder to make sure they were alone. "We're supposed to be in love," she whispered. "You would think he would at least bring me lunch or something."

Morgan barked out a single laugh, then clapped her hand over her mouth.

"It looks suspicious," Marlee said. "That's all. And if he doesn't show up today, then it's really going to look suspicious."

"If he doesn't show up today, there are going to be more than a few disappointed parents," Morgan agreed.

They heard the crunch of tires on gravel and turned to see Matthew's car ease into Decker's driveway. Marlee felt her whole body unclench as she realized he had shown up after all. At the same time, she felt a strange lightheadedness as they watched him come down the hill toward them, his dress shoes kicking up dust in the grass. Marlee could feel, rather than see or hear, an excitement among the parents as he came closer.

"Didn't you tell him this would be casual?" Morgan whispered.

"I did," Marlee said. "That is his version of casual. He's not wearing a tie."

"Sorry I'm late," he said as he got closer to the table. "I had a…new patient." He mumbled the last, as if he was ashamed. But Marlee knew it was just that he didn't want to admit that he had a new patient. Sharing that would mean admitting this wasn't a terrible plan.

"Not a problem," Morgan said. "I don't need you until the kids hit the trail. After I give my spiel about the Pathways program, our sponsors, what to expect, blah, blah, blah, I'll turn it over to you. In the meantime, you're welcome to help your betrothed here." She gestured at Marlee's table.

Marlee looked up sharply. *Betrothed?* she wanted to ask. *Really?* But she didn't have time to say a word.

"Oh," Morgan said. "And it looks like your paparazzi is here."

Marlee swiveled in her chair. Janquil and Tyler had parked in Decker's driveway and were sauntering down the hill toward her tree. She could sense, rather than see, several of the parents turn and watch. With Janquil's little notebook and pencil clutched in one hand and her giant, black-rimmed glasses perched on her face, and Tyler's camera slung around his neck, there was no mistaking that they were reporters. In that moment, Marlee felt the tiniest pang of regret. She hoped that her whole life wasn't about to turn into a circus. More than that, she hoped that her presence wasn't going to upstage Annie and Ben's wedding.

She made a mental note to have a chat with Janquil about blending in. But, deep down, she knew that there was no blending in for a reporter and an accompanying photographer in a town like Haw Springs.

"I'm going to…avoid being on camera," Morgan said, sweeping away and leaving the two of them alone.

Marlee tried to catch Matthew's eye, to somehow get a sense of how he was feeling this morning. She was pretty sure he was about to bust this whole thing wide-open. Her palms started to sweat, and she felt her heart in her throat. But Matthew looked calm and resolute.

"You good?" she asked.

He finally made eye contact. "I have three new patients," he said.

She knew that was his way of saying that he was okay, and that this was okay, although he still didn't love the idea of what was going on. He may have come around begrudgingly, but still he'd come around.

"That's amazing," she said. "Congratulations."

She could see him cast his eyes over her shoulder. He was looking at Janquil and Tyler. She, too, glanced at them. Annie had caught them, and was busy chatting their ears off. They nodded politely as she went on. When Marlee glanced back at Matthew, his Adam's apple was working.

"Do you need to say something?" Marlee asked. Janquil was edging away from Annie, bringing a panicked pinkness to Matthew's cheeks.

"PDA," he blurted.

Marlee stopped, her hands still gently cradling a cluster of violets. "I'm sorry?"

"Public Displays of Affection," he said, clarifying.

"I know what PDA is," she said. "I just don't know why you randomly said it."

Matthew leaned over the table. He looked for all the world like someone who was calm and in control, maybe even flirting. But to Marlee, who had spent plenty of time in his presence when he was flustered, could see something else. "We're not believable without it," he whispered.

"Oh." Now it was her turn to feel flushed. "So you think we should be…kissing?" Her throat felt scratchy and dry, and she could barely get the word out. It sounded like a hiss.

"Well, you don't have to say it like it's the worst thing in the world. But, no, I don't mean kissing. Except…" He glanced at Janquil and Tyler again. They were still caught up with Annie. "Well, they might ask for that. For a photo."

Marlee hadn't even considered that. He was right, and it made total sense. They not only *might* ask for them to kiss for a photo but would very likely ask for that. Marlee hadn't kissed anyone since she last kissed Keith, and she wasn't about to start now. She was all for acting the part, but she had to draw a line somewhere, and it turned out that lips were that somewhere.

Besides, there was something about the idea of kissing Matthew specifically that made her feel a little extra awkward.

"We'll evade," she said simply.

"Evade how?"

"I don't know, but we'll do it." She forced her concentration back to the violets but noticed the tiny petals quivering as her fingers shook when she touched them.

"That doesn't seem like much of a plan," Matthew said.

"We'll change the subject or come down with a cough or… I don't know, maybe it will be more enticing to our followers if we haven't kissed yet and are saving that moment for something special."

"Something special? Like what? Our wedding? That they will surely want to come to, by the way?"

Marlee paused. He was right. She knew he was right. This was a little bump in the road that she hadn't seen coming. She was starting to fear that there would be many bumps that she wouldn't see coming until she was on top of them. Why was she so bad at seeing bumps ahead?

She took a deep breath. She could do bumps. She was great at bumps. Or at least great at pretending she was great at bumps. "We'll cross that bridge when we get to it. In the meantime, I think we can hold hands more. And maybe you could put your arm around me every now and then." She tried not to think about how having Matthew's arm casually slung around her shoulders would feel. She shivered with the effort.

"Yes," he said. "Right. Also…followers? I hate that word."

"Well, that's what they're called."

He scratched the back of his neck, making a *hmm* noise. "I suppose it's just that I hate having them."

Janquil and Tyler finally broke away from Annie, and were coming toward Marlee's table, double-time, their voices getting louder as they approached.

Marlee leaned over her table. "They're not followers. They're three new patients," she whispered. "And you don't hate having those."

Matthew grinned, holding back a chuckle. An unusual sight on him. He nodded, his hand still resting on the back of his neck. Marlee noticed dimples creasing the edges of his cheeks for the first time. The sun, which had begun to rise in earnest, lit up the right half of his face. He stole one last glance at Janquil and Tyler, made sure they were watching, then swooped in and quickly gave her a peck on the cheek that sent waves of warmth throughout her while simultaneously freezing her completely.

And in that moment, holding a cluster of violets loosely in her palm, watching him there, all dimples and discomfort and sunlight and uneasy smiles, the soft warmth of his lips lingering on her cheek, Marlee was struck with a thought: Feeling his arm around her shoulders felt comforting and familiar. Maybe not bad in the least.

CHAPTER FOURTEEN

SHE WAS A STAR.

A true star.

Maybe or maybe not on social media—Matthew didn't know and didn't care about that. But at her little folding table strewn with flowers, Marlee West was the brightest star in the solar system.

After Decker got the camp started, he broke the kids into groups and they rotated through several stations, some learning how to tack a horse, some learning about helmets, some playing games. There seemed to be endless things for them to do, and most of the kids looked like they were having the time of their lives.

He lowered himself to the ground under a tree and watched but, time and again, he found himself turning his attention to Marlee's table. Listening to her melodic voice talk about safe and unsafe foliage and answer impossible questions. *What happens if I eat poison ivy? What kind of flower would it be if you mixed this flower with that flower? What about this one? And this? Can you write my name in flowers? What was the very first flower ever?* She seemed to know everything about flowers. Either that, or she was great at making stuff up.

He heard the snap of a camera and spun around just in time for Janquil to join him, her ever-present notebook in hand.

"She's got her hands full, huh?" Janquil asked, nodding toward Marlee's table.

"She's amazing," Matthew responded, trying to lay it on thick, but finding that he didn't really have to. She *was* amazing. Anyone could see it.

"It's also pretty amazing that you just come to sit here and watch her. Do you do this every year?"

"I have a thing with the parents later." He sidestepped, feeling a prickle of wariness. Did he do this every year? What would Marlee have said if they asked her the same question? Suddenly, he didn't want to be there. Being interviewed alone felt like a trap. How could he possibly ensure that their answers would match?

"How long exactly have you two been together?" Janquil asked.

Oh, no. There it was.

"Not long enough. Feels like a lifetime. In the best possible way." He silently commended himself for another artful sidestep.

Janquil arched one eyebrow and pursed her

lips, sneaking a glance at him over the top of her glasses. "Don't you know your anniversary?"

"Of course I do." He felt irrationally stung by this accusation. There was no anniversary, yet how dare she insinuate that he wouldn't know it? He had been great at that sort of stuff with Tamara.

Fat lot of good it did him in the end.

"So it's…?"

Focus, Matthew, focus.

He got an idea. "Could we not share that? It's just that, you know, a lot of people aren't good with boundaries. And I really don't want to receive a thousand teddy bears or little heart trinkets. I'd prefer to keep our actual anniversary date private." There. That sounded good. Very believable. And then he doubled down, in a terrible way. "Same with our wedding date."

Now both of Janquil's eyebrows flew up. "Oh, so there *is* a wedding date!"

Instantly, he knew his mistake. He was going to either have to ride it out or he was going to have to double back on what he'd just said. And he didn't have any time to consider his options. Every second spent mulling things over felt like an hour. The longer he took, the greater chance that Janquil would see through his lies. Once again, he regretted his decision to go along with this plan.

Three new patients, Matthew. Three. In one day.

He nodded. "We are engaged, yes."

"But… Marlee isn't wearing a ring."

"It's being sized," he explained. "I, uh, got the wrong size. Too big. She didn't want to take the chance of losing it."

"So this was recent if the ring is still being sized."

"The jeweler is behind. It's going to take a while."

Janquil's whole face twisted in confusion and doubt. "So weird that Marlee didn't say anything about a wedding date. I guess I was under the impression that you hadn't proposed just yet. Tell me, how did you do it? I'm sure it was incredibly romantic, given how romantic your first date was."

This was getting too deep, and Janquil was pushing too hard. Tyler's camera lens felt like a magnifying glass concentrating sunlight directly onto Matthew's face. He began to sweat under its glare. He glanced at Tyler, who gave him a cocky, gum-chomping smile.

Matthew was beginning to fear that he'd weave a story of which he wouldn't be able to remember all the details. That Marlee would be asked these questions later and would give different details. That they would be caught just because he was so bad at lying. Exactly what he'd feared would happen.

"We can reenact it," he blurted. "I mean, in case you want photos." He gave Tyler another glance, and the photographer returned it with another *Sure thing, bud* smile and a perfunctory nod.

What did he mean, in case they wanted photos?

They were media—of course, they would want photos! Dangling that in front of them was like dangling a steak in front of a starving dog. Janquil's entire existence lit up. He could practically feel her joy emanating beside him.

"Yes," she said. "How about tomorrow?"

This was getting out of control. Every cell in Matthew's body was backpedaling. "I think it's supposed to rain tomorrow," he said, shrugging his shoulders regretfully, as if that explained everything.

"Oh, did you do it outside?" Janquil asked.

"Yes."

Decker's ranch sat on top of a hill that offered an incredible bird's-eye view of all of Buck County. Matthew's eyes landed on a spot on the ridge across from where they sat. He knew the spot well.

He pointed to the horizon. "There's a hiking trail that opens up onto a ridge right where you see that grove of pines. You can see all of Buck County on this side and all of Deerfield County on the other. If you take a pair of binoculars up there, you can just about see all the way to Riverside."

He didn't guess this; he knew it. He'd done just that more times than he could count. He'd spent countless hours sitting on a rock up there, legs dangling over the edge of the ridge, feeling like he was literally on top of the world, looking down at the trees below, soaking in the beauty of nature and feeling rooted in the place where he'd grown up. Feeling sure that he would never leave that spot, never leave Haw Springs, never leave his roots. Dreaming of the future, savoring the welling excitement in his chest, the balloon feeling of possibility. But he hadn't been there alone, hadn't been dreaming alone.

In fact, it was the spot where he'd once proposed to Tamara.

The spot where she'd denied him. So, actually, he realized after, he had been dreaming alone. He just hadn't known it at the time.

He hadn't been back since that fateful night. Since he pointed out all the things he'd changed about himself in order to be the perfect partner for her. Since she told him that she'd never seen him that way, not in a permanent sense. Since she told him that no matter what he changed, he would never be that for her.

It was not a good spot. In fact, he sort of hated it.

But it was a spot that he knew well. And he didn't have time to indulge past hurt feelings right now. He had to come up with an outdoor spot that he didn't need to think about.

"It's the perfect spot," he said, somewhat lost in the nostalgia of it all. "Living in Haw Springs, you tend to look up a lot." He gestured toward the lush greenery in front of them.

"It's very picturesque here," Janquil agreed.

"So when I was ten or so, I got my first bike, and I wanted to go to the very top of that ridge right there. I wanted to be in the place where I'd set my eyes my entire life. So I did. And it became a refuge. I hiked or rode my bike up there every chance I got. I brought guidebooks. I could name every tree, every bush, every bird. When I was at the top of the ridge, I felt like I could see an entire lifetime laid out in front of me, and it was…it was beautiful. I wanted to share it with Marlee. Not just the spot, but all of it. The swooping birds, the sunshine, the hum of nature, and the future. Especially the future."

This was exactly what he had been thinking when he'd proposed to Tamara, and the memory of it brought a lump to his throat that dried up his words.

"Wow," Janquil said. "So beautiful. You really are romantic, Matthew." She was scribbling words in her notebook, as if trying to capture everything he just said, and he wanted to take all the words back. Somehow, telling her the truth felt worse than lying to her. The idea of the public knowing real things about him brought him a feeling of empty dullness. What if Tamara read this article? Would she recognize her own experience? Would she come forward? "We'll keep it short."

He snapped out of it. "What?"

"Because of the rain. A few romantic shots. Quick reenactment. We can touch up the photos to include a ring, no worries there." She tilted her head to one side. "Tomorrow. We'll just beat the rain."

"Beat the rain?"

She shrugged. "It can't rain every second of the entire day. Can we drive? Looks like a long way to hike with Tyler's equipment."

"There's a service road that will get you most of the way there," he said through numb lips. "Might be hard with a car. Especially if it's wet."

"We'll rent an ATV. We'll go in the morning." She stood, brushed off the back of her pants. She checked the time on her phone. "What time is your little presentation? It's getting hot… I would kill for an iced chai. I don't suppose I can find one around here?" She paused, dipped to look him in the eye. "Hello? Iced chai?"

"Huh?" Matthew felt far away, trapped from himself. Was he really proposing to Marlee tomorrow? In the same place he'd proposed to Tamara?

The same place where his heart had been shattered and he'd sworn off love and relationships forever?

"Oh, uh, yeah. Down on Main Street. It's called, uh, The Baked Bean."

Janquil snapped her fingers at Tyler. "That's where you got those homemade Pop-Tarts this morning, isn't it?"

Tyler nodded, still chomping his gum. Matthew had begun to see the gum-chomping thing as smug. As if Tyler was so uninterested in all of this, he had to chew gum to keep himself awake and upright.

"Okay, I'll be back in time for your—" she flailed her fingers toward him, a similar smugness to the gum habit "—your…whatever. Let's go, Ty. It's so hot here."

Matthew watched them go, Janquil talking to Tyler, gesturing toward the ridge that they'd be visiting in the morning, then turned his eyes to Marlee.

She was watching him from her table, which was swarmed with kids. Her nephew, Archer, was perched in her lap, patiently plucking flowers off their stems and letting them drop into splashes of glue on a piece of paper.

She gave him a tentative smile, as if to ask if everything was okay.

He nodded and smiled back.

He would break it to her later. Why interrupt her happy moment now?

CHAPTER FIFTEEN

"THAT WAS GREAT!" Marlee said as soon as she saw Matthew.

"We need to talk," Matthew responded, blinking as his eyes adjusted from the dim lighting of the indoor arena to the late afternoon sunshine. He grabbed her hand and glanced over his shoulder but didn't pause. Marlee could see Janquil and Tyler weaving through the crowd of parents.

"I think they're trying to catch up," Marlee said, but her words were whisked away as he pulled her along at a fast clip. "Whoa!"

But he didn't slow down. He simply glanced over his shoulder again and kept going, his feet kicking up dust. He was pulling her toward the pasture, where Ben and Annie were tying up the horses. "Let's take a ride. Do you think Ben would mind?"

"No, but what about Janquil and Tyler?"

One more glance. "They'll get great sunset pics," he said. "Our *followers* will eat them up."

Okay, that had a bite to it. Something was eating at him. She pulled against him, and when he didn't stop walking, dug her heels into the dirt. "Stop," she said.

He took two more steps, then turned back.

"What's going on?" she asked.

"Wait up, you two!" Janquil called.

Matthew let out a breath. "I need to talk to you before you talk to them."

"What? Why?"

"Can we just take the horses out and I'll tell you then?"

But it was too late. Janquil was trotting to catch them, her big messenger bag bouncing against her hip. "What's the hurry, lovebirds?"

Marlee felt Matthew let out a frustrated breath. She gestured toward the pasture. "Sunset ride."

"So romantic," Tyler said. Was Marlee crazy, or did she hear a tinge of sarcasm behind those words?

Janquil had closed the gap. Out of breath, she asked, "So we're on for tomorrow?"

Marlee felt Matthew stiffen next to her, his hand squeezing just a little tighter around hers, as if to convey a message. She squeezed back as if to lob a message his way in return: *Gotcha. I'll let you take point on this.* Whatever Matthew wanted to talk to her about, it had to do with what was happening tomorrow.

"Yep," Matthew said. Marlee could tell that he was trying to sound light and carefree, but there was a clipped edge to his tone that she recognized from the million times he tried not to sound irritated about her parking choices. "Ten?"

"Ten is perfect," Janquil said. She turned to Tyler. "That'll give us time to go back to The Baked Bean. It's such a sweet little place. We're thinking of doing a little side story about how finding the perfect, cute coffee shop is a little romance all its own. Or how you can create a romance with a favorite, cozy café. Or maybe something about the love of hearts in coffee cream. Or, I don't know, the adorable owner. Surely she's got a romantic story we can lean into. What's her name again? Ellen?"

"Ellory," Marlee said. "And she does. She met her husband, Rowan, there. He got stuck in a blizzard on his way through town at Christmas. She took him in, because her heart is the biggest. They got snowed in and fell in love. She's my best friend, and The Baked Bean is her baby. She's worked hard to give it the exact vibe you're describing."

Janquil gave a little noise and clutched her hand to her chest. "So perfect. A shop owner who fell in love *with* her shop, and then fell in love *at* her shop. What a spin! Why is Haw Springs so adorable, Tyler?"

"Some towns," Tyler said, as if that explained everything.

"Some towns," Janquil agreed, apparently picking up his message. "Okay, great job today. We're going to go back to Riverside and get some much-needed hotel air-conditioning. We'll see you at ten tomorrow!" She pointed high up on the ridge opposite the ranch. Marlee followed her finger. Why on earth could they be wanting to go up there?

"See you there," Matthew said, the tightness in his voice growing even tighter.

Holding hands, Marlee and Matthew watched them go, offering a little wave as Janquil and Tyler got into their car and took off. They let go as soon as the car was out of sight.

Marlee ignored that her hand felt funny without his in it. Cold or something. Only then did she realize that this was the first time they'd really held hands, and it hadn't felt as uncomfortable as she'd imagined it would feel. Actually, it had felt quite natural.

"Do you still want to ride?" she asked him.

"Uh, sure. It's been a minute," he said. Some of the parents who had been congregating by the arena doors had started to saunter toward them. "It would be nice to get some privacy."

"Let's go," Marlee said. This time, she grabbed his hand.

And tried to ignore the fact that it settled her.

MATTHEW SWUNG UP onto Tango, Decker's powerhouse of a horse, like it was nothing. Marlee, who hadn't ridden in a while, had taken two tries to get up on Morgan's much smaller horse, Tweety.

"What?" he asked when he noticed her staring at him with her mouth hanging open.

"Are you just naturally good at everything?" she asked.

"I grew up here, if you recall," he said. "Horses are hardly a mystery to me."

"So did I," she countered. "And you heard me grunting while trying to get up here, right?"

"Well," he said, "you're pretty small."

"Need I remind you that there are literal children riding these horses all day? They get up with no problem."

He shrugged. "It's about practice. I rode a lot when I was a kid." He paused. "Is everything a competition with you?"

"No," Marlee said, defensive. "I was just making an observation. You're good at a lot of things. Observation."

"So are you," he mumbled. "Especially observing. Let's just get moving." He used his heels to get Tango going.

"Why does literally everything turn into an argument with you?" she asked to his back, but he didn't respond.

For a while, they just rode as the sun started to set around them, the sky turning orange and pink. Marlee began to see the twinkle of lightning bugs down in the valley, like glitter splashed across the town. It was beautiful. And, if she were to believe in such a thing, romantic.

She watched Matthew, who rode in silence, his body moving fluidly with the horse. She saw his eyes sweep the valley floor, and wondered if he, too, felt enchantment press thick and heavy around him. Did he think the lightning bugs looked like glitter? Like tiny, knowing winks?

She felt a pang of wistful desire. She was with a handsome, strong, talented man, and she'd even begun to suspect that he wasn't a myth.

But he wasn't her man.

She was next to him by design, her own cockamamie plan set into action. He was a lie. Her lie. Which made him a myth of her own making.

She had to break the tension before she began to lose her head, get emotional, begin professing things that were likely invented solely in her mind and shouldn't be professed.

"So, what's the deal?" she called out.

He slowed to a stop, then turned Tango so that they were facing each other. Ben had given him a cowboy hat to wear, because he just couldn't stand the thought of someone riding a horse without one, and in the shadow under the brim, his eyes shone bright. He looked tan and rugged under the evening sky. In this moment, one could imagine him a true cowboy.

"You said you needed to talk to me. But you've been mum this whole ride. What gives? I'm assuming it has something to do with whatever we're doing tomorrow at ten."

"Getting engaged," he said, as if this was the simplest fact in the world.

"Excuse me?" She felt a zip of energy. "What did you say?"

"We're getting engaged tomorrow at ten."

The energy quickly turned into an electrifying curl of fear. "What?" She had heard him, loud and clear, twice now. But she couldn't process what she'd heard. *What?* was all she could think to say. The only word her brain could form, over and over again, turning the answer this way and that, hoping to make sense of it.

"We're getting—"

"I heard you," she snapped. She slid off Tweety and held the reins. Her legs felt shaky beneath her, so she lowered herself to a crouch. "How did this happen?"

"Well," he said, dismounting Tango, "you invited a magazine to come cover our lives but didn't have a plan and have, so far, left all of the lying up to me. Some of my lies are better than others. But all are better than yours, because you have offered no help whatsoever."

Her head snapped up. "You're blaming me?"

"Not entirely. I'm also blaming myself for going along with this crazy plan of yours."

She stood, hands on hips. This was the Matthew she knew. Yes, he was just naturally good at so many things. But being obstinate, cranky and difficult to deal with was what he was best at. "You went along with it because you wanted new patients."

"I went along with it, but I never thought I would get waylaid into scheduling a reenactment of our nonexistent engagement."

"I didn't ask you to do that!" Marlee yelled. Tweety huffed, and Marlee patted her neck apologetically.

"What else was I supposed to do? You were busy with the kids and she asked!" he yelled back. Tango didn't so much as twitch, but Tweety shifted her weight.

"You could have told her you hadn't proposed yet. You could have told her you were waiting until after Annie's wedding or said you hadn't yet worked up the nerve to ask my parents' permission or that you had bought plane tickets to do it in…in… Jamaica or…or Las Vegas, or…or I don't know… Honduras. You could have said you were waiting until Christmas Eve or our anniversary. There were so many things you could have said." She held up her left hand. "I don't have a ring. How did she even buy the story?" A recent memory wanted to tickle the back of her brain—something about that photographer—but she didn't let it.

"I told her it was being sized," Matthew said. "And I want to remind you that I was up front with you, from the beginning, that I am uncomfortable with lying."

"I thought you just meant that you didn't like to do it. I didn't know that you meant you were horrible at it."

"Well, I am."

"Clearly."

Tweety gave a whinny and shifted her weight again. Marlee took a breath. She didn't want to upset her sister's horse. More than that, she didn't want the horse to be agitated and take off or throw her off or who knew what. She wasn't a strong rider, but she knew enough to know that she needed to take her voice down a notch.

Besides, Matthew looked completely defeated. She felt guilty. She had been the one to invent the entire scam, and he was correct in that he had voiced his discomfort with lying from the get-go. He'd done his best in the lurch and now she had to do her best to carry out his story.

"Okay," she said, measured and calm. "Where are we doing this?"

"Up on Hawthorne Ridge," he said, thumbing over his shoulder.

"I've never been up there," Marlee said. "Is it pretty?"

He paused, and for a moment, she thought maybe he wouldn't speak at all. "It's the most beautiful place I've ever seen," he said. "It's perfect for a proposal. Or...at least I once thought so."

She opened her mouth to ask what that meant, but things between them weren't exactly easy at the moment, and she doubted he was in a place for sharing.

"Okay. How should I dress?"

He studied her; she felt his gaze all the way to her bones. When did this start happening?

"Everything you wear is perfect," he said.

Warmth washed over her. She shifted uneasily. *Get a grip, Marlee. This is your fake boyfriend that you're about to get fake engaged to. The last thing you need is to start catching feelings.*

"But we'll have to hike a little, so you might want to dress for a hike. And it's probably going to rain on us."

"Got it. Something cute and magazine-worthy, but also practical and waterproof. You've got to be kidding me, Matthew."

"Well… I surprised you."

"Yes, this is definitely a surprise."

"No, I mean, when I proposed to you, I surprised you."

"Ah, I see. Go ahead, weave the story, Nicholas Sparks. How did it go?"

"I asked you to go hiking with me, which you normally aren't big into. In fact, you argued with me a little, asked if we could just go for a quick jog instead. Or maybe even forget about exercise and go get burgers."

"So far, the last one is the most accurate."

"But I talked you into it by promising to get burgers after we were done."

Marlee giggled. "Somehow, you actually know me pretty well."

"So, we hiked. You tried to get me to stop and turn around a few times, but I refused. You were kind of a little irritated at me by the time we crested the ridge. A little pouty. But I thought it was cute."

"No one has ever called me cute when I pout. Also, I don't pout."

He continued, taking a step toward her. "But when we got to the top, you saw that I had already laid out rose petals in the shape of a heart—"

"That's what you bought those roses for. I was so mad that you bought roses and wouldn't tell me why," Marlee teased with a wink, but he was too into his story to be stopped now.

"I'd drawn a heart with the petals on top of the flat rock where I most loved to sit and dream about the future when I was a kid."

"The rock you'd told me about so many times."

He took another step in her direction. He was close enough for her to smell the leather of his hat, to see the shadow of stubble that had sprouted on his chin. She held her breath, unsure what was going to happen next, half delighted, half terrified.

He was still holding Tango's reins, but he lightly encircled her wrists and drew her hands up to her face. "You were so surprised, you put your hands over your mouth, like this. And I wanted to pull them away so I could kiss you, but instead, I..."

He pulled her hands away from her face and held them as, in one swift movement, he lowered to one knee.

She gasped. She couldn't help it. Even though she knew it wasn't real, it felt real. Way too real.

"I told you that I loved you and that the only thing in my entire life that even came close to the same beauty as the spot we were standing in was the light in your eyes. I told you that I wanted to spend the rest of my life standing in that light, soaking it up. And then I said, 'Will you do me the honor of being my wife?'"

"And I said yes," Marlee breathed. *Because who wouldn't?*

For a long moment, or maybe it just seemed like a long moment, Marlee and Matthew stayed frozen in each other's gaze, him holding her hands, the sun all but gone behind the very ridge where they got engaged in another, make-believe life.

Matthew moved first, dropping her hands and getting back to his feet. Marlee cleared her throat and went back to stroking Tweety's neck to break the spell.

"And I gave you a ring—whatever kind you like best—but it was too big, and you were afraid you'd lose it. So, we took it to get sized at a shop in Kansas City. But they're swamped, so it'll be a few more weeks before we get it back." He pulled himself up into Tango's saddle.

"Princess," Marlee said.

"Pardon?"

"Princess cut," Marlee said. "If I were ever going to get engaged—which, obviously, I'm not—it would be a princess cut diamond."

He gave a single nod. "So, can we agree that's the story?"

"We can," Marlee said. She made her first attempt to get into Tweety's saddle, let herself slide back to the ground, then tried again with a mighty grunt. No such luck.

"Here, let me." Matthew started to swing his leg around, but Marlee stopped him.

"No. I've got it."

She placed her foot in the stirrup, and with a grunt so mighty she could hardly believe it came out of her, she somehow inched her way up onto the horse.

"Piece of cake," she said over her shoulder, and began to lead Tweety back to the barn.

Once she got going, though, she couldn't help but stare up at Hawthorne Ridge. It had darkened with the pressing evening, but she could still make out the giant rock at the top. The one with the fictitious rose petals in the shape of a heart.

Fictitious, she reminded herself.

Made up.

Just like always, a myth.

CHAPTER SIXTEEN

THE SKY GRUMBLED OVERHEAD. Matthew gazed up into the darkening rain clouds.

"You sure you don't want to turn back?" he heard from behind him. Sounded like quite far behind him. He needed to slow his pace.

He turned. Marlee had split the difference between sporty and magazine-worthy and wore a stylish, pink, off-the-shoulder top and a pair of cutoff shorts with hiking boots, her shoulder-length hair drawn into jaunty pigtails. She squinted up the trail at him through the gray glare.

"It's going to rain. They're not going to show."

"They are. They knew it was going to rain, and they didn't care."

Another grumble of thunder vibrated the ground beneath them. Marlee turned her palms up as if to say, *Do I need to say more?*

"Come on, we're almost there. If we hurry and get the photos right the first time, we'll be on our way back down before the first raindrops fall."

"They'll be bad pictures," she said. "No sunlight."

"I assume they know that," he insisted, feeling impatient. "Come on."

"Has anyone ever told you that you're stubborn? They're not going to show," she muttered, but picked up the pace and surpassed him on the trail so that he had to jog a few steps to catch up.

In fact, many people had told him he was stubborn. It was his stubbornness that made him successful, as far as he could reckon. But it was borne of something else. A flexibility that had gotten him hurt. He wasn't naturally stubborn the way he was—as Marlee suggested—naturally good at things. His stubbornness was protection. As long as he stayed true to himself, he would stay insulated from hurt.

Yet, somehow, Marlee managed to break through his stubbornness time and again. He found himself feeling light around her, smiling. Which was crazy, given that theirs was a relationship entirely built on conflict.

He also found himself sneaking little looks at her, practicing things he wanted to say to her, hoping that he was pleasing her—or at least not displeasing her. He found himself wanting to treat her as a girlfriend, when he wasn't even sure he would classify her as a friend.

He felt cracks clicking their way through the walls he'd built around himself, little pieces of gravel falling on the ground at his feet, tripping him up as he tried to walk, to follow her lead.

Turned out, they did show. In fact, they beat Matthew and Marlee there, and had already set up the camera, ready to go. An ATV was parked on the trail. Only after he saw it did Matthew realize there had been tire tracks along the trail. He stood on one.

"We rented that in Riverside," Janquil said. "Long, bumpy ride, but at least we'll beat the rain to the bottom. You didn't come all the way up here on foot, did you? Oh, boy, you're going to get wet."

Marlee shot a glare at Matthew, who ducked his head to hide his smile. He didn't care if they got wet, but apparently Marlee cared a great deal. Or at least cared that she gave off the impression of caring a great deal.

"Lighting's bad," Tyler said, snapping some practice photos. "Too dark. We should have picked a better day."

Again, Marlee glared.

Janquil waved her hand. "It's fine. We can touch them up in the studio."

"No matter how many times you say it, we can't touch up every little thing in the studio," Tyler snapped.

Janquil shot him a look. "We can try."

"We should just get it over with," Marlee said, grabbing Matthew's hand and pulling him toward the rock. She gasped when they got close. "Rose petals." Hands in front of her mouth, she turned to him. "How…?"

"This is my second time up the mountain this morning," he said. "I wanted it to be right."

Though, even as he'd been doing it, he hadn't been sure exactly what *right* meant. He supposed he was putting on the show for Marlee's sake, once again trying to please her even if he was unsure why.

"Let me see the shots you're getting, Tyler," Janquil said. She'd returned to the ATV and was rummaging through her messenger bag.

"So romantic," Tyler said, his voice droll as he snapped photos of the flower petals. "Too bad they'll get washed away later." He gave Matthew a wink before going to Janquil.

Matthew chose to ignore the comment, ignore the wink, and climbed up on top of the rock. He held out his hand for Marlee, who took it and climbed up beside him.

"Wow," she whispered, looking out over the valley. "This view is even better than the view at McBride Ranch. Look! You can see the shop! And your clinic!" She pointed. Matthew leaned over her shoulder to follow where she was pointing.

"You're parked in front of my clinic. Why?"

Marlee threw her head back and laughed with such glee, he couldn't help joining her. For the briefest pause, he was lost in the moment, forgetting all about Janquil and Tyler. For the briefest pause, this was real.

Suddenly, there was a boom of thunder that made Marlee jump and cower in Matthew's arms. Only then did he become aware of the click-click-clicking of the camera. Marlee must have also been aware, because she backed away from him and cleared her throat self-consciously.

"We should probably get pictures now and catch up on the story when we get back down there," Janquil said, abandoning her search in the messenger bag. She looked a little worried.

Tyler went into overdrive, instructing them to pose this way and that. Even had it been real, Matthew was struck by how stripped of actual romance the moment was. *Just tilt your head this way and hold your hands this way, not that, and now pretend you're speaking, pouring your heart out to her...that's right. Can you switch knees, by chance?*

There was nothing romantic or real about these candid shots. All Matthew could think of was getting off the ridge before the rain started up.

They didn't.

At first, Tyler was insistent that they stay until they got drenched, and then capture some stills of them kissing in the rain. *Very motion picturesque*, he'd said, but Marlee had demurred, claiming to have a fear of lightning, and Matthew had been glad. He wasn't ready to kiss her—not even a fake kiss.

Maybe especially not a fake kiss.

The rain intensified from a sprinkle to a patter.

"We should go!" Janquil yelled. She was holding her messenger bag over her head. Raindrops had collected on her glasses. "If your equipment gets ruined again, they'll have our hides."

Tyler looked as if he wanted to argue. He ping-ponged between Janquil and the two of them, still standing atop the rock. Matthew knew what he was thinking: he hadn't gotten a single good shot.

Thunder shook the ground beneath his feet. Marlee leaned into him, although Matthew thought there was a strong possibility she wasn't even aware she had done it.

"We've got to get out of here," Janquil said. "Come on!"

Without waiting for Tyler to make up his mind, she trotted to the ATV, her bag still over her head.

Tyler cursed under his breath, then followed her, stowing his camera in a pouch around his waist as he went.

"What about us?" Marlee yelled, but neither Tyler nor Janquil so much as paused as they got on the ATV, secured their belongings, and raced down the trail.

As if to punctuate their departure, there was a flash of lightning so bright it illuminated the forest around them, followed by thunder that they could feel coming up through the rock. As if someone turned on a faucet, the rain began to pour down, instantly drenching them.

"Come on," Matthew said. "I know where we can go."

He jumped off the rock, then turned and held out a hand for her. Instead of taking it, she put her hands on his shoulders and let him ease her down off the rock. Then she grasped his hand and let him lead her to a place he'd only taken one other person in his whole life.

Hawthorne Ridge might have been Matthew's respite, but this place felt even more private.

Instead of turning back down the trail the way they'd come, he went in the other direction, where the trail bent around the ridge and out of sight of Haw Springs. They ran, their feet splattering in the mud, and then swerved off the trail onto a weedy, overgrown gravel driveway, which wound back toward the tree line.

At the end of the driveway were the bones of a house that had, at some point before Matthew had found it, burned to the ground. Next to it, pushed nearly into the trees themselves, was a decrepit greenhouse with a broken door.

Matthew led Marlee through the brush and weeds to the door and pushed it open.

It still smelled the same as it had when he was twelve. Green and sweet and musty. Some of the timber frame had begun to warp, and there were a few holes in the ceiling—Matthew guessed from a long-ago hailstorm. Otherwise, it was warm and dry. A good place to wait out the rain.

It seemed to take Marlee a few seconds to realize where they were. She spun slowly, taking it all in with childlike wonder.

"Whose is this?" she finally asked.

He shrugged. "I've never known anyone to live here."

She picked her way down what used to be a center aisle, occasionally reaching out and stroking a leaf or bending to inspect a plant buried under the weeds that had overtaken it. He felt rooted in place, watching her in her element.

She was strong and elegant at the same time. Knowledgeable. Inquisitive. Beautiful. He didn't want to look away.

No. No, no, no. You're getting carried away. This was the worst spot to choose for your so-called fake engagement, and now there are consequences, that's all. You're getting your emotions all mixed up. What you're feeling is just a holdover from Tamara and nothing to do with Marlee West.

Yet, as she crouched to examine a purple cone-shaped flower, water dripping from her hair down the open back of her shirt, it felt real, and it felt about her.

"They grew vegetables here," she said. "But

they also grew some interesting flowers. This is a foxglove."

"Pretty," Matthew said, trying to distract himself by noting the purple flowers with the dark insides. He started to lean in to pick one, but she knocked his hand away.

"Pretty poisonous," she said. "I don't know why anyone would grow them alongside their food." She stood, brushing her hands off. "Though I suppose they might not have. Could have been carried in here another way."

"Could have been serial killers who got rid of their victims one salad at a time," Matthew said.

She gazed at him. "You have an odd sense of humor, did you know that?"

"Who said I was joking?"

There was a clap of thunder. Marlee jumped, folding herself close to him again. Instinctually, Matthew encircled her with his arms. They both briefly looked up, as if awaiting instructions from the sky, and then awkwardly stepped apart.

"You're afraid of storms," Matthew observed.

Marlee shivered and glanced up again. "Not usually. It's just that we're way up here. The storm seems closer to us somehow."

"I get that," Matthew said, following her gaze to the water streaking down the dirty windows. "But I think we're pretty safe up here. Dry, at least."

Marlee pulled her pigtails loose and ruffled her hand through her damp hair. There was a brightness about her. Her eyes pierced through him, her skin dewy and pink and alive. When she moved her hair, tiny water droplets landed on him. She grinned. "What were you saying about being dry?"

"Fair enough. Drier than we would be out there," he amended. "Better?"

"Better."

The air, already greenhouse-thick, grew even thicker around them as they stood in each other's space, eyes locked, words evading them. A rivulet of water cut loose from a strand of hair and snaked its way down her cheek; Matthew wanted to brush it away, but held back, confused and disconcerted about where his feelings were going.

It's just sentimentality. It's just the location, he repeated to himself. *It's not real.*

But somewhere in the back of his mind, a little drummer who had gotten out of sync with the rest of him piped up: *But why not with her?*

He wanted to ask if she was feeling the same pull. He wanted to broach the subject, lay it to rest. Or...maybe wake it up, bring it alive? He opened his mouth, closed it and opened it again.

She broke away, wandered down the path, her fingers outstretched to brush against the plants that spiked up this way and that.

"So, you've been here before," she said. A statement, not a question. "In this greenhouse."

"I have." His throat felt scratchy, his voice a croak.

She turned. "Alone?"

"Why?"

She shrugged and continued walking. "Just curious. I have a feeling I'm not the first girlfriend you've let into your secret little garden here."

"Technically, you're not my girlfriend."

She turned again. This time, her smile was tight. "So you keep reminding me. And I'll take that as confirmation that I'm right."

"I told you. I like to come up here to think," he said.

"Hmm." She narrowed her eyes at him, tilted her head. "You're pretty set in your ways, aren't you? Have you always been that way? Were you one of those forty-year-old ten-year-olds?"

He didn't like the mocking tone in her voice. "I'm comfortable with who I am," was all he said.

"Don't fence me in," she sang softly.

"It's not about that."

"Then what's it about?"

How could he explain his heartbreak to her? Why should he have to? Suddenly he was filled with resentment over this whole situation. Baring himself to the public, to her. Who was she, anyway? A pain in the neck who refused to park where she belonged. A charismatic con artist who caught him in a vulnerable moment. She wasn't his girlfriend, and he owed her nothing.

At the same time, he wanted to let her in.

"You want to know? I'll tell you. Yes, I did bring someone here once. She hated it. She didn't know a foxglove from a fire hydrant. She called it oppressive and said it made her throat itch. We didn't stay. I never even got a chance to tell her about the time I spent in here as a kid, sketching the flowers in my little notebook, hoping to find them later in the *Flora and Fauna of Missouri* guidebook my parents got me."

"You did that? Cute."

"She didn't know why this spot was important to me, and she didn't care enough to ask. But I was so head over heels in love with her, I was willing to let that part of myself go. I let every part of myself go, just trying to mold myself into the man I thought she wanted me to be." This was the first time Matthew had really let this all out, and he found that once he started talking, he couldn't stop. He began to walk the aisle, feeling a little as if he was walking backward through time. "I became someone I didn't even recognize anymore. I hid the parts of me that embarrassed her. I told myself that they embarrassed me, too, even though they didn't. I pretended to dislike things that I liked and to like things that I didn't." He whipped around. "You know what? I hate tofu. There, I said it. I hate tofu and I don't enjoy matchmaking reality TV shows, and I think matcha tea tastes like dirt."

Marlee walked toward him. “Matthew. You don’t have to… I was teasing you… I’m sorry if the teasing got too real.”

He held up a hand to stop her. “No. I want you to hear this, because sometimes I think you find me rigid without reason.”

“A little rigid, maybe. But I never considered for what reason. Or even if you had one.”

“Well, I did. And I do. I changed myself for her. I told myself that it was worth it because I loved her so much and I wanted to spend the rest of my life with her. I convinced myself that everyone makes sacrifices when they find love. I ignored that I was the only one sacrificing. And you know what it got me in the end?”

Marlee gave her head the tiniest shake. Suddenly, Matthew was very tired. He didn’t know exactly why this was all coming out now. He hadn’t thought about Tamara in years. Hadn’t thought about that day or the crushing sensation he’d carried in his chest for months after.

Oh, Matthew, Tamara had said, her lips turning down at the corners while she stared dubiously at the ring. *I don’t know what to say.*

His heart had deflated, knowing that whatever she was about to say next wasn’t going to be the yes that he’d hoped to hear.

I just don’t think you’re my forever person, she’d said.

So it had been about him. After all the ways

that he'd changed for her, in the end, it hadn't been enough.

"It got me nothing," he said quietly. "In the end, all I learned was that I wasn't good enough, no matter what I did."

"I'm sure that wasn't it," Marlee said. "How could you be not good enough?"

"It doesn't matter," he said. "The end result is the same. I decided I would never change myself for someone else again. No matter what. I stay true to me. I know that I've got…quirks. I know I'm idiosyncratic. And I'm great with it. I can be alone forever. I don't mind."

"Matthew—"

He turned and paced back to where he'd started. "No, it's true. Like you said, I'm pretty set in my ways."

"Matthew—"

"And, like I said, I like it that way. I intend to stay that way. Whether you like it or not. Which you clearly don't."

"Matthew!"

He spun to face her. "What?"

She pointed. "I was just going to say…you're standing in poison ivy."

He jumped back, away from the foliage, just as the storm ended and a ray of sunshine shone down on the path where he was standing.

CHAPTER SEVENTEEN

ANNIE BUZZED WITH excited energy during the entire drive to Kansas City, talking a million miles a minute. She sat in the front seat with Morgan, who was driving, but spent most of the drive turned sideways so she could hold court with the back seat, where Marlee sat, squeezed between Janquil and Tyler.

Annie's wedding was only days away, and she was the most excited bride-to-be that Marlee had ever encountered. When she'd asked Annie if she wanted to come along to the wholesaler to buy her flowers, she'd had to pull the phone away from her ear; she could practically feel the squeal rolling down off the ridge into the valley. Annie had immediately asked if she could bring her matron of honor, Morgan.

Truth be told, Marlee didn't mind the excessive chatter. It gave her time to think. And time to not talk, as she pondered what Janquil had said as they piled into Morgan's car—that she was hoping to get some good, candid shots of Marlee. *The romantic florist in her element. Show the world that you're swoon-worthy, too.*

Swoon-worthy, too. Marlee knew exactly what that *too* meant. With every new post that *Modern Vow* put out there, the fervor over Matthew grew. And after the reenactment of the fake engagement, it had reached a fever pitch. Which, of course, meant the internet had begun to turn on Marlee just the tiniest bit.

He's so cute. I hope she knows how lucky she is. I'm not sure she does.

Why isn't she smiling from ear to ear? Does she not see him???

She looks terrified. Girl, forget the heights and focus on what's happening in front of you.

If a man proposed to me like that, I wouldn't leave that spot until we got a preacher up there to marry us right that minute. She's crazy if she came down off that mountain without a ring on her finger.

She looks like she's going to throw up. Meanwhile, I volunteered to take my sister's kids to the doctor just so I could meet him. One of us has our priorities wrong. LOL

She better be careful with that lukewarm reaction. Someone might just steal him away. That someone might be me.

Marlee tried not to look. Tried to readopt her previous attitude about social media, which was that she wasn't interested. But it was hard to stay away, mostly because the photos were amazing. They did look like they were in love.

But the commenters were right—she also looked terrified.

What they were wrong about was that it wasn't the height that was scaring her. She was afraid because in that moment, she could see what a catch Matthew was. She felt the pull of him. The tiniest pinpoint of longing deep within her. It was new, but it was also old and familiar, something she'd locked deep inside herself when she'd gotten hurt and swore would never let out again.

She hadn't let it out. At least she was safe there. But it was knocking against the walls of her chest, begging to be released. Just as much a myth as a dragon breathing fire against her rib cage. And she was tempted.

You're in love with the romance, she tried to tell herself. Modern Vow *is in the business of selling romance, and they're good at it. You're buying in, even though you know it isn't real.*

"...common?"

Marlee swam up from her thoughts, bursting

into the moment when she realized that Janquil had been asking her a question.

"I'm sorry," she said. "I didn't hear you."

Janquil cleared her throat. "I said, is that color combination common? For a wedding, I mean. Seems like maybe not."

Marlee glanced at Annie, wondering if she'd changed her mind again. *I just love all colors*, she'd said more times than Marlee could count. *Can't we do rainbows?* Ben had said no to rainbows, Marlee had to remind her time and again.

"I'm sorry," Marlee repeated. "I guess I was daydreaming. What colors?"

"You know. Purple and blue," Annie crowed. "Purple is my favorite color, and blue is Ben's favorite color. And I want them to be shimmery." *Relief.* The colors hadn't changed.

"Not super common, especially for a summer wedding," Marlee said. "But not unheard-of. It's going to be beautiful. Right, Miss Annie?"

Annie beamed. "Like mermaid scales."

Marlee tried to ignore the slight sneer that she saw Janquil and Tyler exchange through the rearview mirror. She was growing weary of the sneer. "Like the best, most beautiful mermaid," she agreed.

They arrived at their destination. Morgan found a parking spot and they all piled out. Annie wrapped her arm through Morgan's and led them inside, walking on her toes the entire way. Not only was Morgan Annie's matron of honor, she was also just always there for whatever Annie needed. Watching them made Marlee wish she had brought Ellory along for moral support, too. Ellory would have told her that she didn't look like she was going to throw up in those pictures. She would have assured Marlee that she, too, was swoon-worthy.

Yet something in the back of Marlee's mind told her that wasn't exactly what she needed to hear, anyway.

Something told her that what she most wanted to hear was that Matthew was *not* swoon-worthy. That she wasn't missing out on something that was right under her nose. That the myth was still a myth, and that she was getting caught up in the undertow of social media popularity that swept so many people away.

She would assure her that this was surface-level, just for business, and still a good idea. She pulled up her order app to peruse new orders that had come in. Just three. Only three yesterday, too. And two the day before.

Is it really worth it? the back of her mind prompted once again. *Yes, it is. For the long game*, she tried to answer, but being so deep in her thoughts, she tripped over nothing, stumbling forward into Janquil. She mumbled an apology.

"Sweet nothings?" Janquil asked, pointing at

her phone. Marlee had been doomscrolling again without even realizing it.

Marlee quickly thumbed it off. "Yes," she said, trying her hardest to sound as if she'd been exchanging syrupy texts with her soulmate, not pondering whether the dismal orders coming in and the snarky social media comments confirmed what she'd come to think: that she was doing herself a disservice rather than a favor.

"Aw." Janquil tilted her head to the side. "You two are just hopeless romantics, aren't you?"

Marlee gave an affirming smile, trying her best to be convincing.

After the rain had let up, and she and Matthew had ventured out onto the trail, the safety of the greenhouse had evaporated just as quickly as the steam from the plants. They'd walked the entirety of the trail in silence, with only the occasional *Watch your step here* or *Don't veer off into the poison ivy there* to break it. Businesslike. Formal.

When they'd reached their cars at the bottom of the hill, they'd simply gotten in and driven away, not even a wave or a look backward. Marlee had felt as if she'd somehow stumbled onto information that she shouldn't have. But he'd shared it freely. Openly.

That was what made it so unsettling.

Yet at the same time, it made her feel soft inside, as if she understood him a little better now. As if they had something in common. It was something that she could draw upon when having to be believable in their romance. But it was also more than that.

She'd wanted so badly to question him. To find out more about his heartbreak. To learn about his failure. To get his thoughts about her theory that falling in love was a big, old myth. She suspected that he would agree. It would have made her feel better about her own feelings in a way that she couldn't quite identify.

The poison ivy had bailed them both out. But especially her. Because she was starting to feel, and she didn't know what to do with that.

How could bonding over their mutual distaste for love make her start to feel as if love was possible? It made no sense.

"I'm surprised he didn't take off work to go with us today," Janquil said.

"Oh…he's swamped," Marlee said. "He's got so many new patients." She hoped this was true, and she suspected that it might be. And instead of feeling jealous that her scheme had made her business die and his flourish, she couldn't help feeling a little bit happy for him.

"I'm not surprised to hear that. He's all anyone can talk about," Janquil said. "You've got yourself a very desirable fiancé."

"Hmm," Marlee said, pasting a smile on her face and hoping the sick feeling she had inside wasn't showing.

But, clearly, it was. Janquil stopped walking and tugged on Marlee's arm with the hand that was still holding the pencil. "Everything okay?"

Marlee took a breath and deepened the smile very deliberately. *Big nod. Big, big nod.* "Mmm-hmm," she said. "Great."

Janquil frowned, tilting her head—her signature reporter move—and studying Marlee more deeply. "Is there something going on, Marlee? Something wrong between you and Matthew?"

Marlee hoped that her aghast look was better than her placating look. "Of course not! No, nothing's wrong! We're both just really busy is all."

"It seems like you two are only together when you have to be together for us," Janquil said.

Everyone had stopped walking now. Annie and Morgan gazed over their shoulders curiously while Tyler moved in with his camera. *Money shot*, Marlee imagined him thinking. She wasn't sure what it was about Tyler, but there was something about him that made Marlee think he would love nothing more than to uncover them as frauds.

Marlee felt everyone staring at her, the camera lens taking her in. She felt the weight of the entire terrible plan on her shoulders.

"I don't know what you're talking about," she said. "Everything's totally fine. This is an adult relationship. We both have adult responsibilities that come first. We prioritize."

Janquil had somehow opened her notebook

without Marlee even seeing it happen. She scribbled a note. “Are you saying that your relationship isn’t high on the priority list?”

“What? No, I’m not saying that. You’re twisting my words.”

Janquil looked up from her notes and grinned, looking kind of like a shark. “I’m only repeating what you said.”

Marlee closed her eyes, took a deep breath, tried to silence the little voice in the back of her mind that was imploring her to just out the whole lie and put an end to it. Go back to life as normal. *It’s not like Dad is asking you to pay back that loan right now, Marlee. You don’t have to put yourself through this.*

Morgan tore herself away from Annie and in two strides had her arm around Marlee’s shoulder. “Annie’s wedding is super important to us all,” she said. “Marlee just wants to get everything right, so she’s focused. And Matthew is building his practice, which takes a lot of time and effort. They’ve both worked very hard to get where they are, and they respect each other. They respect each other’s time and responsibilities. And because they know they will always be there for each other, they don’t sweat it when they have to be apart. It’s beautiful to witness, really.” She gave Marlee’s shoulder a squeeze. “It’s true love.”

The relief that Marlee felt from Morgan bailing her out of the conversation, combined with the little dig about true love, almost made Marlee laugh out loud. She tilted her face to the ground to keep Janquil from seeing her struggle to keep it in.

"I say we focus on Annie today and leave Matthew to his work, huh?" Morgan squeezed Marlee's shoulder again, gave Janquil a perfunctory nod and skipped back to Annie. Arm in arm, they led the way into the warehouse.

Tyler turned and began snapping photos of Morgan and Annie. Janquil gave Marlee a shrewd look.

"You've got a great sister," she said.

"I know."

"She seems very smart."

"She is."

They stared at each other, something passing wordlessly between them. Marlee willed herself not to break eye contact, not to flinch or lick her lips nervously or do anything that would betray the groundwork that Morgan had just laid.

Finally, Janquil closed her notebook, slid her pencil behind her ear and said, "They left us behind. We should get moving." She didn't wait for Marlee, who hung back and watched everyone head into the warehouse.

She hated this.

She hated lying. But more than that, she hated that she was no longer sure if she was lying. Not entirely.

Because the truth was, she, too, had been thinking about Matthew at the exact moment that Janquil had asked about him.

And realizing that she'd been doing more and more of that lately. Without even meaning to.

CHAPTER EIGHTEEN

MATTHEW'S ANKLES ITCHED.

He had been a Boy Scout, for goodness' sake. How could he just be standing right there in poison ivy and not even notice?

Because you weren't really standing there. Your body may have been there, but you were lingering in the past. Reliving things best left alone.

He wasn't sure what had come over him, why he'd decided to open up to Marlee about what had happened with Tamara. But he was sure that his itchy ankles were natural consequences for acting rashly…er, so to speak.

With every scratch, every application of calamine lotion, he promised himself that he would never open up like that again. Not to Marlee, not to anyone. He had to focus, that was all. Let this fake romance play itself out and then go on with his life.

He pulled up to his parents' house—meat loaf night—and groaned out loud when he saw Lynette's car in their driveway. She had worked alongside him all day and hadn't said one word about being there tonight. Whatever was currently being cooked up along with the mashed potatoes couldn't be good.

His mother met him at the door, hands on hips.

"So, I have to hear about your engagement from someone other than you?" she asked.

"Hi, Mom." He gave her a kiss on the cheek. He knew this would happen eventually. He'd tried a thousand times to come up with a way to talk to her about it and couldn't think of anything. It was one thing to lie to the world—it was another thing altogether to lie to his mother. He wasn't built that way. He'd never lied to her, not about anything serious.

Even if he could make himself say the words, she would know. She would see right through him and know.

In the end, he'd gone with saying nothing and hoping that Lynette would also forget.

Mistake. Big mistake.

He supposed he knew that all along, too.

"You have nothing to say for yourself?"

He tried skirting past her into the living room where his dad watched a ball game on TV, but Lynette appeared out of nowhere, holding her phone in one hand, her other hand on her hip to match his mother's stance.

"Traitor," he mumbled.

Her eyebrows flew up. "Who is the traitor here?

I told you in no uncertain terms that I would tell her." She held her phone out to show a photo of Matthew on one knee on the rock, facing Marlee, her hands covering her mouth. The sky behind them was somehow brilliant blue with rays of sunshine bouncing off Marlee's hair.

"That's faked," he said, glad that he'd been able to lead with a true statement at least.

"So, you're not engaged?" Lynette turned the photo back to herself and brought it to her face, squinting. "Because that looks like you. And that looks like the florist across the street from your clinic. The one that you just can't seem to stay away from."

His mom slapped her chest and threw her head back dramatically. "My only son, engaged without so much as a word to his mother."

"Mom, I'm not engaged." He held up his left hand as if that proved it, while also knowing that it proved nothing. "Can we sit down?"

"You would think you would have at least told me after you'd done it, but no. The whole world gets to know first." She edged to the side to let him through.

"There's nothing to know. Hey, Dad." He tossed a wave at his father on his way through the living room.

"Hey. We're down two. Bottom of the third."

Lynette was obviously targeting her approach and had only told his mom. At least there was that.

Maybe he could squash the story before it even reached his dad. Just as Matthew bent to retrieve a soda out of the refrigerator, the front door banged open, followed by his sister's bugling voice.

"So gross!"

Footsteps, and then she, too, was shoving a phone at his face.

"I can't even relax without seeing your face."

"Love you, too, sis."

"You're engaged? *Engaged?* We've never even met this woman, have we?" She said this last to their mother, who took it as another chance to throw her head back and wail.

"Okay," he said. "Okay, that's enough. I'm not engaged! You shouldn't believe everything you see on social media. The photo has been altered. It wasn't even sunny that day. We got stuck in a rainstorm on our way back down the mountain." He used the toe of his shoe to scratch the back of his other ankle.

"So that is you, then? And that's her? You were up there, and down on one knee? It's just that it wasn't sunny?" his mother asked. "Is that what you're telling me? How is that any better?"

"I'm saying the whole thing was faked. *Is* faked. It's…ugh. It's complicated." He sank into a chair at the kitchen table and rubbed his face with the hand that had just been holding the soda, streaking cold condensation down his face. "This whole thing has gotten out of hand."

"What whole thing?" Sarah sat across from him. Lynette and his mother flanked him on either side, leaving behind the theatrics for a second.

"I'm not supposed to tell anyone at all," he said. "But I can't do this anymore."

"This what?"

"This lying," he said. "Mom, I promise you, we're not engaged. We're not even in love. Or dating." *We can barely stand each other*, he wanted to add but found that he couldn't. Somewhere along the line, he'd grown fond of his time spent with Marlee, and had found himself thinking about her when they weren't together. "It's all for show."

"Why on earth would you do that?" his mom asked.

Lynette sucked in a breath. "All those new patients." She turned to his mom. "We've been swamped. Lots of single moms and aunts and best friends bringing in their kids. It's been the strangest thing."

"I still don't understand. What does standing on a rock, proposing to this woman, have to do with new patients?"

His sister let out a bark of a laugh; he hung his head. He should have come out with it sooner, sworn his mother to secrecy. It would have been difficult for her, but she would have honored the secret. But now that his sister knew, it felt very public, and very dangerous.

"You perpetrated an internet hoax?" Sarah

asked, then continued to laugh uproariously. "*You?* Dr. Straight-and-Narrow are fooling the entire interent?"

"It was an accident at first," he said. "I just happened to be in the wrong place at the wrong time, or maybe it was the right place at the right time—I don't even know anymore. A kid caught a photo of me catching Marlee as she fell off a ladder. It went viral, and Marlee concocted a plan. I went along with it, but I never wanted to."

"Well, then, why did you?" his mom asked.

"Because of the new patients," Lynette said.

He nodded, miserably. "*Modern Vow Magazine* got ahold of the photo and now all sorts of good things are happening for both of us, and I can't just call it all off now. We're going to let the story play out. Let Annie Allbrook's wedding happen. And then the reporter will go away and that will be the end of it."

His sister continued laughing. "You have no idea how many of my friends are crushing on you right now. The minute you 'break up' with her, you're going to be mobbed."

He hadn't considered this, that the people walking into his office knew him as someone different from who he really was. That they might consider him fair game when the story died down. That he wouldn't be rid of the romance dilemma even after the public part of it ended.

How was he going to end this?

"Please," he implored, "don't say anything to anyone. If we get discovered now, it will ruin everything. It could even ruin Annie's wedding."

The three women were silent.

"Please," he said. "At least until the *Modern Vow* story has been published."

"Okay," his mom said. "But I still don't understand what you hoped to achieve with something like this. I'll have to explain to all my friends why I never mentioned the engagement. I'll have to explain it at church, Matthew. *At church*. Lying at church."

His sister started laughing again.

"Please, Sarah, do this one thing for me? For Marlee and Annie, really."

She nodded, her face going red with giggles. "I won't out you, bro. But you have to let me plan your next date."

"No way."

"That's the price I'm charging," she said.

"That's extortion."

"Don't be so serious. I'm just kidding. I'll keep your secret."

He looked at Lynette, who gave a solemn, singular nod.

"Thank you," he said. "Can we let this go now?"

"Well," Lynette said, "yes, of course. But now that Sarah mentions it, where is your next date going to be?"

“I don’t have any idea. The wedding is coming up. I guess that’s the next date.”

“How about a carnival?” his mother said to Lynette. “I’ve always thought carnivals were so romantic.”

“That’s because you met Glen at a carnival a million years ago,” Lynette said. “They’re not inherently romantic. A tearoom, now that’s romantic.”

“A tearoom?” Sarah said. “Where would you even find a tearoom?”

“There’s one in Kansas City,” Lynette said defensively. “Tea and quiche and a delicate little chocolate torte for dessert. Lovely.”

“I don’t know if she even likes tea. Or quiche,” Matthew said. “I don’t think that’s the best option.”

“Everyone likes tea and quiche,” Lynette said, offended.

“I don’t like tea or quiche,” his mom said.

“But have you had it in a tearoom?” Lynette asked.

“You know I haven’t.”

“You might have.”

“Well, I haven’t. I think he should find a good carnival. Instead of tea and quiche, they can fall in love over popcorn and frozen lemonades.”

“We’re not falling in love,” Matthew said, trying to keep this conversation from steering any further off course. But it was no use.

"Because you haven't had tea and quiche," Lynette said, as if that settled everything.

"He's right," Sarah cut in. "He's not actually looking to fall in love. It's all about optics."

"Thank you, sister."

"For best optics, it needs to be somewhere that their tender love stands out. Someplace loud and public and dangerous. Like a drag race."

"A drag race?" both Lynette and Matthew's mom said at the same time, their faces drawn down.

"What's so wrong with a drag race? People fall in love at the races all the time."

"No. No drag race," Matthew said, but it was too late. The argument over whether or not fast cars were romantic had begun in earnest. He watched them for a moment, but it had become obvious that his presence was no longer required in this discussion about his life. He got up from the table and joined his dad in the living room.

"Down four now," was all his dad had to say.

"Been a rough season," Matthew said as he eased onto the couch.

Matthew knew that it was impossible for his dad not to have absorbed the big scandal that had the ladies going in the other room. It was easier to ignore from out here, but words kept floating through, balloons of outrage that popped over his head.

Finally, a commercial came on and his dad lowered the footrest of his recliner. He turned to face Matthew, earnest and serious, but not scandalized. Matthew was grateful.

"I suppose you know what you're doing," he said.

Matthew shrugged. "I think so."

His dad nodded. "And you're prepared to deal with the consequences on the other side of that *think so*?"

"I am."

"Getting good business from it?"

"I am."

"Feeling good about it?"

Matthew shook his head. "Not at all."

"Can you look at yourself in the mirror?"

Matthew grimaced, every ounce of him shriveling inside himself. That was one question he'd been avoiding asking himself. He was afraid of the answer, although he supposed he knew exactly what the answer would be, even without asking it.

His dad gave a contemplative nod and chewed his bottom lip, as if Matthew had answered him. He gazed at the TV screen—a shaving cream commercial.

"Mmm-hmm," he said. "That's what I thought. Are you going to be able to walk away from her when this is all over?"

That was the other question Matthew hadn't asked himself.

Because he hadn't needed to. He'd started to

feel it in his chest when she was around. He'd opened up to her because he'd wanted her to know him. It was a question that answered itself before it could even be asked.

Was he falling in love with Marlee West?

Maybe.

And he didn't want to know, because he knew that he had to stop it. Right now. Before the feeling really got hold of him and it became too late to go back.

He'd been in love before, and it hadn't worked. It couldn't work, because love changed people, and he didn't want to be changed.

No. Whatever he thought he was feeling for Marlee West, he was wrong and he needed to reverse course right away. Shut it down and shut her out.

Again, he stayed silent.

"Yikes, son," his dad said, standing. "*Yikes.*"

CHAPTER NINETEEN

MARLEE WAS JUST putting the finishing touches on the last pew marker when Ellory came through the door, holding two coffee cups.

"Vanilla almond frosting," she sang. "In honor of the big day tomorrow!"

Marlee's assistant, Kimberly, who'd uncharacteristically shown up for work early, dropped the tulle she was holding. "Yes, yes, yes!" she said, racing toward the coffee. She grabbed one and took a sip. "Mmm!" She closed her eyes and held the cup against her chest. "Tastes just like wedding cake and happiness."

"Sounds delicious," Marlee said, holding her hand out for the other cup, which Ellory handed over. "And I could definitely use the happiness. And the caffeine."

"Burning the midnight oil again?"

Marlee took a sip. It was warm and sweet and tasted exactly like the world's best wedding cake. "Oh, my. You're putting this on your regular menu, right?"

"I am. Seems like the whole town is going to be at the wedding. Everyone's super excited about it. I'm donating all tips to Annie and Ben's honeymoon fund."

"That's so sweet," Kimberly said. "It makes me want to cry." She drew an invisible tear down one cheek. "Mar, I'm going to take five to enjoy this coffee and a good sob."

"Gotcha," Marlee said. Seemed like Kimberly was always *taking five* to do something that looked an awful lot like sitting around on her phone doing nothing. And it was never anywhere near five minutes. More like fifty.

Kimberly disappeared into the back room. Ellory watched her leave, then winked at her friend. "Since you're not doing anything, seems like a good time for a break. This place looks like the bottom of the ocean."

"Right?" Marlee spun in a slow circle, taking in the purple and blue flowers and bows that were taking up every square inch of space. She hadn't noticed it while she was putting it together, but it did give Blush & Bloom a certain aquatic aesthetic. "I just want Annie to be happy."

Ellory frowned, taken aback. "What was that?"

"What was what?" Marlee glanced over each shoulder, trying to ascertain what her friend was referencing.

"That sad little downturn on the word *happy*."

"I didn't downturn."

"You did downturn. 'I just want Annie to be *happy*,'" she mimicked. Marlee hadn't realized it in the moment, but she had to admit, if Ellory's impression was accurate: she had definitely downturned. Ellory sat on the bench, and Poppy, who had been snoozing on her bed, got up and slowly meandered toward her, tail wagging sleepily. Ellory bent to pick her up and plop her in her lap. "She downturned, didn't she?" Ellory said to Poppy. Poppy yawned and flopped down, instantly going back to snoozing. "That's her way of saying you did. So, spill. What's behind the downturn?"

Marlee let out a sigh and opened her mouth to answer but was interrupted by the door opening before she could speak.

Matthew strode in, white lab coat and tie in place, and came straight to the counter, all hurry and intensity. Marlee felt that weird sliding feeling in her gut again, and her cheeks began to burn. "Oh, hey," she said, but her voice was caught, tiny.

"I haven't seen you in days," he said.

"I've been busy." She held up a shimmery, purple pew bow. "The wedding."

"Nice," he said, glancing at the bow. "I would like to see you before the wedding."

"Okay?" She realized that it came out as a question. He was acting weird, and she wasn't sure where this was going. She wasn't even sure where she wanted it to go. "Why?"

"We're engaged," he said. "I would like to see my fiancée."

Marlee could feel Ellory's eyes bug out from across the room. She employed every ounce of effort at her disposal to not look over at her.

"I…we're not really…are you okay, Matthew?" He looked a little sick, a little sweaty.

"Without them," he said. "Just us."

She blinked. "Like…a real date?"

His misery deepened right in front of her eyes. "I was thinking we could practice dancing. Before the wedding. This evening at six?"

"Sure," Marlee said without even thinking, excitement blooming in her chest. "Okay."

"Okay. See you…see you then. Just, you know, casual. Dance practice." He patted the countertop lightly with his palm, still looking a little waxy. "Oh, and can you do me a favor?"

"Sure."

"Move your van."

He tapped the counter twice more and was gone. Marlee and Ellory watched him jog across the street and disappear inside his clinic.

"Oh, I see now," Ellory said.

"What? What do you mean, *you see*?"

Ellory pointed at her. "You're grinning. You went from downturn to grinning."

"I'm not grinning."

"You're *trying* not to grin, that's true, but you are most certainly grinning. You downturned because you're not happy. But you know what would make you happy. And that makes you unhappy."

"Anyone ever tell you that you don't make sense?" Marlee asked, picking up the pew bow and fiddling with it some more. It was finished and didn't need anything else. She only fiddled to keep herself from unwittingly grinning again.

"Anyone ever tell you that you're a horrible liar?" Ellory settled back on the bench and stroked Poppy's ears, looking smug, as if she'd cracked a code that nobody else could figure out. "Can I give you an outside observer's opinion?"

"No." Marlee took a long swig of her coffee, knowing that Ellory was going to provide said opinion no matter what she said, and also knowing that she wanted it.

"You should just let yourself grin. Enjoy the date. Stop the lie. And I don't mean the social media lie."

"You're funny," Marlee said. "You're not nearly as wise as you want to make yourself out to be." She held up the coffee cup. "But you make a very mean wedding cake latte."

"Thank you. And you are excellent at denial." She had stroked Poppy's fur until it shone, neat and sleek. The dog looked like she was in heaven and had commenced to happily licking her paws. "Where do you think he'll take you for this little dance practice? Somewhere romantic?"

Marlee shrugged. "He said casual." But she

felt anything but casual on the inside. Her limbs hummed with excitement. Her hands felt far away and soft, floaty, like two clouds bobbing through the air, plucking at flowers and tulle.

Ellory set Poppy on the floor and got up. She walked to the counter and took the bow out of Marlee's hands, then put her own hands on top of her friend's, trapping them. "I know that you've got a past that haunts you. But I think it's time for you to let that past go. Let yourself be swept away. That's just my opinion, of course."

Marlee pulled her hands out of Ellory's and gave her a reassuring nod and smile. "I've got a date to get ready for," was all she said.

MATTHEW WAS EXACTLY on time, breezing through the front door of the shop at 6:00 p.m. on the dot. Marlee had been there for a while already, too excited to be fashionably late. She busied herself with Annie's centerpieces to make it appear as if she was casually awaiting his arrival. No big deal, just another date. As if she went on dates all the time.

In reality, she'd gone home and changed into a gauzy little dress, perfect for an early summer evening out at…wherever it was they were going to go.

To her surprise, Matthew had also changed. In place of the typical slacks, button-down and tie under a lab coat, he was wearing chinos, a maroon tee and a knit jacket.

"Hi," he said simply, standing just inside the doorway, his hands pushed into his pockets. Marlee had taken Poppy home and fed her dinner. The result, surprisingly, was that she felt awfully alone in the shop with him, without Poppy as their regular chaperone.

"Hi." She slid the centerpiece to the side and brushed off her hands, grabbing her purse from under the counter.

He nodded toward the centerpiece. "That's pretty."

She turned to admire it. "Thanks. I think Annie will be pleased."

"Definitely."

"When you say six, you mean six," Marlee said, coming around the counter.

"I'm always punctual, yes."

"I, however, am almost never on time, and this is a miracle," Marlee said, shouldering her purse as she made her way around the counter. "Usually, I'm a little late and coming in hot, one shoe on and one shoe off, my earrings still in my hands."

"Is it bad for me to say that doesn't surprise me?"

"Not at all."

"Then that doesn't surprise me." He opened the door to let her go first. "I'm honored that you chose to be on time today."

She locked the door. "Don't let it go to your head. This is a one-off."

They started across the street; he stopped abruptly. "Wait. Is that why you're always parked in the wrong spot? You're in a hurry because you're late?"

She shrugged. "Maybe it used to be. Now, I just like to make my neighbor gripe."

"Speaking of. You didn't move it, even though I griped."

"I was busy getting ready. I had a date to be on time for. Where are we going, anyway?"

"Not far," he said, grabbing her hand and pulling her across the street.

It wasn't until they stepped inside that Marlee realized she'd never been in his clinic before. She stood in the waiting room and surveyed the area around her. It was just like Matthew—equal parts traditional and disarming, with dark blue vinyl chairs in a line along one wall, a corner strewn with toys on the other.

She found herself lingering at a table near the reception desk. On top of the table were two microscopes and some slides. Marlee leaned over the microscope and peered inside.

"Hair," Matthew said, picking up the slides and inserting them, one by one, into a tray, a neat line. "This one is sand. It's my favorite."

Marlee took the slide from him and replaced the hair slide. She squinted into the eyepiece and fiddled with the knob until a scattering of tiny, differently shaped, colored pebbles and shells came into focus. "Whoa. It's like a tiny treasure trove."

"We just walk on it, with no idea what we're walking on. Cool, huh?"

Marlee straightened. "I think it's cool that you have this here. I've never seen one in a doctor's office before."

He tapped the last slide into place inside the tray and closed it. "I remember the first time I ever looked inside a microscope. It blew me away. I couldn't wait until I could do it again. I asked for one for Christmas, and my grandparents got me a really nice one. Powerful, and it came with all these cool slides. Blood, hair, skin." He pointed to the microscope in front of her. "Sand. I was obsessed. I think it was then that I knew I wanted to create a life around biological science."

"Meant to be," she said.

"Meant to be," he agreed. "And if I can ignite that same passion in another kid, why wouldn't I? Lynette doesn't love that she has to monitor the table. Just to make sure the eyepiece gets wiped down, no glass gets broken, that kind of thing. But most kids are really respectful. They seem to know that they've been given something special here."

He was sharing a piece of himself with every kid who walked into his clinic. That *was* special.

"I could give you some petals and stems and

such," she said. "If you wanted to add them to your slide collection."

"I would love that," Matthew said. "Although it's the spider legs and blood that most kids are attracted to."

"Ew, really?"

Matthew shrugged. "Can't say I was any different. You think you know what something looks like. Blood is a great example. You know what blood looks like without a shadow of a doubt. It's a deep, red liquid, right? But you get closer and it's all these pink and purple circles. Look at it dried, and it looks almost brain-like, with all these squiggly lines. There's the whole other world that we can't even see unless we stop to study it. It looks nothing like what we're accustomed to. Yet at the same time, we're living in it. We're living in both the deep red liquid world and the pink and purple circle world, and the brain-like squiggle world, all at the same time. I must have been about eight when I first came to that realization." He placed his fingers on his temples and made a soft explosion sound as he flicked his hands open and drew them away from his head. "It blew my mind. I guess I wanted to be the one who could crack this strange code, who could understand all the worlds—the far away and the up close and the somewhere in between—all at the same time." He ducked his head. "I suppose it sounds silly, now that I say it out loud."

Marlee shook her head, entranced. "It's not silly in the least."

They gazed at each other for a long time. She suspected something could happen between them, but she didn't know what, and she didn't know whether or not she was supposed to let it happen. Or if she even wanted to.

And, maybe she was crazy, but she could have sworn Matthew was thinking the same thing.

"Anyway," he said, his voice loud to break the spell. He threw up his arms. "This is the reception area. Lynette works there, of course." He gestured toward the reception desk, which looked dark and abandoned. He took a few long strides and opened a wooden door. He stepped aside and gestured for her to go in.

It was just like any other doctor's office. A scale in the hallway, some rolling blood pressure machines stuffed with cuffs of all sizes, some exam rooms. And an office.

She lingered in the office doorway, unable to tear her eyes away.

It was crammed from top to bottom with books, skeletons, models of body parts, old-fashioned medical instruments, paintings of the brain, the lungs, the heart, a couple of college pennants, and a whole slew of degrees, diplomas and awards. On one leather chair sat an old-fashioned medical bag—the kind doctors used to carry when they made house calls. She remembered now that

Matthew had shown up with that bag before, during a fundraiser that Morgan had organized for Pathways.

She also remembered that the cute doctor with the old-timey bag had stuffed said old-timey bag with balloons for making balloon animals.

"Have you read all of these?" she asked, pointing to one of the many bookshelves lining the walls.

A singular nod. "I like to read."

"Me, too, actually," Marlee said, wandering into the room and running her finger down the spine of a book. "I just never really know what to read."

"Take one."

"Just take a book?"

"Sure. They're not all textbooks, you know." Matthew swept toward the shelf, leaning over her as he pulled a book out of its spot, then thrust it toward her. "This is a good one."

Marlee turned it over in her hands, at once curious and confused. "I didn't mean for you to be my personal library."

Matthew rolled his eyes. "After you're done reading it, we can talk about it over lunch. Like a book club. Just take the book, Marlee. It's not that big of a deal."

But staring at the empty space on his bookshelf, it felt like a big deal. She had a feeling that Matthew didn't loan his books out to just anyone. She'd broken into some inner circle without meaning to. Which would be fine, except she was beginning to have all these conflicting feelings about him, and for some reason, taking this book, leaving this empty space on his shelf, felt like a step too far.

She pushed it back into its spot and gave him a warm smile. "I'll grab it another day. We've got a date to get to."

Matthew looked disappointed. Marlee hated being the one to let him down. If her thoughts could just stop swimming when she was around him, this would be so much easier.

"Right. The date," he said. "Come on."

Once again, he grabbed her hand, and they were on the move. She didn't want to leave his office. There was something about it that was very comfortable and inviting to her, even in the chaos. She knew, without a shadow of a doubt, that Matthew kept a mental catalog of each and every item in that office, and that he could likely recite an inventory, if needed. That office was Matthew personified. Chaotic and humble and reservedly warm.

She followed along with a little yelp, having assumed that they were only at his office for him to pick something up or maybe show her around. He led her out the back door, which, like the back of her shop, butted up against a modest neighborhood, a small metal swing set separated from his back lot by a chain-link fence. He let the door close behind them and pulled her toward a rolling safety ladder, which had been pushed up against the building.

She followed him up.

And gasped.

Sunflowers, lavender, daylilies, petunias, geraniums, nasturtiums, hydrangeas, the standards, just as he'd described to Janquil that first, disastrous night. Only it was so much more beautiful than she ever imagined.

She propelled herself forward on leaden legs, lowering her hands to brush against the leaves on either side of her as she walked—lamb's ears and hostas and blue star junipers in pots and on stands, pressed in so close, she was confined to a narrow walkway. The walkway led to a clearing, in which Matthew had placed a table for two under a pergola strung with twinkling lights. There was a picnic basket resting on the ground next to the table and a small makeshift dance floor overlooking Main Street.

"What do you think?" he asked, his voice warm and buttery.

"This isn't real. It can't be real." She spun to face him. "You did this?"

He shrugged like it was no big deal. "I've been working on it ever since I talked about it at our dinner party slash interview."

"You told Janquil that the landlord made you

take it down. Why did you go ahead and build it, anyway?"

He hesitated. "Because I saw the look on your face while I was talking about it."

She touched her chest. "The look on my face? I was so irritated that night. I can only imagine what the look on my face must have been."

"That's the thing. You were irritated. But, when I was talking about it, you got this faraway look, like it would be a dream come true to have such a space."

"So, you built one."

He shrugged again. "So, I built one."

"Matthew, do you know how much work it's going to take to upkeep this?"

"I'm aware. I've been tending to it. I find it relaxing, actually. And it's the perfect spot for dance practice. Does this mean you like it or hate it? I can't tell."

She spun a slow circle, arms outstretched to feel the plants. The town she grew up in, spent nearly every day of her life walking through, looked totally different from up here. Smaller, more romantic. "Are you kidding? I love it. Oh! Look! There's a ball on top of my shop." She pointed and laughed, walking onto the dance floor. "And a shoe. How does a single shoe end up on the roof?"

He joined her. "I had a Frisbee on mine. I haven't seen anyone throw a Frisbee since I moved in."

"Maybe because the person who threw it only owned one Frisbee and it got stuck up here," Marlee said. "Also...that person might have been me. Don't ask. Archer is a terrible catcher."

"It's in my office. In the file cabinet. Filed under *F*."

"Of course it is."

"Um...oh! I almost forgot." He reached into his pocket and pulled out his phone. Poked around on it a little and soon, music began to play over a speaker hidden somewhere in the hydrangeas. He slipped the phone back into his pocket and offered Marlee his hands. "Care to dance?"

Marlee couldn't help herself—she took his hand and gave a little curtsy. "What a great idea! Yes, please." She pulled herself closer to him to place her other hand on his shoulder—trying not to feel like a big goofball for curtsying—and let him wrap his free hand around her waist. He felt extraordinarily warm, but in a good way. They moved together easily and seamlessly, surprising her. Turned out, they didn't need practice. But Marlee wasn't about to break away anytime soon. She felt too comfortable. She gazed up at him. "I can't believe you did this. How long do we have before Janquil and Tyler join us and ruin it all?"

She could have sworn his eyes actually glistened. "That's the best part. They're not going to."

Marlee's eyebrows flew up. "You shook them?"

"More like artfully avoided."

Marlee threw her head back and laughed. Matthew took that as an opportunity for a wild spin and a dip. Marlee squealed, feeling as if she were on a roller coaster. The sun was sinking, throwing shadows over them, the twinkle lights growing brighter, and when Marlee came back up from the dip, she felt herself pull in tighter. She wanted to be closer to him. Less friends and more…something else. She began to hear Morgan's voice in her head. *It's not a myth. Not everyone is Keith.* She didn't want to believe these things. She'd invested too much of her time and mental energy convincing herself that love and romance weren't a thing.

She didn't want to get hurt.

Yet, how could someone who had built this rooftop garden just because she lit up when he described it ever hurt her? Ever hurt anyone?

She felt herself sliding into territory she knew nothing about.

She was so deep in her thoughts, she didn't realize the music had stopped until Matthew pulled away. "Should we eat?" he asked.

"You made food, too?"

"Why else would there be a table?"

Marlee couldn't help laughing. This pragmatism of his was what normally drove her up the wall. He was no-nonsense, empirical, obvious. What you saw with Matthew LaSalle was what you got. But tonight it didn't bother her. It charmed her. Of course there would be food, because there was a table. Simple. Self-explanatory.

"Well, when you put it that way, how can I say no?"

They made their way to the little table under the pergola. He'd even thought to cut a small bouquet of lavender and pop it into a vase.

Wait...not a vase, a beaker.

Of course.

Marlee had to resist letting out another delighted laugh. If she kept this up, he would surely think she'd lost her mind.

"The lavender is a really nice touch," she said. "I always think it smells so nice."

"My grandmother was a big fan of lavender." He bent to pick up the picnic basket as he settled into his chair. "The smell reminds me of her."

"What was she like?" Marlee asked, her stomach rumbling as she watched him pull food out of the basket and lay it out—a charcuterie board filled with meats and cheeses, a bowl of fresh fruit, olives, thick slices of tomato, a loaf of crusty bread, artisan crackers. He'd spared no expense.

"Oh, I thought my grandma was everything," he said, laying a plate and silverware rolled in a cloth napkin in front of her. "She understood me better than anyone else in my life ever has. And accepted me exactly like I was. Please." He gestured toward the food. Marlee reached out and took an olive, popped it into her mouth. "She was a scientist, too. A nurse, because back when she was growing up, that was about her only option. But, at heart, she was a research scientist."

"What about you?" Marlee asked.

He glanced up. "What about me?"

"At heart," she said. "What kind of scientist are you?"

"A doctor."

This, too, elicited an internal *of course* from Marlee. Matthew was who he was, inside and out.

"Anyway." He filled his plate with food and smoothed the napkin over his lap. "She always encouraged me to embrace my passion. We talked about science for, literally, thousands of hours. She was great. I miss her. What about you?" he asked. "Who was your champion? As a kid, I mean."

"Morgan. Definitely," Marlee said. "My parents are amazing people, and my grandparents were great, too, but Morgan is my otherme."

"Your otherme?"

Marlee ate another olive. "You know. The one person out there who totally gets you. Doesn't expect more out of you than you can give. Sees your flaws and loves you, anyway. Cheers you on and holds your hand and lets you cry actual wet tears all over the front of their shirt. Your otherme."

"Ah," he said. "I see."

But Marlee could tell that he didn't see. Not entirely. Her heart ached for him. She suspected that maybe his grandmother was as close to an otherme as he'd ever had. She wondered if he would even be capable of having another one. Despite herself, she wondered if there was a world in which she herself was Matthew LaSalle's otherme.

She felt a strong desire to change the subject. "This spread is amazing, Matthew. Thank you. I can't believe you did all this."

He shrugged, the tips of his ears going red. "I think I owed you. And I owed myself. I don't know about you, but, since the start of this, I've been having a hard time feeling like I can get away from it all, just have some alone time. You know what I mean?"

"Yeah," she said. "Although, after prom it kind of died down for me. I'm not the cute pediatrician that everyone wants to fall in love with."

The tips of his ears grew even redder. "I've had people bring in kids with fake maladies this week." He raised his voice to falsetto. "What? She doesn't have pink eye? Well, I could have sworn…" He batted his eyelashes dramatically.

Marlee burst out laughing. "You're kidding! People have really done that?"

"Oh, and that's not all. One woman brought her nephew in with stomach pain, and when I lifted his shirt to palpate his belly, her phone number was written across it in red marker, with the words *Call me*."

Marlee laughed so hard her own belly hurt. "You're making that up."

"I'm not!" he said, laughing along with her. The redness had drained from his ears as they giggled and laughed and told tales of the strange things they'd seen and heard since inviting *Modern Vow* and social media into their lives.

"This is good," Marlee said, sitting back in her chair and gesturing at the garden surrounding them. Twilight had fallen in earnest, stars beginning to dot the sky above them. The lights strung around the pergola really seemed to be blinking now. "I needed this."

He bowed his head. "Feel free to come over anytime. You don't even have to come inside. Just walk on up. It's yours. Maybe I'll even have a sign made—Marlee's Garden."

She shook her head. "I think we should call it BL Gardens."

"BL? Who is that?"

She shook her head, leaned in, and snagged a piece of cheese. "Not a who. A what." She stuffed the cheese into her mouth and reached for another olive. "Belly laugh. Belly Laugh Gardens."

"I love it. Everyone should have a place to belly laugh." He grinned and reached for more food as well, adopting a goofy, overexaggerated British accent. "I thus declare it so. This space has been christened as, and shall henceforth be known as, BL Gardens." His hand accidentally brushed up against hers as he hoisted a cracker with cheese up high in a toast. Instead of feeling awkward and weird, she felt warm. Butterflies coursed through her belly. She was content here.

And it was 100 percent real.

Nothing fictional about it in the least.

Forget what happened with Keith.

She was falling for Matthew LaSalle. There was no stopping it now.

CHAPTER TWENTY

MATTHEW WAS GLAD to see that his morning was going to start with a regular patient. In fact, one of his initial regulars who got his practice off the ground in the first place: Archer West, Marlee's nephew. Only, when Matthew started seeing Archer, he didn't even know yet that Marlee was just across the street, making weddings beautiful and parking her van right in front of his office.

Morgan was a couple of years younger than Marlee, so Matthew hadn't even known about her in school. If he had, they might have been friends, or at least in the same study groups. She was a serious, driven type, like him. Only her drive led her to advertising instead of medicine. When she'd introduced herself by appealing to him to help fundraise for McBride Pathways, he'd found himself giving free checkups to kids at a carnival. It was fun and it made sense. He fit there.

Oh, but you fit with Marlee, too, he thought miserably. *Your little rooftop project says it all. You just don't want to admit it.*

True. He did not want to admit it. In fact, not admitting that his feelings for Marlee were changing was occupying most of his waking thoughts. He was so not into her, she was the only thing he could think about.

He rolled his eyes at himself and strode down the hall. He pulled Archer's file from the chart holder on the door, knocked twice and went inside.

Archer lit up when he saw Matthew. Matthew's heart soared. "How you doing, buddy?" he asked, as the child barreled into his legs, headfirst, for a hug. Matthew ruffled Archer's hair, then offered his hand to Morgan. "How are you, Mrs. McBride?"

She beamed and shook his hand. "I'm doing great. We're doing great."

Matthew extricated himself from Archer and hoisted the child up onto the exam table. "My notes say you're here for a checkup. Is that okay?"

"Yes," Archer said.

"Yes? That's excellent!" Matthew glanced at Morgan in surprise. Archer was on the autism spectrum and largely nonverbal. The last time Matthew saw him, the only word he really knew was *no*, and he loved to use it.

"He's made a lot of progress," Morgan confirmed. "His vocabulary is growing. Archer, tell Dr. LaSalle what you made at camp."

"A friend," Archer said without pausing.

Matthew pulled himself up onto the exam table so he was sitting side by side with the boy. "Is that so? What's your friend's name?"

"Isabella," Archer said, carefully and proudly.

"Whoa! Isabella, huh? That's amazing!" He directed the last at Morgan, who looked like she might launch right out of her chair and fly with pride. "Sounds like camp is going great. Should we go ahead and check you out to see how much camp made you grow?"

Archer looked down at the floor but nodded his head. Matthew slid off the table and quickly and efficiently went through the checklist, asking Morgan questions as he went along, while also "playing" just enough to disarm Archer. He was finished quickly, as he knew he needed to be when it came to kids with sensory issues, and sank onto his rolling stool.

"Well, Archer. You look healthy as a horse. Are you a horse?"

Archer giggled. "No."

"Are you sure? Have you tried whinnying?" He made his own whinnying sound. He'd spent a good amount of time in college mastering all of the animal noises, correctly guessing that knowing all the best animal noises would come in handy during the course of his career. He found himself pulling out a realistic elephant trumpet more times in a week than he could count.

Archer giggled again and shook his head, but then gave it a try.

"Hmm," Matthew said. "That was pretty good. You may be part horse."

"No," Archer said, but he jumped off the exam table and galloped circles around the room, whinnying over and over again.

"Do you have any questions for me?" Matthew asked Morgan.

"I don't think so," she said. "He's grown so much in every single way. More than I could have ever predicted. A year ago, when Annie asked if he would be the ring bearer at their wedding, I was really on the fence. But now I have no worries at all."

"He's going to do great," Matthew said. "And we'll all be there to cheer him on. Won't we, buddy?" Once again, he reached over and ruffled Archer's hair. He stood, ready to make his exit.

"We're all excited about it. I'm most excited for a chance to spend a whole evening with my sister. She always works herself to the bone before a big event like this, and we've been too busy on the ranch for me to help her. I feel like I haven't had any solid sister time in ages." Morgan stood, following his lead. "I was glad to see that you and Marlee found some time to wind down last night, though. Or maybe it was work, since you were with the magazine, huh?"

He froze. "What do you mean?"

"Last night? On the roof? You guys really outdid yourself on that, by the way. I hope the magazine helped you out. Seems like a lot of time and money went into it."

Her words were sinking in slowly. The roof… winding down…the magazine…*the magazine*. He must have looked as confused as he felt, because she reached into her back pocket and pulled out her phone. She tapped around on it and then turned it for him to see.

There, on her phone screen, were the silhouettes of him and Marlee in each other's arms, dancing, the sky the new gray of evening, the twinkling lights on the pergola behind them. The photo was clearly taken from the ground across the street. He and Marlee had never seen Janquil or Tyler. They'd never thought to look. They'd thought they were alone.

There was a caption above the photo: *We don't think they need any practice before the wedding, but we think it's adorable, anyway. #dancepractice*

He tried not to gawk. But he was gawking.

"Is something wrong?" Morgan asked.

"We didn't know they were there," he said.

Now it was Morgan's turn to gawk. "Wait. You were…? This was an actual date? I thought… I mean, Marlee had told me that this was all… Well, I guess maybe I misunderstood that—"

"Fake," he said. "No. I mean, yeah. It's all fake."

"I don't understand."

He ducked back into the exam room. Morgan grasped Archer's arm and followed. They shut the door.

"The whole thing is faked, yes. But this." He pointed at her phone. "This was not fake."

"It was a date? Like, a real date?"

"Yes. No. I don't know," he said miserably. "We were practicing for the wedding. That part is true."

Morgan sucked in a breath and then let it out with a smile. "Oh, I see."

"No, you don't see," he said. "Or, maybe I should say, if you see, can you clue me in? I have no idea what I'm doing."

"You're falling for my sister is what you're doing. And you're very smart to do so."

"I never said anything about falling," he said.

"You didn't have to. Look at the photo. Look at how romantic this is. Did you build the garden together?"

"No," he said. "I surprised her with it."

Morgan bit her bottom lip and scrunched up her nose and shoulders, as if to say, *See what I mean?*

Archer had flopped over the rolling stool on his belly and was using his feet to spin the stool in slow circles. Matthew sank onto the chair Morgan had been in earlier. She perched on the edge of the chair next to him. She put away her phone.

"Okay, this isn't my business, and you didn't ask, and she would disown me if she heard me say what I'm about to say, but I'm going to say it, anyway." She reached over and squeezed his hand, which was resting on his knee. "My sister doesn't believe in love. She thinks it's a myth. She was burned—like, seriously burned—in the past, and never put her heart all the way back together. It's fear. She's afraid to really open up to someone out of fear that what happened to her before could happen again. And I suppose it could. That's the chance anyone takes with love, you know?"

"Oh, trust me, I know," Matthew said.

"Right. Everyone knows. Nobody gets through life without experiencing heartbreak. It's not about avoiding hurt, it's about putting yourself back together afterward. I had to risk being hurt when I admitted that I loved Decker. But I'm so glad that I did." She let go of his hand and placed hers on her chest, as if to feel her own heart swell. "As Marlee's sister, I've been waiting for her to open herself up again. She deserves love, and I want her to experience the kind of life that I'm experiencing. I want her to have everything. Including the romantic moments that people repost or like or love or whatever. I want her to actually have a magazine-level romance. But I want it for her, not for fame or business or whatever it is she's doing right now. I want the rooftop dance to be real."

"It was real," he said.

"Now that I know it wasn't set up by the magazine, I can tell by the look on my sister's face that it's at least partly real for her, too." She placed her palm against his chest, tenderly pressing. "I think it is real here. I think you want to have it, too. I think you actively want it."

There was a short rap on the door and it cracked open. Lynette's face popped in. "Your next appointment is in room two," she said.

"Okay, thank you," Matthew said. "I'll be right there."

"We're ready to hit that lollipop jar, anyway, aren't we, Archer?" Morgan said, standing and tucking her purse into her side as if she had been just any other mother of a patient. "We'll see you at the wedding tomorrow night, Dr. LaSalle?"

He stood. "Absolutely. I'll be there."

Lynette led them out into the hallway, Morgan shutting the door behind them. He needed a minute to compose himself.

Because, of course, he already knew that she was right. He was starting to fall for Marlee.

But where she was wrong was that he didn't want it to be real. He desperately wanted the opposite.

He closed his eyes, still seeing the photo behind his eyelids. That moment with her in his arms had felt so good. The entire evening had been easy and peaceful and blissful.

The photo robbed it all away, made him feel like an ant under a magnifying glass. It felt dangerous, and he felt far too exposed.

When he let himself really think about it, that's how he had felt every time he met with a new patient since the ruse began. It didn't feel earned. It felt like he was someone else in a Matthew suit, pretending. Just pretending. Always pretending.

Which was his biggest fear.

Would he and Marlee ever be able to be real? How could they possibly know? They'd already taken that away from themselves. When you start out as a lie, how do you even know when you've found the truth?

He felt nauseous. The garden was right over his head right now. He'd spent days working on it, dripping sweat into the flower boxes and pots. It was almost as much him as this building beneath it.

Yet, it now felt as if it belonged to someone else.

It felt like it belonged to everyone else.

But not to him. And, if he was smart, he would make sure it stayed that way.

CHAPTER TWENTY-ONE

Now that the big day was here, Annie was a giant knot of nervous energy, buzzing around the ranch, double- and triple-checking every tiny detail to make sure it was perfect. She'd chosen an outdoor wedding at the ranch. Paying homage to the camp where she and Ben met, the reception would feature "elevated camp chow at the bridal mess tent"—dainty peanut butter and jelly finger sandwiches, crystal bowls filled with chips and Goldfish crackers, vats of trail mix, and, of course, potato salad. Ellory had been commissioned to make the cake, and had done a brilliant job of duplicating a striped snack cake that Ben had shared with Annie back when they were teens—the first kindness meant to express his feelings for her.

The "mess tent" had been upgraded to a white bridal tent with a dance floor, the picnic tables given a fresh white paint job. Marlee had decked out the entire tent in blue and purple, with flowers, bows and accents everywhere the eye could see, leaving a vibe that felt like a mash-up of *The Little Mermaid* and Mardi Gras.

Marlee stood back and admired her handiwork, hands on hips, feeling joyful in a way that she couldn't quite define. It was more than the jubilance of camp and young love. It was more than the elegant cheer of a wedding.

It was the simmering she felt inside. Something had shifted between her and Matthew, but mostly she'd felt the shift inside herself. It was a shift away from the hurt that Keith had left her with. It was scary, but in a good way, to admit that maybe, just maybe, love wasn't always a myth. Maybe, just maybe, Mr. Right and Mr. Perfect could be real, and could be one and the same.

Could be Matthew LaSalle.

Marlee had decorated more than her fair share of weddings and receptions. Usually, the task made her feel like an outsider. She was providing a service for the insiders, the people who could and did have what she could never have.

But today, the flowers seemed perkier, more jubilant. The colors were more vibrant. The air filled with a hopefulness that she'd never experienced before.

Even though it frightened her, she found that she didn't mind it. She was more frightened by the idea that she might never feel it again.

She stood on the empty dance floor, scanning for things to fix. Every so often, she would drop her hands, bustle to a centerpiece, rearrange an imperfection that only she could see, then go back to her post on the dance floor. She was already dressed for the wedding. The sun was lowering in the sky. By the checklist, she was ready.

She heard footsteps approaching and turned to see Ben coming toward her. He was gussied up in a tux, but wearing his usual brown cowboy hat, darkened on the brim where he constantly clutched it with his fingers. He tipped his head forward just slightly.

"Ma'am."

"Ben," she said, stretching out her arms to give him a hug. He stopped several steps away, though, demurring, as he always did. She dropped her arms at her sides. "It's your big day. Are you ready?"

"The word *big* is an adjective used to connote size, ma'am. Since days are simply a concept, one cannot be bigger than another. But I understand your intent in meaning that this day will carry more importance in my life than other days. I will be tasked with awareness of this date every year and will be expected to acknowledge it with gifts. Based on this acknowledgment, I will agree with your claim. It is a big day, so to speak."

Marlee grinned. This was Ben's style, and she loved it about him. He never tried to be anyone he wasn't. "And you're ready?"

He looked over his clothing. She could practically see him going through a checklist. *Slacks, check. Shirt, check. Coat and bow tie, check and check.*

"I mean, in here," she said, touching her chest with her fingertip. "Are you nervous?"

"Oh," he said. "Yes, ma'am, I am."

"Ready or nervous?"

"I am dressed, and I have rehearsed my tasks many times, so in the strictest regard of being prepared, I am. *Ready*, as you put it. But, as a human being who is not a robot and cannot be programmed to never make a mistake, I can make errors that might feel embarrassing. I don't like feeling embarrassed. Sometimes when you do something embarrassing, people laugh at you. I don't like that."

"Oh, Ben," Marlee said. "No matter what happens today, nobody will laugh at you. Everyone who is coming today loves you and loves Annie. It's going to be wonderful. The best day of your life."

He shifted his weight and scratched one ear, thinking. "Technically, we could only make the claim that it is the best day of my life up to this point. We don't know if I might have better days later in life. And we also don't know that something catastrophic won't happen on this day."

"Well, I can't argue with that," Marlee said. "Let's just say I'm hoping that this day turns out to be the best day you've ever had, and that you may have some days in the future that are almost as good as this one, or maybe even better."

"Yes, ma'am," he said.

They stood side by side and surveyed the tent from the dance floor together.

"What do you think?" Marlee asked. "Do you think it's pretty?"

He gave his head a quick dip. "Yes, ma'am, I think it's beautiful."

"Do you think Annie will love it?"

"Yes, ma'am, she will love it very much."

"That's exactly what I was hoping for," Marlee said.

"Ma'am?" There was an uncomfortable tremor in his voice.

"Yes?"

"Which flower do you think is the prettiest?"

"What do you mean?"

He nodded his head toward the tables. "In this tent. Which flower do you think is the prettiest one?"

"Oh." Marlee bit her lip, her brow scrunching. "There are a billion flowers in here, Ben. I couldn't possibly choose a prettiest one."

"Beg your pardon, ma'am, but unless you counted, it is highly unlikely that you have placed exactly one billion flowers in this tent. It might be better to estimate hundreds, or even an approximation of one thousand."

"Well, that's true, but it doesn't change the point that I can't choose the prettiest one."

"Could you try, ma'am?"

Marlee turned toward him again. He'd removed his hat and was holding it at his side. She noticed only then that he had scrubbed himself so clean the back of his neck and tops of his ears were red. On top of that, he was flushed now, too, the whole effect rendering him very beet-like. "Do you mind my asking why?" Marlee asked.

He stared at his boots, which he began scuffing along the ground. There were many aspects of Ben that were so innocent, it was as if she could see the little boy still lurking inside. "I was hoping to take it," he said. "If that's okay with you, ma'am."

"Why? I mean, you can do whatever you wish with these flowers. You paid for them. But I'm just curious why you want to take one flower out?"

He scratched his ear again. "I'd like to give it to Annie when she comes down the aisle to greet me," he said. "She's the most beautiful girl in the whole world. Mr. Decker says I can still say that, even though I, technically, haven't seen every girl in the world and can't assess their beauty against hers, because I am biased in a good way and I should keep it that way. And since she's the most beautiful girl in the world, I want her to have the most beautiful flower at our wedding. Just for her. If that's okay."

Marlee felt tears instantly push forward. "Oh, Ben," she said, reaching over to touch his arm. "That is so romantic. Annie is such a lucky girl."

"Luck doesn't have anything to do with it, ma'am. We each exhibit qualities that make us compatible with each other. That's all."

That's not all, Marlee thought. But she knew that it was no use arguing with Ben about…well, anything. So, instead, she said, "Let's find the prettiest flower."

They wandered through the room, pointing here and there, stopping to admire a big bloom or a bright color. Finally, they agreed on one that just happened to be in the centerpiece of the bridal table. Marlee pulled it from the vase and handed it to Ben, then fussed with the other flowers to compensate for its absence.

"If you want, I can take it to the house and wrap it in some paper and ribbon," she said.

"No, thank you, ma'am. I like it just the way it is." He took a deep breath and let it out. It was shaky. "I suppose I should get back."

"I'll see you at the ceremony."

He tipped his hat, touched the brim. "Ma'am."

Marlee was left standing alone on the dance floor again. In just hours, it would be packed. She would be dancing with Matthew, Janquil and Tyler nearby snapping photos and asking questions about their own upcoming wedding. She knew that Matthew was tired of them. He'd been incensed that they'd been caught dancing up on the roof. He'd stormed into the shop to show her the photo, but she'd pretended to be too busy with last-minute wedding preparations to attend to it. But the truth was she didn't share his anger.

She didn't mind that they looked like they were in love.

She didn't mind that the magazine had captured a tender moment.

The fact that he did mind, and that he minded so very much, only pointed out to her that, to him, this was still an act. He wasn't in love with her. Even though when they were together, it very much felt like he was.

After all, he hadn't given her the prettiest flower at the wedding; he'd given her an entire, beautiful garden.

She never meant to actually fall for him, but here she was. Falling, falling, falling so hard, all she could think about was being in his arms on this very dance floor in just a few hours.

She suspected he was falling, too, and that was the real source of his angst. But she was going to need to pry it out of him.

And she intended to do just that.

Tonight.

She would tell Matthew how she truly felt about him, and hope to hear what she wanted to hear—that he felt the same about her.

CHAPTER TWENTY-TWO

MORE THAN ANYTHING, Matthew didn't want to go to this wedding at all.

He was going to have to tell Marlee that he wasn't falling in love with her.

He was going to have to look her in the face and lie.

No. It wasn't a lie. He wasn't in love. He was experiencing a little infatuation, that was all. It was the lie that he was currently caught up in, and as soon as he extricated himself from it, it would be over, and he could go back to his regularly scheduled business of being happily alone.

But you weren't happy, were you? Not truly. That's the real lie here. You thought you were happy. But that was until you started hanging out with Marlee. Then you experienced what actual happiness looks and feels like, and you know very well that you weren't feeling happiness before. It was guarded contentment at best.

He took a deep breath and shuttered his mind, tried to concentrate on tying his tie.

"In just a few hours," he said to the mirror, "this will all be over."

He didn't need Janquil and Tyler to point out where Marlee was. He saw her the minute he crossed the lawn to where the ceremony was to be held. She was doing some last-minute fussing with a pew bow.

She was breathtaking. Literally. His breath caught when he saw her, and he had a wild moment of thinking he might just turn around and go back home. Text her an apology later.

No. That's not who you are.

He steeled himself and walked toward her. But it was as if she sensed him. She stood upright, finished fussing and turned toward him, her eyes meeting his with no searching whatsoever. She smiled and waved. He waved back, afraid that his smile might actually look like nausea. It was definitely what was happening in his gut.

She came toward him, her blue-and-yellow floral dress fluttering around her like butterfly wings. They met at the last row of chairs. She swiped her hair across her face and pushed it back behind one ear. His knees wanted to buckle at the sight of her being so casually beautiful.

"You made it," she said.

"I made it. Did you need help with that?" he asked, pointing at the pew bow she'd just been messing with.

"No. At this point, I'm just being a perfectionist. Plus, Tyler wanted to get an action shot of me preparing for the wedding."

Matthew let out a sarcastic chuckle. Of course Tyler wanted to get an action shot. Tyler was so present during every moment of their lives over the past several days, Matthew was beginning to wonder what was real and what was not.

Two teens walked past, their heads bent toward each other, their hands over their mouths. When they reached Marlee and Matthew, they burst into giggles. Matthew thought one of them might have been the girl who started it all. The one who'd been in Blush & Bloom when he'd caught Marlee on the ladder.

"He's so cute," he heard one of the girls say, and then more giggling.

He made a noise deep in his throat, something like a grunt.

"Problem with your fans?" Marlee asked.

"Yes," he said. "The fact that I have fans is the problem. I shouldn't have fans. I don't do anything fan-worthy."

"You don't like calling them fans, and you don't like calling them followers," she said.

"I definitely don't do anything to merit having followers."

"Well, whatever you call them, they're here for you. Look around."

For the first time, he really looked at the crowd, turning his head slowly. The teens were hardly the only two guests talking about him. Plenty of people—mostly women—were looking right at him, barely concealing the fact that they were discussing him, many with the same wide smiles and admiring eyes.

"Can we sit?" Matthew asked, wanting nothing more than to get out of the limelight.

"Sure." Marlee looped her arm around his elbow and started walking, leading him to a spot near the side, somewhat obscured by a pole. "How's this?"

"It's good. It's fine." He found himself slouching down in the chair to avoid being seen, but within seconds of them choosing a seat, he heard the click of Tyler's camera. He rested his forehead in one hand, hoping to casually shield his face and dissuade Tyler.

"Don't worry," Marlee said, leaning in. "They promised me they would stop when the wedding starts."

"And you believe them?" he whispered. "They spied on us on the roof."

"I don't know if it's spying when we invited them to Haw Springs to take pictures of us." She leaned back and studied him, then moved toward him again. "Are you okay? You seem a little agitated."

"I'm fine," he said. "I'm just..." He waved his hand, as if to wave the thought away. "I'm fine."

She took his hand and squeezed it. "Matthew. It's almost over. We will soon fade into the oblivion of the internet. Our flash in the pan will be all sizzled out."

"You're right," he said. "I know."

More guests filled in around them, and soon a preacher appeared, along with Ben, who was carrying a blue flower on a long stem. Ben's best men fell in behind him, and then the music swelled.

At the preacher's motion, the entire crowd stood and turned. Annie stood at the end of the aisle, grasping tightly to her father's arm, her smile so wide, it looked like it hurt. Ben tipped his hat at her, and she laughed loudly and waved. Her father had to slow her a couple of times as she practically raced down the aisle to her groom. When she got to him, he handed her the flower, which she quickly tucked into her bouquet. The stem was three times the length of the stems in the bouquet, so the flower jutted awkwardly away from the rest of them. Yet it seemed right. It looked perfect. Matthew gave Marlee a quick glance. She was smiling from ear to ear. Not a single worry about what the wayward flower had done to the shape of the bouquet she'd painstakingly arranged.

After she tucked the flower in, Annie leaned over and gave Ben a peck on the cheek.

"Now, now, not yet," the preacher admonished, and the crowd laughed. Annie laughed the hardest of everyone, briefly putting her hand over her mouth in mild embarrassment.

To be so absolutely certain, Matthew thought.

To be so open. Their lives were going to change forever. They would cease to be two individuals and become one unit. Ben and Annie, Ben and Annie, BenandAnnie. And they looked utterly thrilled about it.

The ceremony wasn't long. The vows were short and sweet, and when Ben thanked Annie for being the one person in his whole life who understood him and didn't ever, not even one time, call him a know-it-all, everyone in the audience sniffled and wiped their eyes. Matthew had a strong desire to wrap his arm around Marlee, but he fought it with everything he had.

After the ceremony, they all filed to the tent for dinner, cake and dancing. To accommodate the neurodivergent guests, the DJ had agreed to a silent disco, greeting each guest with a set of headphones.

Marlee gasped as she eagerly took the headphones. "Fun!" she said. "Dance with me?"

"I don't know. Everyone's watching," Matthew said, but he was cut short by the appearance of Janquil and Tyler. For the briefest moment, he had forgotten that they were there. He struggled to keep from rolling his eyes at their presence.

"We need some dancing photos," Janquil said. "The headphones are going to be the cutest addition to the Marthew journey."

"Marthew?" Matthew asked.

"Matthew plus Marlee. Marthew. Sort of like Brangelina or Bennifer."

"They're celebrities," Matthew argued.

Janquil leaned in conspiratorially. "Look around, Dr. LaSalle. You've got more than a little bit of celebrity surrounding you, too."

"This is someone's wedding," he said. "I don't want the attention."

"Too bad, buddy," Tyler said, snapping a photo of the headphones hanging from each of their hands. "You don't get a choice in the matter."

Matthew pleaded with Marlee with his eyes, but she only gave him an apologetic shrug. "It's the last night," she said, and while that was supposed to make him feel better, it didn't.

"Well, then, let's get this over with."

Matthew crammed the headphones down over his ears, grabbed Marlee's hand and led her to the dance floor.

THE MOMENT HE touched her hand, he didn't want to let go. They made their way to the middle of the floor as a slow song started piping into his ears. All of his frustrations drained away as he took her into his arms and began swaying with her. She smelled like powder and perfume, and everything about her was soft. They moved together easily, without counting or directing or any of the things couples have to do to keep from tromping all over each other's toes. She rested her head against his chest, and he couldn't help it; he dipped his nose down and buried it in her hair. It was like resting in a flower patch.

The headphones made it so they couldn't speak but had to let the tenderness of the way they fit together do the speaking for them. Matthew felt as if maybe he'd known Marlee for an entire lifetime. That seemed like the only possible way that this could be so easy for them.

The slow song ended, and a fast one started up. They stepped away from each other awkwardly, an unspoken question hanging between them: *Should we keep dancing?*

Tyler orbited around them, answering the question for them. Matthew began moving his hips and bending and bopping, as self-conscious as anyone could possibly be.

About halfway through the song, Marlee's mouth began to move with words. Matthew shook his head and pointed at the headphones. She repeated herself. *A faraway water toothache?* Matthew thought. What did that mean? He pulled his headphones away from one ear, surprised by how silent the tent was. Just the low murmuring of conversation, the tapping of dress shoes against the wooden dance floor...and Marlee's scream over music that only she could hear.

"I said I've always wanted to do this!" she yelled. Every head that wasn't covered with headphones turned and stared.

Matthew couldn't help himself. He let out a hearty laugh.

"I thought you were saying you had a faraway water toothache," he said.

She shook her head and turned her palms up. Of course, she couldn't hear him.

Even though he knew it would do no good, it was still second nature. He raised his voice. "I thought you had a toothache!" Now the faces were turned to him. Which only made him laugh harder.

Finally, she pulled one headphone away. "Tuesday?" she asked, though she was still yelling. She winced and lowered her voice. "What's happening Tuesday?"

Matthew laughed harder and grabbed her hands, whirled her in a circle. "We're terrible at this," he said.

"Speak for yourself," she yelled back. "I'm doing great!"

She twirled away from him, her skirt flaring around her, and then, as the music changed to a new song, really started to go for it. She danced exactly the way he imagined she would. Carefree and flowy and with feeling. As if she was daring the song to resist her. After a moment, it almost seemed as if her dance was creating the music, rather than the other way around.

Tyler snapped photos. Janquil watched, smiling,

her pencil poised over her pad. A crowd formed around the two of them.

But, like the rest of them, Matthew could only stand and watch.

He couldn't take his eyes off her.

He felt leaden, knowing that he was only hours away from saying goodbye to her, for his own sake.

CHAPTER TWENTY-THREE

THEY DANCED UNTIL Annie and Ben took their leave. And then they danced some more. Marlee felt breathless and tired and warm and damp as the cloying summer evening air clung to her skin. Matthew had shed his jacket and rolled up his sleeves and taken off his tie. He looked younger, like the high school boy she had known, and he smiled more than she'd ever seen him smile.

When the DJ finally called it a night and collected the headphones, Marlee walked up the hill to the restroom to freshen up. Her mom was there, washing her hands.

"You sure did cut a rug," she said, leaving the water on for Marlee while she grabbed a paper towel.

"We did." Marlee changed the water to cool and let it flow over her entire arm, and then the other. It felt like diving into a pool.

"You looked very natural out there."

Marlee splashed some water on her cheeks.

"It almost looked real," her mom said. "You and Dr. LaSalle. If I didn't know better, that is."

Marlee froze, looked at her mother in the mirror. "Morgan told you? You haven't told anyone else, have you?"

Her mom shook her head. "Archer told me. And no."

Archer. Well, there was a little development she hadn't counted on. Morgan had told her that his speech was getting better, but she'd been so busy tending to her own…whatever this was… she'd neglected her nephew. She had no idea his speech had gotten this much better.

"I wish you had told me, Marlee. I would have tried to talk you out of it. When I asked Morgan about it, she said you were doing it to pay off the loan? Honey, we don't need you to do that. Not at the cost of your privacy."

Marlee spun and bent to make sure nobody was in one of the bathroom stalls. She wasn't comfortable having this conversation in public. "Mom, it's fine. I know what I'm doing."

"I don't think you do," her mom said. "I think you did when this started, but it's gotten out of your control. A magazine is here, following you around."

"I know. I invited them."

A drop of water dripped off Marlee's chin onto her dress, reminding her that she hadn't yet dried off. She grabbed a paper towel and ran it over her face and arms. Her mom reached out and cradled her cheek with one soft palm.

"Honey. I saw it in the way you danced with him. This isn't fake. Your feelings for him have become real, and now your heart is on the line. Your sister swears it's a good thing. She says that even if he breaks your heart, at least it means that you allowed him in, which is a huge step. Honey, I had no idea you were still carrying around the pain of what you went through with Keith."

Marlee closed her eyes and let out a breath. "Mom, it's fine."

"It's not fine if you won't let anyone love you. If you won't fall in love. Honey, I don't want you to be alone and lonely because you're scared."

"I'm not scared, Mom. And I'm not lonely. And Matthew and Keith are two totally different people. You have to trust me. I know what I'm doing."

Her mom searched her face for a long time. "Okay," she said. "If you say so."

"I do." She leaned over and kissed her mom on the cheek. Just like her palm, the skin on her mom's cheek was soft and powdery. She had a pang of regret that she'd never talked to her about any of this. Because the truth was, her mom was right. She'd been spending all this time alone and lonely, afraid of getting hurt again, just like Keith had hurt her. It might have been nice to have her mom in her corner, along with Morgan and Ellory. Her mom would have encouraged her the way they did, but she also would have understood. She would have been a soft place to land at the end of it all. She would have called her *my sweet girl* and clucked her tongue and made grilled cheese sandwiches and bowls of ice cream when it hurt the worst.

Her mom threw away the balled paper towel she'd been holding. "We're going home. Your father didn't break in his new shoes before tonight, and his feet are killing him. We're taking Archer so your sister can help clean up. She's got a long night ahead."

"I'll help her." *And have a word with her about not telling me that our parents knew what was up. And fill her in that her son is maybe the tiniest little bit of a snitch.*

The door flew open and Janquil pushed into the restroom. "There you are! I've been looking all over for you."

Marlee gave a thin smile. "Just freshening up a little."

"I'm sure you got hot with all that dancing. Your fiancé is fending off fans as we speak."

"Oh, no." Marlee couldn't help laughing just a little. "Is he okay?"

"He'll be just fine." Janquil turned to Marlee's mom. "It was a cute wedding, don't you think?"

"The cutest," her mom said, giving a tight smile meant to indicate that she would be nice to her, but she didn't trust her in the least.

If Janquil caught the meaning behind the smile, it didn't faze her. "The flowers were beautiful."

"Marlee has a gift."

"Thanks, Mom. Give Dad a kiss good-night for me?"

"I will, honey. And call if you need anything?" Marlee could have sworn she gave a knowing look as she stressed the word *anything*.

"Of course."

"Good night," Janquil said as Marlee's mom brushed past her on her way out. Alone, she returned her focus to Marlee. "Anyway. I was just looking for you to tell you that we're leaving."

"Okay. It's been a long night. Get some sleep and we'll see you tomorrow."

"No, we're *leaving* leaving. Heading out bright and early. We were only sticking around for the wedding. We've got more than enough material."

"Oh. Sure. Absolutely. Thanks for everything. It was good getting to know you."

"Yes. Same. Um, here." Janquil thrust a business card at Marlee. "Give us a call when you've scheduled your wedding. We'll come back."

Marlee felt something warm blooming deep in her stomach. The idea that there could be a wedding for them to come back to was ridiculous, but at the same time, not entirely unwelcome.

Well…except the last thing she would want on her wedding day was that superior sneer of Tyler's and Janquil's skeptical questions. She could do without those.

"Great. Will do," she lied, taking the card.

"Is there anything else?" Janquil asked. "Anything we didn't ask that you want us to? Anything we forgot to talk about?"

Yes, this was all a lie, until it wasn't. And what I'd been hoping for hasn't panned out. But something I'd never planned and actually have really resisted for a long, long time happened, anyway. I lied about being in love with a fiancé who wasn't actually my fiancé and then fell in love with him for real. Isn't life funny that way?

Marlee twined her fingers together and shrugged. "Nope. Nothing I can think of. This was fun!"

Might as well end on another lie.

"BETTER?" MATTHEW ASKED when Marlee rejoined him at the table.

"Much."

"You worked up quite a sweat."

"It was fun, don't you think?" she asked.

"Sure. Yeah. Of course."

He had cleared the table, and now all that was left was to gather their own items and go. Marlee had planned to stay behind and help Morgan and Decker clean up, but it looked like enough people had done their part to make for quick work. Everything was done.

Morgan walked past, carrying a cooler filled with leftover PB and Js.

"Y'all can go ahead," she said. "We're about finished here for tonight. I don't know about you, but that dancing all but did me in. I'm pooped."

"It's past nine, which is when my pumpkin turns into a pumpkin," Decker joked, holding a tub of his own, filled with leftover chips. He held the box up. "Still hungry?"

"No, thank you," Marlee and Matthew said together, although she'd barely eaten anything. Her nerves were too wired.

Morgan glanced at Decker. "I guess it's PB and Js and chips for dinner every night until…" She glanced at her watch. "Oh. Eternity."

"Archer will be thrilled," Decker said.

"Tell you what," Morgan said. "I'll happily eat peanut butter forever if it means I can sit down for a few minutes. Get out of here, you two. Come see me tomorrow. *Late* tomorrow. I'm not getting out of bed until I absolutely have to. I don't think I've slept since Annie said yes."

"Okay, okay." Marlee gave her sister a peck on the cheek and whispered, "I've got something to talk to him about, anyway."

Morgan arched one eyebrow and gave her sister a hard stare. Marlee nodded, biting her bottom lip anxiously. Morgan's eyes grew wide—a whole conversation transpiring between sisters without a single word spoken.

"I'll text you," Marlee said, then turned on her heel.

She reached for Matthew's hand as she walked by. She'd been forcing herself to reach for him so much, it had become second nature to her. Yet now that Janquil and Tyler had gone, it felt different. Exciting and full of promise.

"Let's go," she said.

Matthew waved goodbye to Morgan and Decker and followed Marlee without a word. But he didn't need to say anything.

Because he let her hold his hand.

He didn't pull away.

They were on the precipice of something big, and Marlee was about to push them both over the edge.

CHAPTER TWENTY-FOUR

NEARLY EVERYONE HAD gone by the time Marlee and Matthew crunched over the gravel parking lot toward their cars. There were only a few stragglers—some lingering in the parking lot, chatting, reliving some of their dance moves. Others were likely still hanging around the ranch, maybe cleaning up or tucked away under a tree somewhere to float on the romance of a summer, outdoor wedding or maybe still sitting at a bare picnic table in the tent, unwilling or unable to let the evening go. Decker wasn't the kind to kick anyone out before they were ready. In a place like Haw Springs, where everybody knew everybody, he knew whether or not he could trust the guests lingering on his ranch.

Marlee and Matthew walked in silence, hand in hand, as Matthew scanned the small crowd of parking lot lingerers for phone screens. Who was watching? Who was recording them? Who was looking for their own fame by jumping on the wave?

But he didn't see any phone screens. Nobody lurking around their cars. Nobody creeping up behind. He willed himself to relax.

"I haven't seen our shadows in a while," he said.

"You mean Janquil and Tyler?" Marlee asked. "They're gone."

"They already left for the night?"

"No, they're gone," Marlee said. "Went back to their hotel and leave tomorrow morning to go back to the city. They're done." Matthew stopped walking, forcing Marlee to stop, too. "I'm sorry, were you wanting to talk to them some more? I got her card. We can call her. Maybe they didn't get too far, and they'll come back."

"No." He dropped Marlee's hand, then wrapped his arms around her waist and lifted her up and spun her in a jubilant circle. "Woo-hoo!" he cried.

Marlee laughed. "Put me down!"

Now some of the lingerers were looking in their direction curiously. *That's what you get for attracting attention to yourself, LaSalle*, he thought. But, in that moment, he didn't care. Let them look. The press was gone.

He set Marlee back on her feet. She smoothed her dress around her thighs. "Wow, if I'd known you'd be this happy, I would have told you as soon as I got out of the restroom."

"We're free," Matthew said. "We're finally free. The lie is over. We can go back to living our separate lives again."

"Oh," Marlee said. "Yep. We sure can. But..."

"But what?"

She looked like she would just as soon have the world open up and swallow her whole than continue wherever that sentence was going.

"But what?" Matthew asked again.

She shrugged. "Forget it."

"No, I don't want to forget it. What was that *but* about?"

"It's really nothing, Matthew. Ignore that I said anything."

Wanting Marlee to feel the same sense of freedom that he felt, he reached down and grasped her hands, began spinning her around. "But we're free!" he said. "Can't you feel it?"

"No, I—"

"No more nearly burning down the kitchen trying to make romantic food. No more recounting fake engagements or spinning cute tales. No more *sweetums*."

"But, I... Matthew, stop spinning me."

"No. More. Limelight."

"Matthew, stop. Stop!"

With the last *stop*, Marlee pulled her hands out of his and stood her ground. For a moment, she swayed, as if she might fall down, and Matthew felt dizziness pressing in on him, too. He felt as if he'd just gotten off a really fast carousel, and took a moment to marvel at the metaphor. *So true, Matthew. So true.*

"Please," Marlee said. "Just stop."

"I stopped. I'm sorry. I got carried away. I'm just so relieved. I was so sick of living a lie." It finally dawned on him that she looked anything but relieved. In fact, she looked quite miserable, standing in front of him, wringing her hands, her entire face drawn down into a sad frown. "Are you…not…relieved?"

"Yes and no," she said. Her voice was tiny. "I'm glad to get rid of our entourage. I didn't like always feeling like someone was watching me."

"Exactly."

"But I'm not…looking for freedom. I'm not excited about that."

"What? Why not?"

She shook her head miserably, as if she couldn't believe what she was hearing from him. As if she'd expected something entirely different from him. "Matthew, I'm falling in love with you." He could see tears glistening in her eyes. "I know I'm not supposed to be. Not for real. And I wasn't when this started. I could barely stand you then. It just happened over time. I started falling and I couldn't stop."

He felt wooden. His feet felt like roots. Or maybe stone, the gravel pressing into his toes—pressing and pressing until his toes began to harden, solidify. He would be marble, or maybe granite. A statue. The statue would be named *Man in Stupor.* How could he have not seen this coming?

"I thought you didn't believe in love."

"I don't. I mean, I didn't," she said. "Until I got to know you." She seemed to be working up courage. She straightened and tossed her shoulders back, jutting her chin. She'd taken him on more times than he could count at this point, yet never had he seen her like this. "I got hurt. I believed in love so fully, and I got hurt. It happens. But instead of saying it happens, I made a promise to myself to never love again. It was a silly promise. But I couldn't see how silly it was until I learned more about you. Matthew, you are decent, and kind and you have such a soft heart. I love that you wear a tie every day. And I love that you have spiders on microscope slides in your office. And I love that you hike and that you know where a secret, abandoned greenhouse is. And I love that you agreed to pretend to be in love with me to help me get more business. And I love that you don't want to move away from your parents. I love all the things that make you *you*."

"You don't know me. You know who I was pretending to be." He thought he heard a scuff in the gravel behind him, but saw nothing but shadows back there. It must have been a car pulling out of the parking lot, he thought.

"You made me a rooftop garden," Marlee said. "That wasn't pretend."

Her shoulders had started to shrink, her chin lower. Her voice was getting quieter. She was retreating into herself. He could see tears shimmering in her eyes, but in true Marlee style, she was refusing to let them fall.

He hated doing this to her. But he had to.

"I succeed at assignments," he said. "It's what I do. You gave me an assignment. Be your fake boyfriend. So I took the assignment and succeeded. You're a florist, I built a garden. Test passed."

He said this with all the confidence and conviction he was accustomed to using when speaking of his abilities. So why did he feel so rotten while saying them? It wasn't just that he was hurting her, was it? Because it felt suspiciously like he was hurting himself. He couldn't make sense of it. He was off the hook. He should be walking away feeling great.

"I don't believe you," Marlee said.

"What?"

"I felt this, Matthew. I felt *us*. When we were in the greenhouse, when we were dancing on the roof, I felt *us*. It's not possible for it to be so strong for me, and nothing for you."

"It must be possible, because that's the way it is. This—" he gestured between them with his finger "—was fake. Exactly like you wanted it to be. An agreement was made, and I stuck to my end of it. You may have changed your mind, but I haven't changed mine. I'm sorry."

His chest felt heavy as he watched a single tear break over her bottom lid and streak down her face. She made no move to wipe it away, but he could practically feel her will any other tears to stay put. He could feel her weighing every possible response that she could make to what he'd just said.

"Don't be sorry," she finally said, her voice cold and husky. "It happens."

She turned, her back ramrod stiff, and went to her car, folding herself inside without another word.

She started the engine and drove away, the sound of the gravel crunching under her tires oddly seeming to be coming from behind him again. *Strange acoustics, this parking lot*, he thought.

He pulled his car keys out of his pocket, but found that he didn't want to go. He wanted to let her put some distance between them.

He stood in the cooling night air, propped against his car, thinking over everything he'd just said.

He had told her the truth. It had all been real. He didn't owe her love just because she felt it. He didn't have to go along with a new plan just because the old one didn't work for her anymore.

He didn't have to change himself just to fit.

He'd imagined himself having to give this speech someday. He'd imagined that, at some point, love would present itself and he would have to demur, to put it in its place.

Tonight was that night, and he executed his part beautifully.

So why did he feel so empty inside?

Why did he feel like he gave the wrong speech?

Why did he feel like it wasn't the truth at all?

It felt like a lie to protect himself.

Because that was exactly what it was.

CHAPTER TWENTY-FIVE

FOR ONCE, KIMBERLY was going to just have to step up.

Or not. Marlee didn't really care.

So, when Kimberly didn't step up, Blush & Bloom remained closed, while Marlee tried to sleep off the humiliation of what had happened the night before. Not that she was sleeping. No, not in the slightest. At best, she was rolling and tumbling, her sheets winding around her, her pillow flattening, as she relived the horrible conversation of the night before.

How had it gone so wrong, so fast?

Dancing with him at the wedding had been such fun. Matthew wasn't the greatest dancer in the world, she would give him that, but he tried, and he looked like he was having fun. He laughed and he watched her—oh, he watched her so closely, she could feel him watching even when she wasn't—and he'd pulled her in for the slow dances without her even having to ask if he wanted to.

They'd shared a piece of wedding cake and giggled when their tussle over the last bite had caused it to land in his lap.

They'd played all the games, and she'd come this close to catching the bouquet. The whole crowd had groaned when it was wrestled away from her, and Matthew had played up the moment with an overexaggerated sad look. She'd heard him tell Janquil that it wasn't going to stop him. *Marlee and I will race that girl to the altar if we have to*, he'd joked.

He'd done all of those things without her asking him to.

Was it really all faked? Was he that good of an actor?

Apparently.

She flipped and turned, kicking off the blanket. She didn't want to relive the parking lot scene. If she kept moving, maybe she could stave it off.

She was vaguely aware of a knock at her apartment door, but she ignored it. Then, about twenty minutes later, another, followed by ten rings of her doorbell. Finally, another twenty minutes or so later, the knock was followed by the sound of a key in the lock.

Marlee groaned. "I'm fine, Morgan. I don't want to talk."

"Not just Morgan," Ellory said, coming in with a coffee. "You weren't answering my texts or calls or the doorbell. I thought maybe you'd died. I was about to have Rowan use his fire axe to break down the door."

Marlee crawled to sitting and leaned against her headboard. She felt physically sore, as if she'd been beaten up rather than just massively let down. "So, you made a dead woman coffee?"

Ellory smiled as she pressed it into Marlee's hand. "I made it extra strong."

Marlee gave it a sniff. "What's the flavor? It doesn't smell like anything."

"Coffee," Ellory said. "I figured you didn't need the distraction, just the caffeine."

"You'd better call Mom," Morgan said, the apartment key that Marlee had given her jingling against its Silver Dollar City key chain as she stuffed it into her pocket. "She also thinks you're probably dead."

"Why is it everyone jumps right to dead when I don't answer the phone?" Marlee asked, cranky. She set the untouched coffee on her nightstand. "Maybe I have the flu."

"To be fair, in Mom's eyes, it's the same outcome. To her, having the flu is as good as dead." Morgan sat on the edge of the bed, on the other side, opposite Ellory. Marlee suspected she was supposed to feel flanked by her troops, but instead she felt trapped. The blanket that she'd been wrapping herself up in now pinned her legs to the mattress.

"And the shop is closed," Ellory said. "It's weird."

"But also because of what happened." Morgan grabbed the coffee off the nightstand and took a sip. She gave the cup an appreciative frown and nod. "I don't know if I've ever had plain, black coffee from your shop before. It's fantastic."

"Thanks," Ellory said.

"You really should give this a try, Mar." She offered the cup. "Then we can talk about what happened."

"Ugh." Marlee forced her legs to slide forward so she could lie back down. She rolled to her side, bringing the pillow up so that it covered her face. She loved her sister and her best friend more than she could ever put into words. But, right now, she just wanted them to go away. "I don't want to talk about it."

"I'm so sorry, Marlee," Ellory said. "If it makes you feel any better, I also don't believe him. I think he was lying about lying."

"Same," Morgan said. "And I would say a solid majority of people agree with us on that."

"Did you see that whole thing that person posted about the psychology of cowardice?" Ellory asked.

"Yes," Morgan said. "I thought it was spot-on. And the one woman who counted the times his eyes shifted left while he was talking. I mean, some people got super extreme about proving their theories, but she wasn't wrong. He looked nervous."

Marlee was working hard on shoving her face deeper and deeper into the pillow, not wanting to see or hear anything. But it slowly dawned on her what they were saying.

She hadn't told anyone about what had happened last night. Not a soul. And she very much doubted that Matthew had confided in anyone. Matthew wasn't a confider to begin with, much less would he be reckless enough to try to confide in the two people on earth, outside of her parents, who would unequivocally take her side.

Plus, they said *people*. They were talking about *people*. As in multiple, unknown people.

She sat up again. Her hair was in her face. She pushed it aside. She could feel it springing wildly from the top of her head, but she didn't care.

"What are you guys talking about? People? What people?"

Ellory waved her hand dismissively. "Oh, just the people on social media who commented on the video."

"What video?"

Ellory and Morgan exchanged glances.

"What video?" Marlee repeated. She reached for her phone. She'd been aware that she was missing calls and texts, but she hadn't realized how many. Her phone screen looked like a novel of missed alerts. "What video?" she said a third time, her gut clenching. She had a feeling she knew exactly what video.

"You haven't seen it?" Morgan asked.

"Maybe you shouldn't..." Ellory said, reaching for Marlee's phone. But Marlee held it out of reach.

"I agree. Stay off social media if you haven't seen it. Why do that to yourself?"

"Yeah. We thought this was the reason you were hiding out. But if you were just having a rest day, then good for you! Healthy habits and all that..." She trailed off as Marlee pulled up social media.

It was the first thing in her feed. She recognized it from the freeze-frame. It was dark, with some orange streetlamps in the distance, some shiny glimmers where cars picked up the lights. The still shot was of Matthew spinning her. Carefree.

Seeing him made her throat want to seize up. Her heart was pounding, and she began to feel sweat dampen her temples. She knew exactly what was about to come out of his mouth in this video, and she didn't want to hear it again.

Yet, she felt like she had to.

Heart in her throat, she tapped the play icon.

After a brief pause while it loaded, the whole scene came at her like a freight train. The darkness, the scuff of their shoes on the gravel, the sound of frogs calling down by the pond. They were standing so close to each other.

It hadn't felt so close last night. It had felt like there were miles between them.

"Matthew, I'm falling in love with you."

She groaned and placed a hand on her forehead, hating this, but unable to look away, as if there was some invisible force gluing her eyes to the phone, and the phone to her hand. *Don't say it, Marlee*, she thought. *Don't say it*. Part of her was hoping that maybe it wasn't as bad as she thought. Maybe she was mistaken in her memory, and she hadn't laid it all out.

"I love all the things that make you you.*"*

"No," she said, making a fist and lightly tapping it against her forehead. "I said it. It was real. I really did that."

In the video, Matthew started talking, and it was even worse than she had remembered. She squeezed her eyes shut and held the phone out toward Ellory, who silently plucked it away. The video stopped.

Marlee felt tears trying to push through her closed eyelids. She didn't want to cry, but there was nothing she could do. They leaked through and down her cheeks. "I'm so mortified," she said. "I can't believe someone got it on camera."

"Oh, sweetie, it's okay." She felt Ellory wrap a protective arm around her shoulder and pull her in. "We've all had moments like these, where we wish we could take it all back."

She felt Morgan's head rest lightly on her other shoulder. "It'll all blow over soon enough."

"Easy for you to say," Marlee said. "You put it

all on the line for Decker and he proposed to you. I put it all on the line, and once again, I got rejected. I told you that love was a myth. But I guess maybe it's only a myth for me. Aren't I the lucky one?"

"I know it feels like that right now. It won't feel like that forever," Ellory said. "I'm proud of you for speaking your truth. Although…"

Marlee waited for her to finish her sentence, but she didn't. "Although what?" she asked, once again feeling like she was several steps behind. "There's more? How can there be more? That wasn't bad enough?"

But then it dawned on her. Her eyes flew open, and she sat straight up.

The video was on social media. She'd been so focused on what the video was, she didn't think about who took it or how it got there.

"Oh, no," she said, snatching the phone from Ellory's hand. "No, no, no."

"Try to remember the internet has a very short attention span," Morgan said.

"That's right," Ellory said. "This time next week…for sure next month…nobody will remember anything about you."

"I'm not… I'm not sure that was comforting," Morgan whispered.

But Marlee only vaguely heard any of what they were saying. She'd pulled up the video again, which was easy to do, given how many times it was reposted.

"Who…?" Marlee said aloud and then tapped on the profile photo of the original poster. A grinning teen stared back at her. Marlee recognized her and then realized she also recognized the background of the photo, as well as the squirming little ball of wavy black fur that the girl was holding. The clandestine video was taken and posted by the teen who'd taken the ladder photo; her profile photo was from the same day. The dog was Poppy. "It was her? How?"

The pieces began falling into place. She remembered seeing the girl at the wedding and vaguely recalled hearing some scuffling in the gravel between the cars behind Matthew while they were talking.

And now, the video was on that girl's social media profile, along with the caption: INTERNET, WE GOT IT WRONG! I'm so sad. They were lying the whole time, and we all fell for it. We've been betrayed, you guys! #fakeflorist #deceitfuldoc

The post had been shared and commented on thousands of times, everything from pity to wishes of terrible things happening to Marlee and Matthew.

She "accidentally" fell in love? LOL serves her right. That's what you get for being a liar, lady.

I'm so bummed. These two were the best part of my day every day. It was all a lie???

They deserve to be sad and alone forever.

I drove over an hour to have my newborn checked out by him. He was so cute. But how do you trust someone who can fool the entire world like that? I'll be finding a doctor much closer to home now. Silver lining: I'll save on gas!

Oh, boo-hoo, Marlee. You accidentally fell in love? Are you serious? You do realize he's a liar. How could you ever trust him? Oh, wait. Doesn't matter because you're a liar, too.

This has been the best free entertainment I've gotten in a long time. I can't wait to see what happens next season. Does someone fall in a well? LOL

"They're not all terrible," Morgan said, rubbing her sister's back. "A lot of people empathized with you."

Ellory placed a reassuring hand on Marlee's knee. "That's right. Matthew is definitely taking most of the heat here."

Marlee let the phone drop down to her lap. "I don't want that, though," she said. "Just because he turned me down doesn't mean I stopped feeling the way I feel about him. I don't want him getting hate."

"He probably doesn't even know," Morgan said. "I doubt he's looking at social media."

"What if it comes to him at his office? You know how people can be."

"I'm sure Jensen has seen it. I'll talk to him about stepping up patrols on Main Street until this blows over," Ellory said.

Jensen Jeffries was a sheriff's deputy and the only officer assigned to patrol Haw Springs. The sheriff's office was housed over an hour away in Riverside, so he wasn't exactly a constant presence in their lives, much to the dismay of all the single Haw Springs females. With his wavy golden hair, baby blue eyes and chiseled jaw, Jensen was indisputably nice to look at.

"I guess you're right," Marlee said. "This will blow over." She shook the phone in the air.

Ellory leaned forward to catch Morgan's eye. Something unsaid passed between them.

"What?" Marlee said for the umpteenth time. "Will you guys stop doing that and just come out with it already?"

Ellory winced and said, "It's just...that magazine."

As if Marlee's heart couldn't sink any further. If her body had a basement, her heart was residing there, fluttering weakly in the dark. "They know?" she asked.

Ellory nodded. "They shared it."

Marlee picked up her phone again. She didn't need to go back to socials. She knew that Janquil had likely reached out to her directly. She was right. There were three Call me asap texts and a voicemail. She went to the voicemail button and hit speaker.

"Hey, Marlee, it's Janquil. So, I saw the video. I have to say, it wasn't really news to us. In fact, Tyler and I had discussed contingency articles just in case something like this happened. There were a lot of weird things about your story. Anyway, now that the world, um…well, now that the truth has come out, so to speak, we can't in good faith run the article we were going to run. Ugh. So disappointing. But we have a ton of good photos from the wedding, and so we're still going to run just a general wedding inspiration article. We've already reached out to Annie and Ben, and they're on board. We, of course, won't be plugging Blush & Bloom. I'm sure you understand." There was a bit of a pause, and then, "On a personal note, I'm sorry you got hurt in this. It sounded like it was your idea from the get-go, but I could tell you were being sincere about falling for him. And who wouldn't? He's cute and charming and he knows how to lay it on thick. The whole world fell in love with him. With both of you. Anyway, take care, Marlee. We'll send copies of the spread when we have it. Bye."

"'He's cute and charming and he knows how to lay it on thick,'" Marlee mimicked. "Yeah, tell me about it. You guys, the whole world is laughing at me."

"No, they're not," Ellory said.

"They are," Marlee argued. "And the worst part is I deserve it. This was my idea. I thought I could fool everyone. It was a bad plan."

"It was a bad plan," Morgan agreed. "But your previous plan of never falling in love was an even worse plan. So, you upgraded plans and it didn't quite work out, but that's okay. And now it's about the plan going forward, right? You can't do anything about the past. You just have to decide what you want to do with the future."

Marlee flopped back against her pillow. "Crawl in a hole and hide for the rest of my life," she said. "That's my plan for the future."

Morgan clapped her hands. "Sounds like a plan that could use some revision. But it's a start. I've got to go pick up Archer. I love you, sis."

"I love you, too," Marlee said.

"Text me later," Morgan called as she headed out.

"I'm throwing my phone away forever," Marlee called in the same lilt. She flopped backward and covered her face with her pillow.

"How would I call you to entice you with new coffee flavors if you threw away your phone forever?"

"You could just bring them over," Marlee said. "Since I'm also never leaving this bed."

"Take the pillow off your face," Ellory said, and when Marlee didn't, she pulled it off for her.

Marlee gazed at her friend with tears in her eyes. "I really like him, Ellory," she said.

"I know."

"And I think he likes me, too. I think he was lying."

"But why? Do you think he knew the girl was recording?"

Marlee sat again and took a sip of her coffee. "No. I think he's lying to himself. I got to know him really well, Ellory. He's scared to love me. He's afraid that if he lets himself fall in love, he'll lose himself."

"So what are you going to do?"

Fight for him. Marlee knew that was what Ellory wanted her to say. *Fight until he sees the truth, that he wants to be with me, and that he wouldn't lose himself. He would grow. We would grow together. Convince him that he can't live without me.*

But she didn't say it.

She couldn't say it.

Instead, she ran her hand through her hair, set her coffee back on the nightstand and let her hands drop in her lap. She shrugged.

"Get over him. That's what I'll do. I'll just… move on."

CHAPTER TWENTY-SIX

LYNETTE WAS WAITING for him in his office, her arms crossed, her phone in her hand.

"'They're both liars, but he's worse than her, because he's also lying to himself,'" she read aloud as soon as he rounded the corner.

He set his bag on the floor. "What?"

"I didn't suspect you'd been online since it happened."

"Since what happened?"

"Since this happened." She uncrossed her arms and turned the phone face out.

"Are you talking about all that social media nonsense that Marlee got us into? It's over and done. The magazine left. I don't want to hear any more about it." He waved her off and picked up a stack of mail that had been left on a small table by the door. He leafed through the envelopes. "I never paid attention to any of it to begin with."

"Normally, I would say that's a good thing," she said. "But as much as I commend you for insulating yourself from the drama, I think today you should maybe pay attention."

He dropped the envelopes on the table and let out a sigh. "Fine. What is it today? I'm not really in the mood."

"When are you ever in the mood?"

"True, never. But I had a rough weekend and would like to just get to work, if that's okay with you."

She handed him her phone. "I'm guessing your rough weekend began and ended with this."

There, on the screen, was a video of Marlee declaring her feelings for him. And him turning her down.

"I knew I heard someone behind me," he said dryly. He handed the phone back without watching the whole video play out.

"You didn't read the comments," Lynette said.

"Why would I do that? I'm sure they're not great."

"No, they're not great. And they're mostly against you."

"Sounds about right."

He walked to his desk and fired up his computer as he settled in his chair, thinking that if he was going to blame someone for how all of this turned out, he would point the finger at himself, too.

He couldn't get Marlee's hurt expression out of his mind. He couldn't unhear her voice. *I don't believe you.* Well, in that moment, and every moment after, he could hardly believe himself.

"You've had two people cancel this morning," Lynette said, sliding into the chair across from him.

He pulled up his scheduling software and gave it a once-over. It was looking a little bare, but nothing like before. "Both new patients?" he asked.

She nodded. "Both coming down from Kansas City."

"Easy come, easy go. They wouldn't have stuck around, anyway."

"Matthew."

"Lynette."

"Matthew. Look at me."

There were times when hiring his mother's best friend seemed like the smartest move in the world. There were other times when he sorely wished he had held out for someone who didn't know the first thing about him. This was one of those times.

He held her gaze. "What?"

"You're being very haughty about all of this. That's not like you. You always worry about the tiniest things."

"Maybe I'm turning over a new leaf."

"Or maybe," she said, getting up to pace the room, slowly bouncing the phone in the palm of her hand while she thought and talked, "you saw this video yesterday and you flipped out just a little. And you made a promise to yourself not to let it affect your day today. Am I right?"

He gave a slow nod. "You could be onto something, yes."

She pointed at him with the phone. "I knew it! I also know that you feel terrible about what happened. You hated turning her down because you were a lot more torn than you wanted to admit to yourself, much less to her. And you weren't even surprised to find that someone was recording you."

"Maybe you should quit working here and become a private detective," Matthew suggested. "Get paid to meddle in other people's lives."

She waved that thought away instantly and kept pacing. "They always say don't turn your hobby into your job or you'll start to hate it. I enjoy it enough to do it for free."

He gave a thin smile. "Lucky me."

She paced back to her chair and perched on the very edge of it.

"So, I'm right?" she asked.

He pointedly glanced at his watch. "We need to get the day going."

"We will. Answer my question first, though. Did you know that someone was recording?"

"I thought I heard someone behind me, but I couldn't see them. I was sort of busy at the moment. No time to go looking around between the cars. But in the end, it doesn't matter. It was only a matter of time before we were outed, anyway. People would have noticed eventually that we spend a whole lot of time not together. For a couple, I mean."

Lynette clicked her tongue. "Oh, Matthew."

"Oh, don't say it like that. Can we get this day started, please?"

"So she's right. You do love her."

"I do not."

"You're afraid to admit it. You're doing this—" she gestured in a circle with the palm of her hand toward him "—as a front. You've seen the video and you felt destroyed by it all over again, and that's why you won't watch it. Because you were there, and you were lying—to her, to yourself—and you don't want to relive that."

He stood, having had enough of this free analysis of his life. "Okay, we've got patients to see today. Let's start letting them in."

Without waiting for her, he strode out of the room and down the hallway to the lobby. *One foot, two foot, step, step, step. This is the easy process. Walking. Just focus on that, and ignore all the things that were going through your mind over the weekend.*

Ignore the desire to pick up your phone and call her. Ignore, ignore, ignore.

He decided to straighten the lobby a little. There wasn't much to be done—Lynette did this every day as part of her job—but he needed something to do with his hands.

"You're ignoring me," Lynette said, coming into the lobby behind him.

"On purpose." He lined up the chairs perfectly.

"But why on earth wouldn't you just give in? Let yourself love her?"

He stopped fidgeting with the magazines and turned to Lynette. "Fine. I wish I could, okay? I wish I was built like that. That I could just take the leap and fall for the most beautiful, vibrant, intelligent woman I've ever known. But I'm not built like that. Maybe I never was, or maybe I was once upon a time, but I'm not now. I would love to be able to say that I love her, but I can't. Not in good faith. Can we please move on?"

She gazed at him as if she still had so much to say. Matthew braced himself for a counterargument. But, instead, she simply dropped the phone into her scrubs pocket and retreated silently to her station behind the reception desk. The phone rang almost immediately, and she picked it up.

The truth was, he'd regretted every single thing he'd ever said or done the minute he'd gotten into his car after the wedding. Everything in his life that had led him to this moment where he'd walked away from the best thing that had ever happened to him. Had Marlee not jumped into her car and driven away before he could change his mind, he might have done just that. In his head, he'd called out for her, made her turn back and swept her into his arms a thousand times.

In his head, he'd done just about everything differently.

Still on the phone, Lynette handed her set of office keys across the desk to Matthew. He took them and unlocked the front door.

"What the…?"

Lynette finished her call and hung up. She strained to look over his shoulder.

"Is something wrong?"

"Yes," Matthew said, blinking as if maybe he was seeing things wrong. "I mean, no."

"You're being clear as mud." Lynette came out from around her desk and into the lobby. She stood behind him and looked over his shoulder. "Oh."

"Yeah."

"I see."

"Yeah."

"Well, silver lining. She finally parked on her own side of the street."

"Yeah." Matthew forced himself to turn away from the door and away from what seemed like the final indicator that his relationship with Marlee was over. He could pretend the conversation hadn't ever happened if he didn't watch the video. He could console himself with the thought that he would still see her due to their ongoing battle over the parking space.

But seeing her parked by her own shop took away any remaining hope that this might not be over for good.

He drew himself up and clapped his hands. “Let’s get started,” he said, although he couldn’t help noticing that he had no patients to get started with. “I’ll be in my office.”

“Matthew, are you all right?” Lynette asked.

“I’m just fine, Lynette. Truly.” He veered toward her desk and gave the schedule a quick glance. It looked like it was going to be a light day. Lots of time for thinking, unfortunately. “Lynette, how’s Charles doing?”

“Pardon?”

“Your husband, Charles. How’s he doing?”

“Fine. Why?”

“No reason. Just checking in. Seems like I’ve been all about myself lately and haven’t asked you about your life. Charles going to retire soon?”

Lynette looked very confused, and a bit wary. Even in the context of what had been going on, this was a highly unusual line of questioning. “My Charles? Oh, he’ll never properly retire. ‘*You retire, you sit down, you die.*’ That’s what he always says.”

“He’s got a lot of spunk. You’ll have to tell him I said hello.”

“Okay,” she said, but it almost came out as a question.

Seven long hours—and only ten patients—later, Matthew found himself sitting on the rooftop, overlooking Main Street, but focused on Blush & Bloom, thinking, mulling things over.

Around him, the garden was starting to sprout weeds, and he could see a close future where it became completely out of control. That was the thing about gardens—you had to tend to them. You had to protect them. You had to be there for them with kindness and good faith. If you did, they would most certainly repay you with beauty. Let your garden go, though, even for a short amount of time, and before you knew it, you were left with a complete mess.

Why did I do this? he wondered. *Why did I build a garden, of all things?* "You know what I don't have time for?" he said aloud. "Weeding. Watering. Fertilizing."

He picked up a pot and launched it over the side of the roof, feeling a slight twinge of satisfaction upon hearing the terra-cotta smash a few seconds later on the ground below. He picked up another and lobbed it over. *Smash.* And then a third. *Crash.*

"Hey!" he heard from down below.

He crept to the edge and looked over. He almost felt as though he was imagining things, seeing her there. Marlee. Standing next to her van on the other side of the street.

"What do you think you're doing?" she yelled.

"Cleaning," he said, but even he had to admit this was weak. He said it sheepishly.

"Well, stop. You're going to hurt someone." She stood with her hands on her hips, in typical haughty Marlee style. She didn't wait for him to respond, just hopped into her van and took off.

But he did stop.

Mostly because he couldn't think of a good reason not to. In fact, he could no longer think of a good reason not to do much. A pretty rooftop garden could be a nice selling point for a piece of choice Main Street real estate.

It might even help him sell the place.

He could possibly make a decent amount of cash that he could use as equity to move someplace new.

In fact, that was just what he was thinking he should do.

CHAPTER TWENTY-SEVEN

"OKAY, MISS MOPE, we're getting you out," Ellory said.

Marlee had just been about to close the shop when Ellory and Annie walked into Blush & Bloom. Ellory stopped to turn the Open sign to Closed and drew the shade down the door, bathing the shop in shadows.

Kimberly let out an audible, "Yesss," untied her apron and tossed it on the counter. "See you tomorrow, boss lady," she said.

Marlee's wide eyes darted between the two intruders. "What's going on?"

"Don't look so panicked. It's just a little outing," Ellory said, coming around the counter and untying her friend's apron for her. Marlee slid it over her head and tossed it on the counter next to Kimberly's, but she resisted letting Ellory take her arm.

"What kind of outing?" she asked.

"Dinner," Annie said, smiling and snickering.

Ellory got hold of Marlee's biceps and tugged;

Marlee dragged her feet, but knew that it was a hopeless fight. "I'm not dressed for dinner."

"You're dressed perfectly," Ellory said.

"I'm not hungry."

Giggling, Annie got behind her and pushed. "You'll get hungry when you get there. They have fried pickles."

"I don't need to get out. Look, I'm already out."

"Work doesn't count," Ellory and Annie said together. With Ellory pulling and Annie pushing, Marlee had no choice. Her feet began to slide across the floor, her shoes squeaking on the tile. She couldn't help herself—she began to giggle right along with Annie.

"Okay, okay," she said at last. "I guess I could eat something."

"Atta girl!" Ellory cheered. "Let's go!"

THERE WEREN'T A whole lot of restaurants in Haw Springs. Most everyone made the trip to Riverside to eat at The Root Cellar Bistro, a well-lit café known for its elevated home-cooking style. It was the perfect choice for everything from Sunday dinner to Monday business lunch.

On the way there, Annie chattered about her honeymoon on the lake, where she and Ben hiked, shopped for hand-pulled taffy and lounged around on a pontoon boat for hours on end.

"It was heaven," she said over and over again. "Ben is the best husband."

Marlee loved Annie, and loved listening to her stories, but after a while her mind started to wander to Matthew, wallowing in the notion that she would never regale someone with stories of their honeymoon. She felt a twinge of something she guessed was akin to jealousy, and kicked herself for ever letting herself get to a spot where she was envious.

The Bistro was hopping, and at first Marlee worried that they wouldn't be able to get a table at all. The food smelled wonderful and now her stomach was rumbling. She prepared herself to be disappointedly eating a burger across the street in the back seat of Ellory's car.

But, to her surprise, the hostess took them to their seats right away.

"Oh," Ellory said, as they approached the table. She bit her fingernail nervously. "I'm wondering if we could have a table over there? By the window?"

"Sure," the hostess said, and they all rerouted.

"What was wrong with that table?" Marlee asked.

"I just didn't want to be in the center of the room," Ellory said.

"This one's more romantic," Annie added.

"I think she means intimate." Ellory gave a shaky smile. "We can talk here."

"Okay…" Marlee said. Something was off. She

just couldn't pinpoint what. She sat in the chair facing the window, her back to the restaurant.

Ellory started to pull out the chair across from her but paused. "Actually, I've got to use the restroom first. Order me an iced tea?"

"Sure," Marlee said.

"Me, too," Annie said. "I'll have a Dr Pepper." She giggled as she walked away.

"Okay…" Something was definitely off. Annie's giggle was too much, even for Annie. And Ellory seemed jumpy, nervous, especially when she asked for the specific table.

But then Marlee heard a familiar voice, and things got even weirder. It was a voice she knew without even looking.

"Oops, hold that thought," Morgan said somewhere behind her. "I've got to take a phone call. We can talk specifics about the fundraiser over an appetizer. Order whatever sounds good."

What were the odds that Morgan would be here at the exact same time, and sitting only one table over?

"Take your time," another familiar voice said. The chair next to her scraped along the floor and a man sat in it.

Marlee spun in her chair. What she saw didn't make sense. Her brain couldn't work it out. Morgan was stalking out of the restaurant with her phone to her ear and Matthew was sitting at the table next to her, so close she could almost touch his elbow with hers.

"What are you—" she started.

"Oh, hey, I didn't expect—" Matthew said at the same time.

They both stopped, staring, as Matthew sank the rest of the way into the chair right next to Marlee.

"You go first," he said.

"I think we have the same question," she said. "But I'll go. Why are you here?"

He smiled. "You're right. We have the same question. Your sister asked me to meet her here to talk over the annual Pathways free health care fundraiser. She's on a phone call. My turn. Why are you here?"

"Ellory and Annie thought I was pouting."

"Were you?"

"Pouting? No. I was working."

"Well, I would ask to move to a different table when Morgan gets back, but she specifically asked for this one."

Marlee screwed her mouth over to one side, nodding. "Are you serious right now? Ellory specifically asked for this one."

It seemed to take him a beat, but then it dawned on him and he let his head loll back. He rubbed his eyes and tried to recover his posture. "We've been set up."

Marlee nodded. "It would appear that we have been."

The air between them felt thick and awkward as it sunk in that they'd both been had by their friends.

"And there they go," he said, pointing out the window.

Marlee looked, and sure enough, there were Annie, Morgan and Ellory, all walking across the parking lot, their heads together. Annie turned and gave Marlee and Matthew a little finger wave. They piled into Ellory's car and left, heading for the burger joint across the street.

"They did not just do that," Marlee said, but she couldn't help laughing.

"I think they did," Matthew said. "Your friends are a little bit diabolical."

This made Marlee laugh harder. "Not just my friends, my own sister! I will have to have some words with them."

"I guess that's what this is supposed to be about," Matthew said. "Having words."

The server appeared, looking a little sheepish as if she, too, had been in on the plan. "I'm so sorry to ask this," she said, leaning over the table. "We had an unexpected overbooking, and it seems like you two know each other? Would you mind consolidating to one table?" When Marlee hesitated, struck silent, the server leaned in farther and whispered, "It's part of the plan. They told me to ask you. But if you don't want to—"

"No, no, it's fine." Marlee gestured for Matthew to sit in the chair on the other side of her table.

After the slightest hesitation, he got up and moved over.

The server, looking pleased that she had accomplished her mission, took their drink orders. "By the way, I loved your social media series," she said before walking away. "We all did."

"Social media *series*?" Matthew whispered after she'd walked away.

"I can feel the cell phone cameras pointed at the back of my head as we speak," Marlee responded. "Do you think we could spin it that it was fiction all along, sort of like a soap opera?"

"You lost me at *Do you think we could spin it.*"

Marlee chuckled. "Fair enough."

The server brought their drinks and a basket of bread. Marlee was grateful for something to do. She buttered a piece of bread and began to break it apart, nibbling on small bites. The Bistro was known for its homestyle baked bread, but in that moment, it tasted like nothing.

"So how have things been over at Blush & Bloom?" he asked.

"Slow," Marlee said. "But it's picking back up. People can be mad, but eventually, when they need flowers, they're going to reach out to the only florist in town. How about you?"

The server arrived with salads.

"Slow," Matthew agreed. "But not that much slower than it was to begin with. It's a lot less awkward now. I was never comfortable with all the 'ear infections' brought in by devoted aunts and best friends and sisters. It was too much. A waste of my time."

They began eating their salads. Marlee wondered if this was what her sister and friends had in mind—the two of them stabbing lettuce-topped forks into their mouths and discussing how bizarre their lives had been over the past month.

"I'm really sorry I got you into that mess," Marlee said. "I guess I didn't think it would grow quite like it did."

"Oh, it grew, all right," he said. "It's okay. I know you didn't mean for it to get so out of hand."

"To be fair, I tried to back out immediately, during that first disastrous dinner."

Matthew laughed. "The charcoal special," he said. "You really did do a number on that poor… what was it supposed to be again?"

"Pot roast. Or maybe it was chicken? I don't even remember anymore. It didn't resemble either one. I had to throw away the pans."

"I could have washed those!"

"You tried to! I couldn't believe you tried."

"I couldn't believe you wouldn't let me. Listen, one of my lesser-known skills is salvaging ruined cookware with nothing but a little elbow grease and dish soap. You don't even know."

"Nobody could have salvaged those." They resumed eating their salads in an amiable silence.

Matthew grinned as he poked a forkful of lettuce into his mouth. "But we salvaged the night. Even though you went with *sweetums*. What are you, a time traveler from the 1920s?"

She pointed her fork at him. "Okay, fair, but don't think you're going to make me forget *sugar cone*."

"I was making fun of sweetums."

"You were thinking on the spot. Not your best skill, by the way."

"I will have you know that I excelled at thinking on the spot during my emergency department rotation."

"I don't think you ever talked about your residency. I bet you have stories."

"Oh, do I have stories."

"Tell me some."

So he did. He talked while they finished their salads, and halfway through their main courses. And then Marlee talked about her college experience and some of her plans and dreams for Blush & Bloom. And for the briefest time, it was good and it was easy and it was fun, and Marlee forgot all about everything that had happened between them.

It was when dessert came that Marlee was reminded of who they were and what that meant.

"A chocolate torte, on the house," the server said, placing a plate and two forks between them. "For your inconvenience. And, also, as a thank you." She leaned forward to whisper again. "For the social media content."

Marlee's mouth dropped open and she turned to look behind her. Seemed the entire restaurant was looking at her. The bartender was blatantly pointing a phone toward them. She gave a sheepish wave.

"Glad to be of assistance," Matthew said, bailing Marlee out. Somehow, he managed to maintain a pleasant tone.

"For what it's worth, I was always team Marthew," she said. "I'm glad to see that you're together."

When Marlee turned around again, the server was gone. Neither of them reached for a fork, which told Marlee that he was feeling as grim about it all as she was.

"Well, that's one way to kill a pleasant meal," she said, tossing her napkin on the table.

"At least this time we'll see it coming."

"That's the worst. The morning-after photos and videos. It feels so… I don't know…violating? You were right from the beginning. I'm sorry."

He wiped his mouth and set his napkin on the table, too. "I could have said no."

"You did say no."

"And then I didn't. I got into this with you because I wanted to. You don't need to apologize. I would say I was being naive, but it was more like willful ignorance. Part of me wanted it."

She gave a weak smile. "You wanted the adventure?"

"More like I wanted the increased business so I wouldn't have to move away."

"Right. Same."

"The adventure was a bonus. Though not necessarily a good bonus."

"That's the part I'm sorry about."

"Well, we both have things to be sorry about, I suppose," he said. "I'm sorry about the wedding."

Marlee winced. "I think that's another apology point for me, but also something we don't need to relive. I acted rashly and totally blindsided you. I didn't give you time to react. And then, of course, I naively neglected the idea that the conversation could be caught on camera and shared with the entire world. The whole thing was just…" Again, she waved her hands. "You don't have to worry about me pining for you or anything."

"But you were right."

He looked like he'd swallowed something dangerous.

"When I said I wasn't interested, you said you didn't believe me, and you were right." His eyes roved above her head. She didn't need to turn to know that he was scanning the crowd behind her to see how many people were recording this catastrophic moment to add to the others. Soon they would have a whole library full of moments they didn't want caught on camera. "Can we…?" He tilted his head to the side to indicate going outside.

"Yes. Please."

"I'll grab the check on the way out."

Marlee stopped in the restroom to splash water on her face. She was a nervous wreck again. It all felt so big, so final. She wasn't prepared for any of this. She thought she'd put the feelings away, but the moment she'd noticed him at the table next to her, they'd all come back. Not rushing back, like they often did in books and movies, but just there. Suddenly and fully. Like a blink.

There was a bench just outside the front door, and Marlee found Matthew there. She glanced up to see Ellory's car still over at the burger place, the three women all standing around it, watching. Marlee never felt more on display than she did at this moment.

Matthew took a deep breath when Marlee sat next to him. She was trembling, unsure where this was going.

"Listen," he said, without any segue. "I should have been more honest that night after the wedding. But, ever since the thing with my ex, I'd always thought that becoming one with someone else would mean losing half of myself. And

I never allowed myself to really challenge that notion, until I met you."

"I already know this. You don't have to rehash it."

"I'm not rehashing. I'm just apologizing for not being honest. The video on the internet is…well, it leaves you holding the bag. And I'll never forgive myself for that. I saw myself in a light that I really didn't like. Hated, actually."

"It's okay, Matthew," Marlee said, although the tremble had moved to her voice. She feared it was more than a tremble—that maybe it was an urge to cry. *Not in front of all of these people*, she thought. *Absolutely not*. "I know you didn't mean for that to happen. You didn't know. I didn't know."

He held out a hand. "I have to tell you this, though."

"You don't." She found herself blinking faster and faster, her body holding back the tears she didn't want to admit to having.

"But I do. I'm telling you before I tell anyone else, actually."

"It's really okay."

"Marlee, I'm leaving Haw Springs."

And there it was. The slamming door in her mind that put an end to all of this. "You're what?"

"I decided that I was hanging on to a past here. And I need to let it go. I've got to stop wishing and waiting for a future and go somewhere that

I can actually create one. I've got to leave Haw Springs."

Translation: Even if he is willing to challenge his beliefs and admit feelings for you, he still doesn't see a future with you.

"I understand." She gazed across at Ellory's car again, trying to figure out a way to convey that she needed to be rescued from the situation they'd put her in. She ended up sending a simple text: SOS. She watched as Ellory read the message, and then all three ladies scrambled to get into the car.

Matthew continued talking, but she tuned him out, nodding as if she was listening. She stood up as Ellory pulled into the parking lot.

And bolted into the back seat before the tears could start anew.

CHAPTER TWENTY-EIGHT

TRANSLATION: I'M TERRIFIED of what I'm feeling, and I can't watch you every day, spending my life literally staring at your shop in hopes of catching a glimpse of you, and not be with you.

Translation: I'm scared of you.

Translation: I'm even more scared of my feelings for you.

Translation: I'm running away, and I know it.

I'm disappointed in myself.

And I know that, too.

CHAPTER TWENTY-NINE

You go on. That was what Marlee told herself daily. In the end, you just go on. You try to forget about him, you ignore the moving van that pulls up outside his clinic, and you go on. You build your arrangements and you pay your loans and you remind yourself that nobody ever died from not marrying the man of their dreams.

In fact, she'd predicted this, long ago. She'd assumed that this would be her fate, had accepted it as a matter of course and convinced herself that as long as she focused on herself, she would be happy.

Now she knew that even when she was happy, she wasn't totally happy.

Total happiness was up on the rooftop, eating cheese and fruit while looking out over the town you loved. Total happiness was dancing at a silent disco, holding solid, warm hands, feeling the strength behind them. Strength that said, *I've got you. No matter what or where, I've got you.* Total happiness was a steamy greenhouse in a rainstorm.

She'd never had it before she met Matthew.

She'd thought she had, with Keith. She'd been wrong. She knew that now.

And it was nobody's fault. Sometimes things just didn't work out. And you moved on.

It had been weeks since her setup lunch with Matthew at the Bistro. Social media had, as predicted, completely forgotten about Team Marthew. The wedding was over and prom was done, and there were only a couple of June weddings and one July family reunion on the books.

Marlee hadn't seen or heard from Matthew, but she'd seen his clinic empty out. She'd heard through the grapevine that he was moving to Kansas City. She'd heard that Lynette and her husband Charles both decided to retire, and they moved to Florida. How horrible for Matthew's mom, Marlee thought, her son and her lifelong best friend both moving away at the same time.

She wanted to know how Matthew's plans were going.

She wanted to talk to him.

But there was no reason. No excuse. No real segue to open a discussion.

Kimberly was late, but Marlee didn't really care. She was busy watching a home remodeling show on her phone when the front door opened and Kimberly showed up.

"Good morning," Marlee said. "Er, afternoon. I thought maybe you were sick…again."

"Ha ha ha, you're so funny. Maybe you should try stand-up," Kimberly said, absently riffling through mail that she'd picked up on her way in.

"I'm about to try lying down, it's so dead in here," Marlee said. She took the mail that Kimberly slapped onto the counter. "Well, at least I have a bill to pay now. Something to do."

"Here, this too." Kimberly handed her a manila envelope. Marlee studied the return address. *Modern Vow Magazine.* She felt a jolt of energy and stood up straight. "Isn't that the magazine that, like, ruined your life?" Kimberly asked.

"They were just doing their jobs," Marlee said. "But, yes."

"Ooh. Open it. What is it? Maybe they're suing you."

"You know, I don't love the delight in your voice at the thought of them suing me."

Kimberly shrugged. "Nothing personal. I'm just bored."

"Well, you could start inventory in the back," Marlee said.

"If that was important to you, you would have done it yourself," Kimberly said. Marlee gave her a stone-faced look, and she sighed. "Fine. I'll go. But if they're suing you, will you at least come tell me?"

"Sure," Marlee said. "Why not? I would hate for you to remain bored."

"For what it's worth, I would have sued you," Kimberly said, sauntering toward the back. "But, again, that's just because I'm bored."

"Poppy," Marlee said, leaning over the counter. Her shih tzu wagged her little tail—*thump, thump, thump*—against her dog bed. "One of these days, we're going to have to do something about her. And I can't tell if I'm looking forward to that day or dreading it."

Poppy, of course, said nothing, but she didn't need to. Marlee was certain that Poppy agreed with her on all things, all the time. She was just nice like that.

Alone, Marlee ripped open the envelope and slid out a glossy magazine. When she opened the magazine, the pages opened automatically to the spread focused on Annie's wedding.

It was stunning.

CHAPTER THIRTY

MATTHEW HAD CLEANED out almost everything.

Almost.

It was weedy and a little overgrown, but the bones of the garden were still there. They beckoned him. Every night, he sat at the table and looked down over Blush & Bloom, watching for Marlee.

Waiting for an excuse that would never come.

Today was the day, though. He had picked out his location in Kansas City. Had applied for an apartment there. It was time to finish the clean out, list the clinic space for sale and say goodbye forever.

He arrived at the clinic with trash bags and brooms and dustpans at the same time that an old, silver Chevy pulled up along the curb. Matthew paused in the doorway, watching.

The Chevy door opened and an older gentleman stepped out, standing tall on the sidewalk, his white hair shining in the sun. He saw Matthew and gave a wave, then shut the car door and loped across the sidewalk toward him, stooping to pick up the mail that had been stuffed into the mailbox just outside the door. Without Lynette there, Matthew kept forgetting to grab the mail. There was quite a buildup.

"Hello," the man said, opening the door and handing Matthew the mail. "I think this is yours."

"Thank you," Matthew said, taking it. "Are you here to see the space? I'd like to call my Realtor if you—"

"No, no," the man said. "Quite the opposite, actually." He looked around. "I'd ask for a place to sit, but you look fairly cleaned out." He gave a smile. "That was quick, son. Do you always give up so quickly?"

Matthew set the mail and the trash bags on the counter and leaned the broom against it. "I'm sorry, and you are…?"

The older gentleman stuck out a hand. "Jerry Tidwell."

"Oh!" Matthew shook his hand. "Dr. Tidwell. I'm so sorry, I hardly recognized you."

Dr. Tidwell chuckled and ran his other hand through his hair. "Well, it's been a couple of years since I last saw you in my clinic. We've probably both changed a little since then."

"Yes, definitely," Matthew said. "Still. My apologies."

Dr. Tidwell shook a finger at him. "I always knew you were a smart cookie. If anyone had asked me, *Who in this town is going to become a doctor someday?* I would have absolutely said, *That LaSalle boy.* And here you are."

"Ah. Well, you're too kind," Matthew said.

"And I would have also said you'd be the one to take all my patients."

"Oh. Well, if some of them started coming to me a while back, you don't need to worry. That's over, and they'll be back to you the next time they need something."

"I know. That's the problem. I was counting on you, and you let me down."

Matthew frowned, confused. "I'm sorry, I don't follow. Is there something I can I do for you, Dr. Tidwell?"

"Yes. You can stop all this packing and cleaning and stay in Haw Springs."

"I'm afraid I can't do that."

"You've got to take over. I've been waiting patiently, but I guess some people need a ton of bricks to fall on their head, and you just may be one of those people."

Matthew laughed uncomfortably. He didn't remember Dr. Tidwell being so…frank.

Dr. Tidwell leaned over him, his face going serious. Matthew only now realized what a mountain of a man Dr. Tidwell was. "Let me retire, son."

"I've already made plans in the city."

"Plans can be changed."

"I've sold all of my office equipment."

"It can be rebought. I'll sell you mine, cheap."

"Sir. With all due respect, I just… I can't. I have personal reasons."

Dr. Tidwell waved him away. "Oh, I know all about those reasons. I may be old, but I'm not completely out of touch. I know all about you and that flower shop girl over there. You two will find your way. I would suspect that you need a fair share of bricks to fall on you where she's concerned, too."

"I don't think it's all as easy as you seem to think it is."

"Listen, son. I've got a tee time in Riverside in an hour. I'm already late. And I want to book a whole lot more tee times. In order to do that, someone has got to take my place. Haw Springs needs a doctor, and you're it." He held up one palm to keep Matthew from interjecting. "Now, I know what you're about to say. You're a pediatrician, not a general practitioner. But I've done a little research, and I also know that your residency was Medicine-Pediatrics. You chose pediatrics, but you could transition to general practice if you want to. And why wouldn't you want to? I can tell you from a lifetime of experience, son, it is so satisfying to be someone's doctor from the moment they open their eyes for the first time, all the way until you retire. You won't regret it, not even for a day. Get your stuff back, rebuild and I'll send all of my patients to you."

"I..."

"Come by my office next week and set up a time to talk. We can iron out the details." Dr. Tidwell opened the door to leave. "As for the other thing..." He tapped his head with his forefinger. "Brick marks. Just ask Mrs. Tidwell." He gave a wink and was gone.

Matthew stood at the door and watched him go, dumbfounded. It wasn't so easy, was it? Could he have just fallen into his way to stay in Haw Springs? Just like that?

No way.

He didn't trust it.

Besides, having the patients only solved part of the problem.

Grumbling, he went back to the mail and threw most of it in the trash. He picked up a manila envelope and opened it. Inside, was a copy of *Modern Vow Magazine*. His reflex was to throw it away, and he almost did. But he paused when he saw a sticky note attached to the front.

Matthew,

In spite of everything, we loved our time in Haw Springs. And for what it's worth, I think you and Marlee made the most adorable couple. I know I said we would keep our article just to the wedding, but there's nothing stop-

ping me from sending you the photos we took (see inside the magazine). I think you need to see them. Best of luck to you. We will forever be #TeamMarthew.
Janquil

P.S. Stop lying to yourself.

He took the magazine up to the roof, and it wasn't until he was sitting at the table that he decided to open it up. A stack of loose photos tumbled out.

Picture after picture of the two of them smiling, holding hands, dancing, looking happy. All candid shots that they weren't posing for, and didn't even know were being taken.

He flipped through them, his heart in his throat. His hands trembled around them. The memories were almost more than he could take. *Put them away. Just put them away and move on.*

But when he scooped them into a pile and shoved them back into the magazine, he noticed one that had gotten stuck in the fold.

He pulled it out.

He and Marlee were dancing on the rooftop. They were spinning in the photo, both laughing.

But it was the angle of the photo that struck him.

Tyler had been standing as close to the base of

the clinic as he could get while still seeing their silhouettes above.

The result was a mirage of them dancing directly above.

As if they were dancing along the edge.

The edge of…a brick wall.

"A whole ton of bricks," Matthew breathed.

CHAPTER THIRTY-ONE

It had been a scorcher, but the sun had finally gone down by the time Marlee returned to Blush & Bloom after her wedding delivery. She pulled up to the curb and threw her van into Park, then jogged into the store. Kimberly had left for the day. Morgan had taken Poppy home. Ellory had flipped The Baked Bean sign to Closed. Main Street was sleepy. It was closing time for her, too.

Not that she had any big plans. Her evening agenda included a hot date with a cold sandwich, some ice cream and a rom-com. Maybe she would invite Annie over to watch with her. She loved the way Annie giggled during rom-coms. Her infectious laugh always made the movie so much more fun.

She had just turned the sign to Closed when she received a text.

Please move your van.

Marlee was pretty sure her heart stopped. She turned slowly and peered out the window. She hadn't seen Matthew in weeks. She had honestly thought he'd moved away.

He stood next to her van.

He waved, then pointed to his phone.

Move your van, please. It's in front of my clinic.

She felt rooted in place. She couldn't make her body move. There he was, right in front of her. And here she was, feeling just the same as she'd felt about him the night of Annie's wedding, the feelings of love and hurt and guilt and hope and dismay all rushing in on her.

She'd prepared a million times for what she might say to him if she were to ever face him again.

But every single syllable was gone. All that was in her head was the buzzing of seeing her otherme standing next to the bumper of her van, beckoning for her to come outside.

Finally, she willed herself to move forward. She grasped the doorknob and pushed the door open.

She lifted her chin defiantly and forced vigor into her step. *Look unintimidated*, she told herself. *Look irritated, if you can.*

"It's not your space," she said, her step growing quicker and more confident as she crossed the street. "In fact, your clinic is closed, so I know for a fact that it's not impeding anyone from getting in there. You're just trying to bully me and I—"

He whipped a bouquet of roses out of nowhere. Smiled. Held them out to her.

She stutter-stepped. Paused. Still too far away to take them.

"What is this?" she asked.

He laughed. "Take them. They're for you."

She took a few more tentative steps. "Why?"

"Because it may have taken a ton of bricks for me to get the picture, but I think I finally got it."

"Huh?"

He went to her and pressed the flowers into her hands. "Marlee, I was so wrong. But I'm not going to be wrong anymore."

She shook her head. "You moved."

"I started to move. I was all ready to go. Then Dr. Tidwell visited me and asked me to stay and take over his clinic. And at first I thought I couldn't do it. That I needed to start fresh somewhere else. I was desperate to leave. But then I realized that the reason I was so desperate to leave was because I wanted you and couldn't have you. I just didn't realize that I was the only thing keeping me from having you. I was afraid of loving you, and afraid of not loving you, and I was running away from that fear. So why move? Why not just…be afraid?"

"You're not making any sense." The roses felt cool and heavy against her palms. He took them and laid them on the hood of the van, then took her hands—his skin, as always, feeling warm and strong against hers.

"I love you." He shrugged. "It's really just that simple. I love you and I want to spend the rest of my life with you."

Marlee's head swam. Part of her worried that maybe she was actually asleep and this was all a dream. A wonderful, terrifying dream. But she could feel his hands in hers. She could smell the roses, warming on the still-warm hood of the van. She could hear the frogs out on the pond begin their call.

And even if it was just a dream, it was a very good dream, and she was going to lean into it.

"I love you, too," she said. "Is this for real?"

Matthew laughed. "Oh, it's for real. No more faking anything."

They gazed into each other's eyes for so long that the sky grew dark around them. Marlee noticed lights twinkling above his shoulder. She gasped. "BL Gardens. It's still there? I thought you threw it all away. Emphasis on *threw*."

"I couldn't make myself tear it down. In fact, I weeded it and planted a few more plants. Replaced some broken pots. Care to see it?"

Marlee grinned. "I thought you'd never ask."

They climbed to the roof, where music was already playing. She set the roses in a vase on the table and fell into his arms, which he held out, a silent invitation to dance. He pulled her in close and they moved together, silently, tenderly. Marlee closed her eyes and laid her head on his chest.

She could hear his heart beating. The sound made her bite her lip and smile.

"Is this real?" she whispered.

"It's so real," he answered. "Terrifyingly real."

"Tell me again," she said.

"I'm in love with you."

"What changed your mind?"

"Being away from you," he said. "Realizing what a fool I was to deny the best thing that's ever happened to me. Realizing that I might change… a little…but that it will be for the better, because you're all the good things I wish I was. Realizing that I want that change."

"I'm glad you changed your mind," she said. "And I love you, too. I love you so much it hurts, but in a good way. It's not a myth. It's real. We're real."

When the song was over, he leaned back to look into her eyes.

"There's just one more thing," he whispered.

"What?" she whispered back.

"I'm still going to need you to move that van." He winked at her.

She swatted playfully at his chest and acted as if she were trying to wriggle free of his grasp. But he pulled her in closer and closer. And she let him.

Her wriggles slowed, her laughter quieted.

And they kissed.

* * * * *

Get up to 4 Free Books!

We'll send you 2 free books from each series you try PLUS a free Mystery Gift.

Both the **Harlequin® Special Edition** and **Harlequin® Heartwarming™** series feature compelling novels filled with stories of love and strength where the bonds of friendship, family and community unite.

YES! Please send me 2 FREE novels from the Harlequin Special Edition or Harlequin Heartwarming series and my FREE Gift (gift is worth about $10 retail). I may cancel anytime by emailing ReaderServiceInfo@Harlequin.com or by calling 1-800-873-8635.If I don't cancel, I will receive 6 brand-new Harlequin Special Edition books every month and be billed just $6.39 each in the U.S. or $7.19 each in Canada, or 4 brand-new Harlequin Heartwarming Larger-Print books every month and be billed just $7.19 each in the U.S. or $7.99 each in Canada, a savings of 20% off the cover price. It's quite a bargain! Shipping and handling is just 75¢ per book in the U.S. and $1.75 per book in Canada.* I understand that accepting the free books and gift places me under no obligation to buy anything—they are mine to keep for free no matter what I decide.

Choose one: ☐ **Harlequin Special Edition** (235/335 BPA G3CD) ☐ **Harlequin Heartwarming Larger-Print** (161/361 BPA G3CD) ☐ **Or Try Both!** (235/335 & 161/361 BPA G3CE)

Name (please print)

Address Apt. #

City State/Province Zip/Postal Code

Email: Please check this box ☐ if you would like to receive newsletters and promotional emails from Harlequin Enterprises ULC and its affiliates. You can unsubscribe anytime.

Mail to the **Harlequin Reader Service:**
IN U.S.A.: P.O. Box 1341, Buffalo, NY 14240-8531
IN CANADA: P.O. Box 603, Fort Erie, Ontario L2A 5X3

Want to explore our other series or interested in ebooks? **Visit www.ReaderService.com or call 1-800-873-8635.**

*Terms and prices subject to change without notice. Prices do not include sales taxes, which will be charged (if applicable) based on your state or country of residence. Canadian residents will be charged applicable taxes. Offer not valid in Quebec. This offer is limited to one order per household. Books received may not be as shown. Not valid for current subscribers to the Harlequin Special Edition or Harlequin Heartwarming series. All orders subject to approval. Credit or debit balances in a customer's account(s) may be offset by any other outstanding balance owed by or to the customer. Please allow 4 to 6 weeks for delivery. Offer available while quantities last.

Your Privacy — Your information is being collected by Harlequin Enterprises ULC, operating as Harlequin Reader Service. For a complete summary of the information we collect, how we use this information and to whom it is disclosed, please visit our privacy notice located at https://corporate.harlequin.com/privacy-notice. Notice to California Residents—Under California law, you have specific rights to control and access your data. For more information on these rights and how to exercise them, visit https://corporate.harlequin.com/california-privacy. For additional information for residents of other U.S. states that provide their residents with certain rights with respect to personal data, visit https://corporate.harlequin.com/other-state-residents-privacy-rights.

HSEHW2603